KILL or be KILLED

IMAGE COMICS, INC.

Robert Kirkman — **Chief Operating Officer**
Erik Larsen — **Chief Financial Officer**
Todd McFarlane — **President**
Marc Silvestri — **Chief Executive Officer**
Jim Valentino — **Vice President**
Eric Stephenson — **Publisher**
Corey Hart — **Director of Sales**
Jeff Boison — **Director of Publishing Planning & Book Trade Sales**
Chris Ross — **Director of Digital Sales**
Jeff Stang — **Director of Specialty Sales**
Kat Salazar — **Director of PR & Marketing**
Drew Gill — **Art Director**
Heather Doornink — **Production Director**
Branwyn Bigglestone — **Controller**

Standard Cover, ISBN: 978-1-5343-0471-0
DCBS Variant, ISBN: 978-1-5343-0773-5
Forbidden Planet/Big Bang Comics Variant, ISBN: 978-1-5343-0772-8

IMAGECOMICS.COM

Publication design by Sean Phillips

Volume Three

KILL or be KILLED

Ed Brubaker
Sean Phillips
Elizabeth Breitweiser

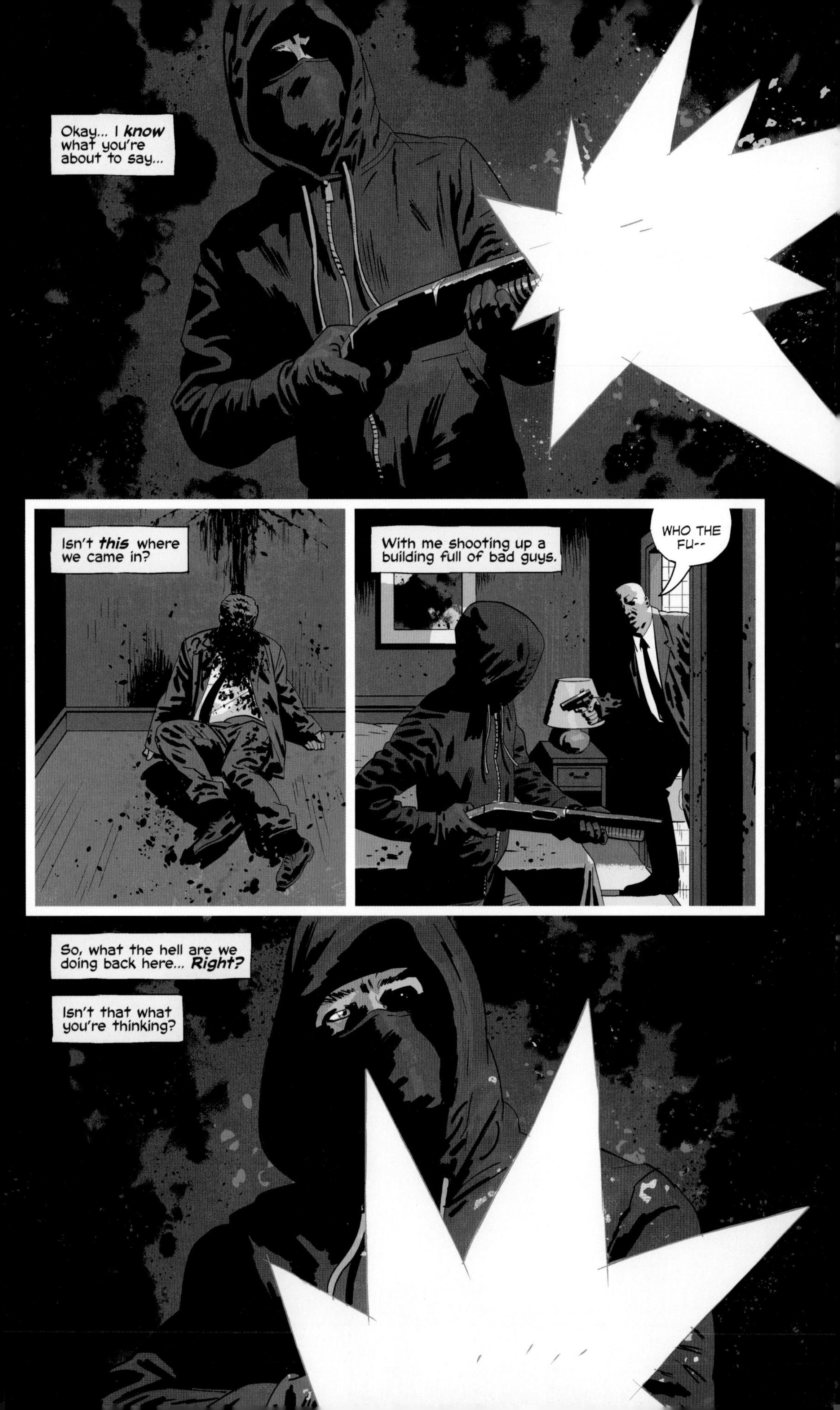
Okay... I **know** what you're about to say...
Isn't ***this*** where we came in?
With me shooting up a building full of bad guys.
WHO THE FU--
So, what the hell are we doing back here... ***Right?***
Isn't that what you're thinking?

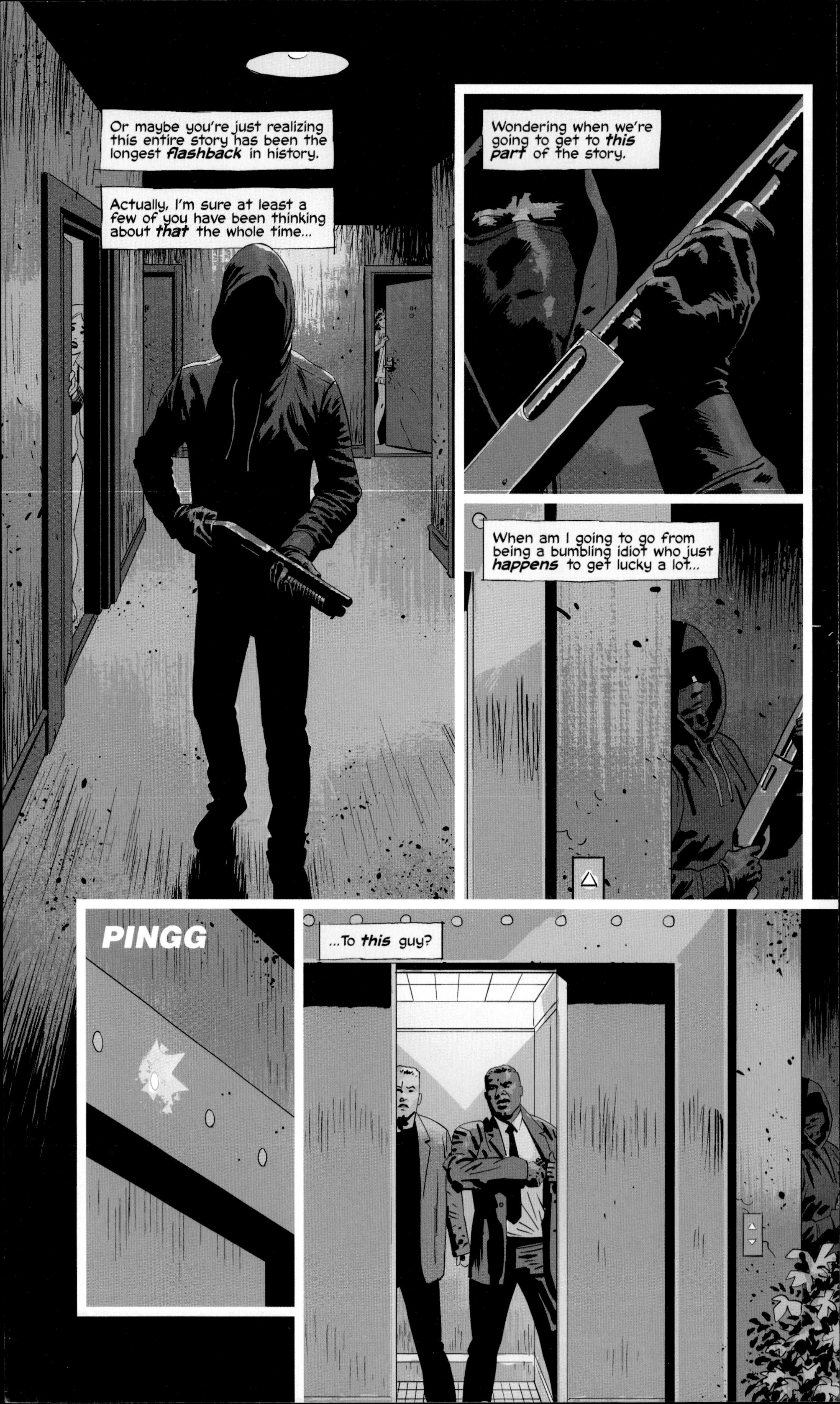

Or maybe you're just realizing this entire story has been the longest *flashback* in history.
Actually, I'm sure at least a few of you have been thinking about *that* the whole time...
Wondering when we're going to get to *this part* of the story.
When am I going to go from being a bumbling idiot who just *happens* to get lucky a lot...
PINGG
...To *this* guy?

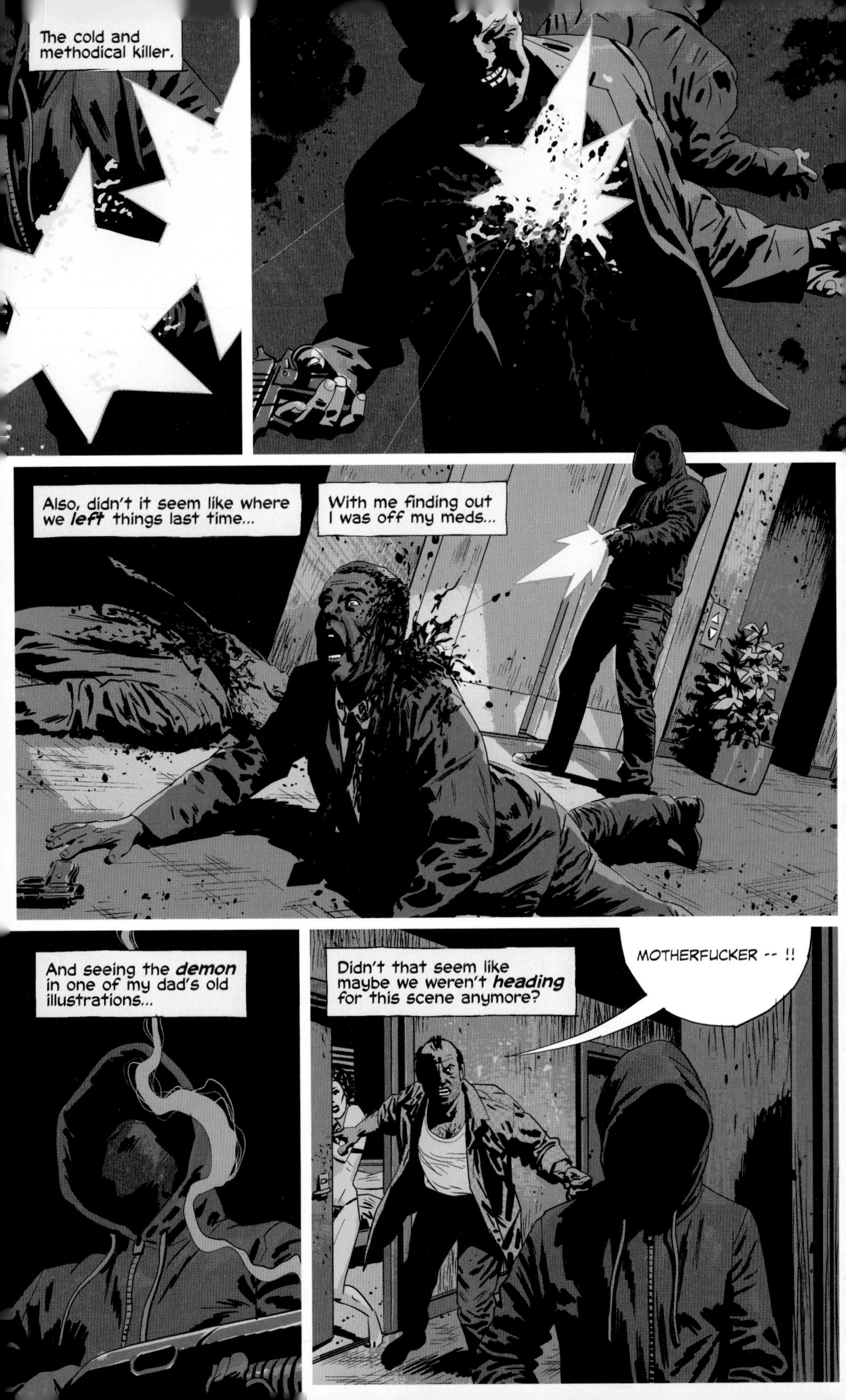
The cold and methodical killer.
Also, didn't it seem like where we *left* things last time...
With me finding out I was off my meds...
And seeing the *demon* in one of my dad's old illustrations...
Didn't that seem like maybe we weren't *heading* for this scene anymore?
MOTHERFUCKER -- !!

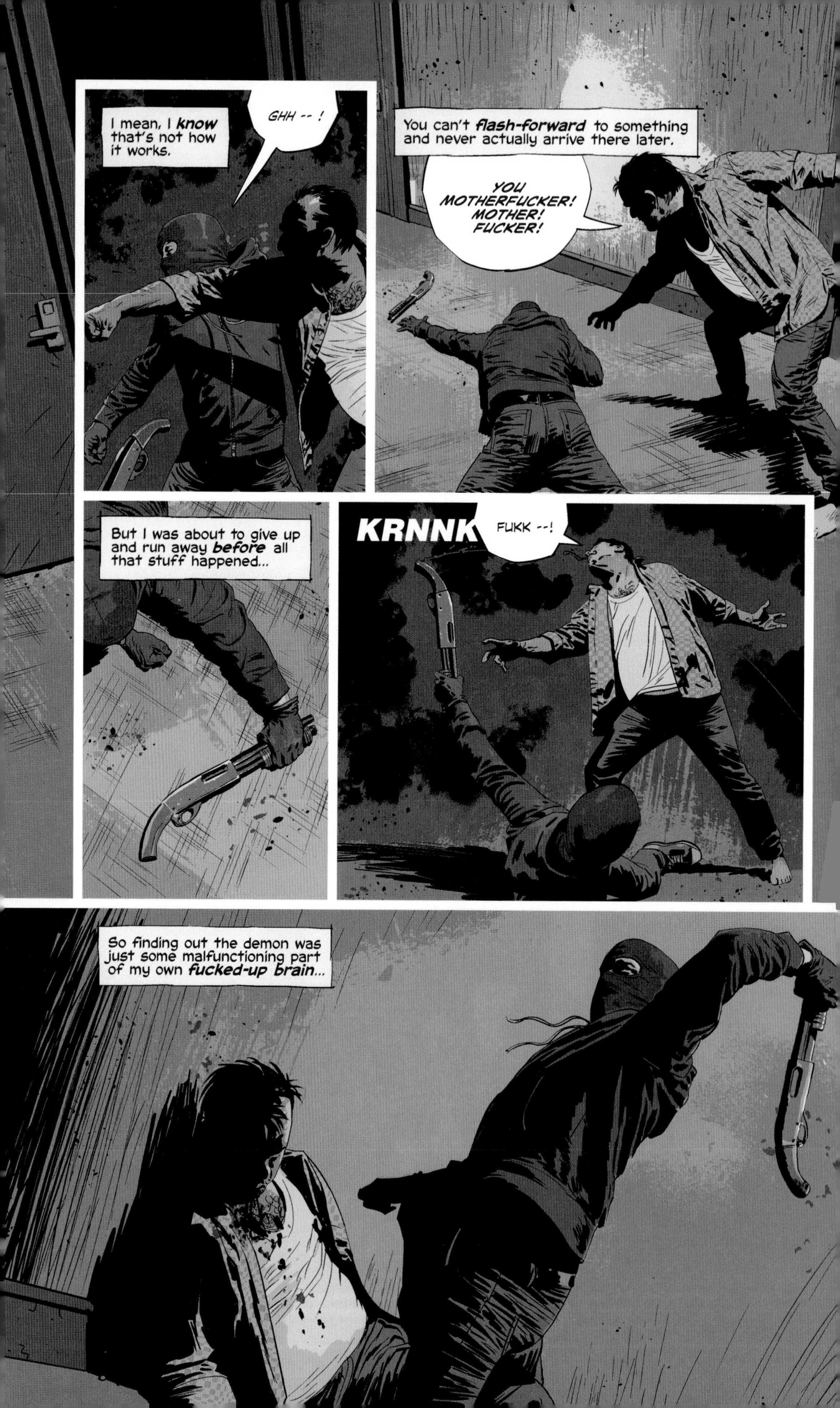
I mean, I **know** that's not how it works.
GHH -- !
You can't **flash-forward** to something and never actually arrive there later.
YOU MOTHERFUCKER! MOTHER! FUCKER!
But I was about to give up and run away **before** all that stuff happened...
KRNNK
FUKK --!
So finding out the demon was just some malfunctioning part of my own **fucked-up brain**...

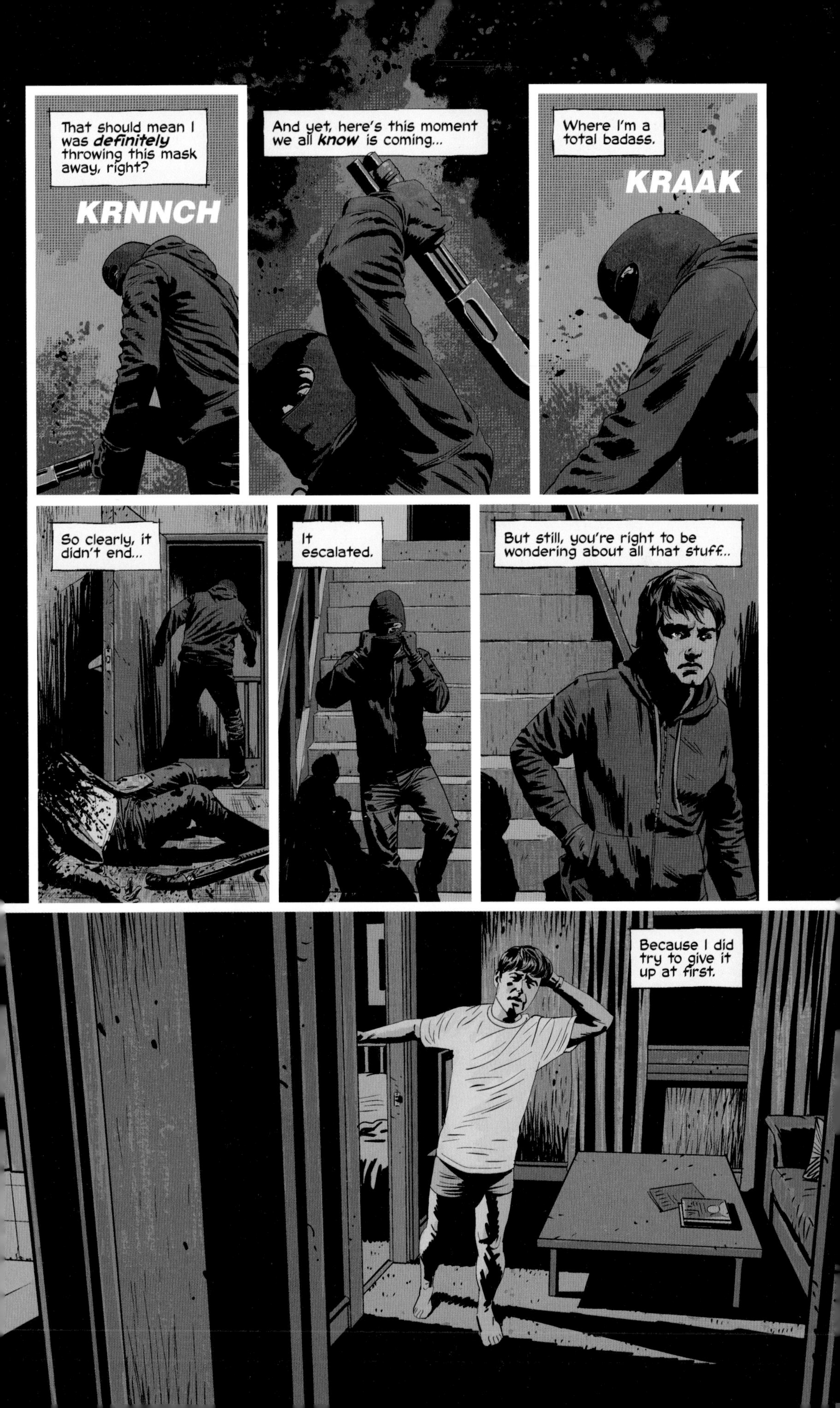

That should mean I was *definitely* throwing this mask away, right?
KRNNCH
And yet, here's this moment we all *know* is coming...
Where I'm a total badass.
KRAAK
So clearly, it didn't end...
It escalated.
But still, you're right to be wondering about all that stuff...
Because I did try to give it up at first.

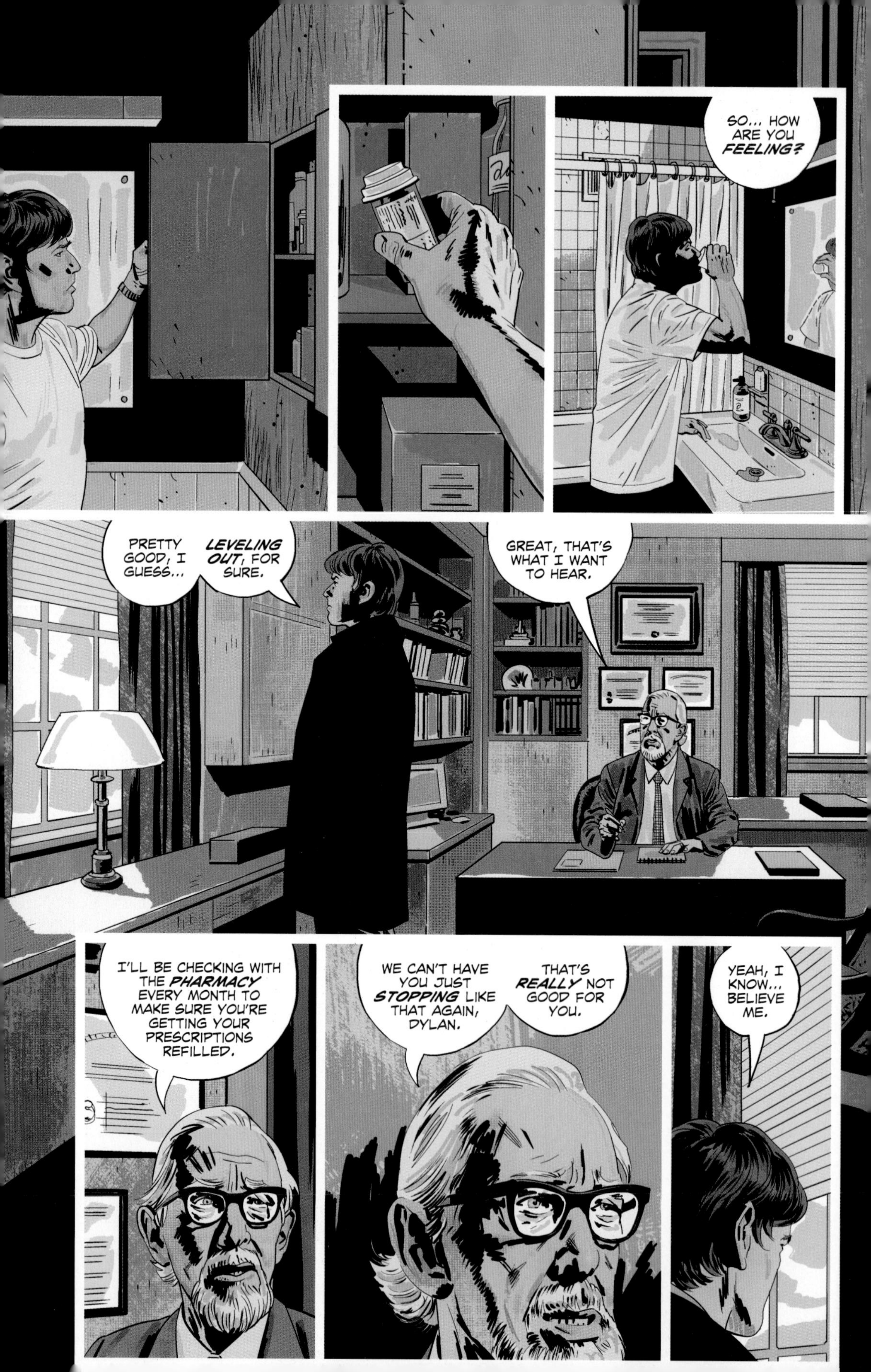
SO... HOW ARE YOU *FEELING?*
PRETTY GOOD, I GUESS... *LEVELING OUT*, FOR SURE.
GREAT, THAT'S WHAT I WANT TO HEAR.
I'LL BE CHECKING WITH THE *PHARMACY* EVERY MONTH TO MAKE SURE YOU'RE GETTING YOUR PRESCRIPTIONS REFILLED.
WE CAN'T HAVE YOU JUST *STOPPING* LIKE THAT AGAIN, DYLAN.
THAT'S *REALLY* NOT GOOD FOR YOU.
YEAH, I KNOW... BELIEVE ME.

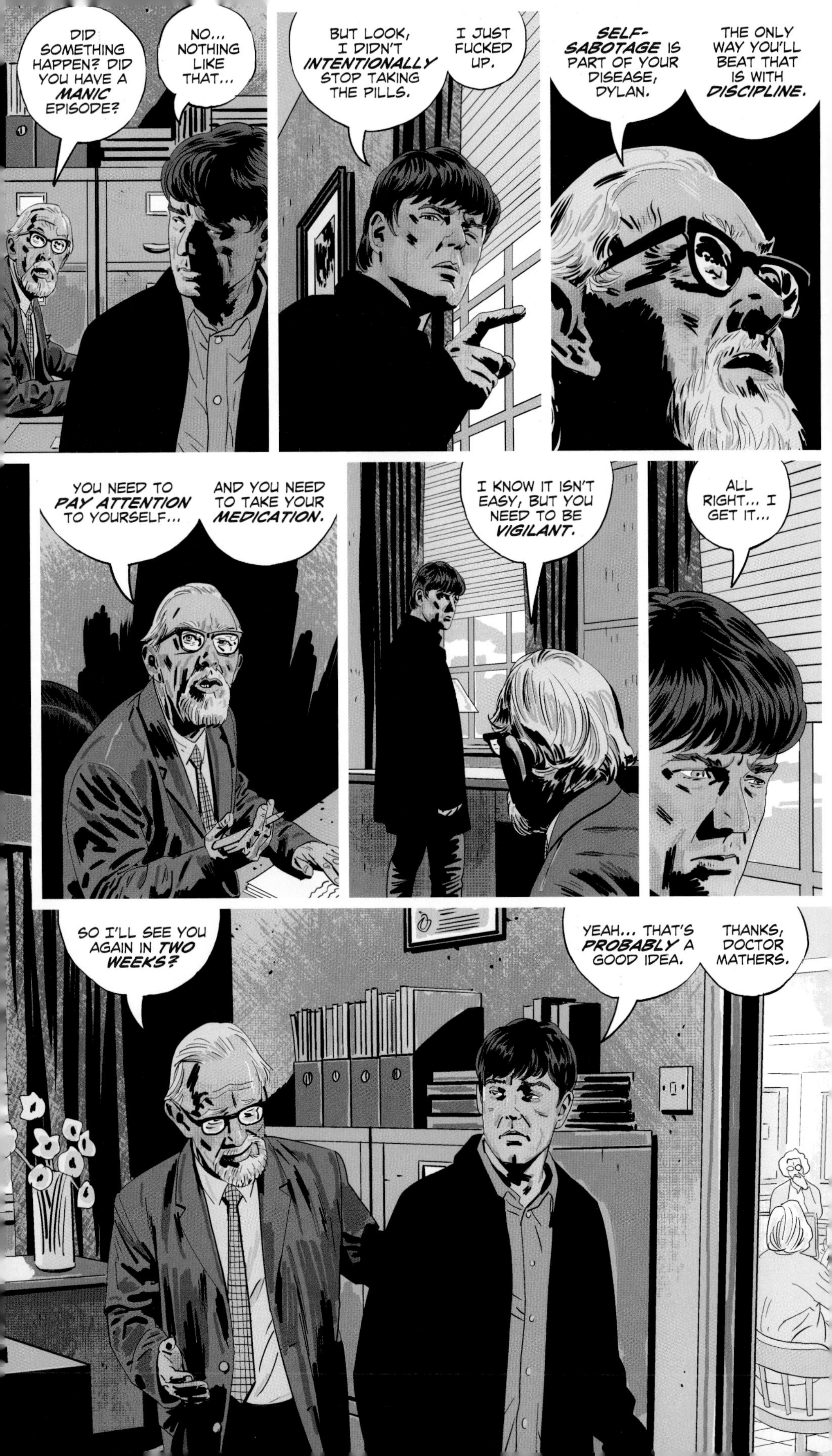

DID SOMETHING HAPPEN? DID YOU HAVE A MANIC EPISODE?
NO... NOTHING LIKE THAT...
BUT LOOK, I DIDN'T INTENTIONALLY STOP TAKING THE PILLS.
I JUST FUCKED UP.
SELF-SABOTAGE IS PART OF YOUR DISEASE, DYLAN.
THE ONLY WAY YOU'LL BEAT THAT IS WITH DISCIPLINE.
YOU NEED TO PAY ATTENTION TO YOURSELF...
AND YOU NEED TO TAKE YOUR MEDICATION.
I KNOW IT ISN'T EASY, BUT YOU NEED TO BE VIGILANT.
ALL RIGHT... I GET IT...
SO I'LL SEE YOU AGAIN IN TWO WEEKS?
YEAH... THAT'S PROBABLY A GOOD IDEA.
THANKS, DOCTOR MATHERS.

So, obviously I wasn't being completely ***honest*** with my doctor.

But come on... what did you expect me to do, ***confess?***

No, I was doing the same thing I complained about everybody else doing... I was trying to get away with it.

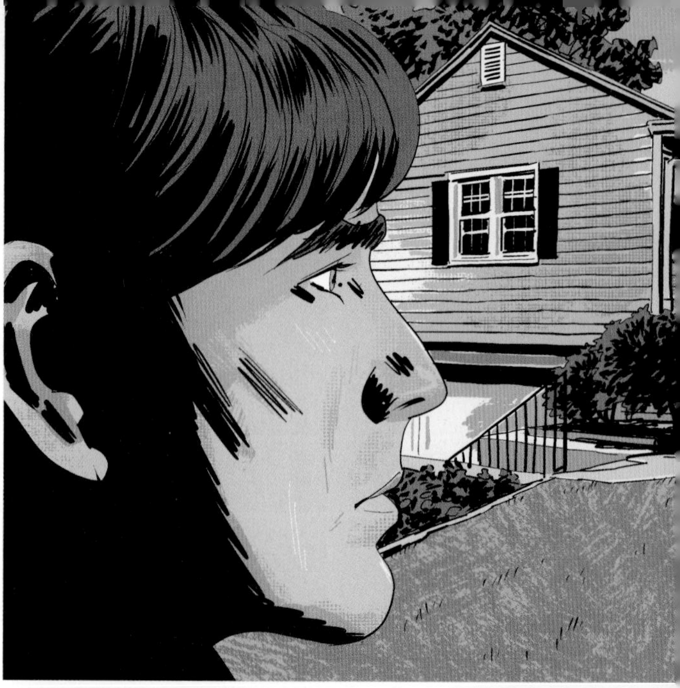

I mean, I already ***knew*** murder was wrong... and I wasn't going to do it again (or so I thought)...

So I figured I'd let my mental anguish be my punishment.

And really, if I'm being honest, I figured ***that*** would fade over time... Probably sooner than it should.

Because other than Rex, all the people I had killed were pretty ***awful*** human beings.

And it's hard to lose a lot of sleep over a dead child molester.

So, time passed and summer turned into fall... and I tried to get back to some semblance of my normal life...

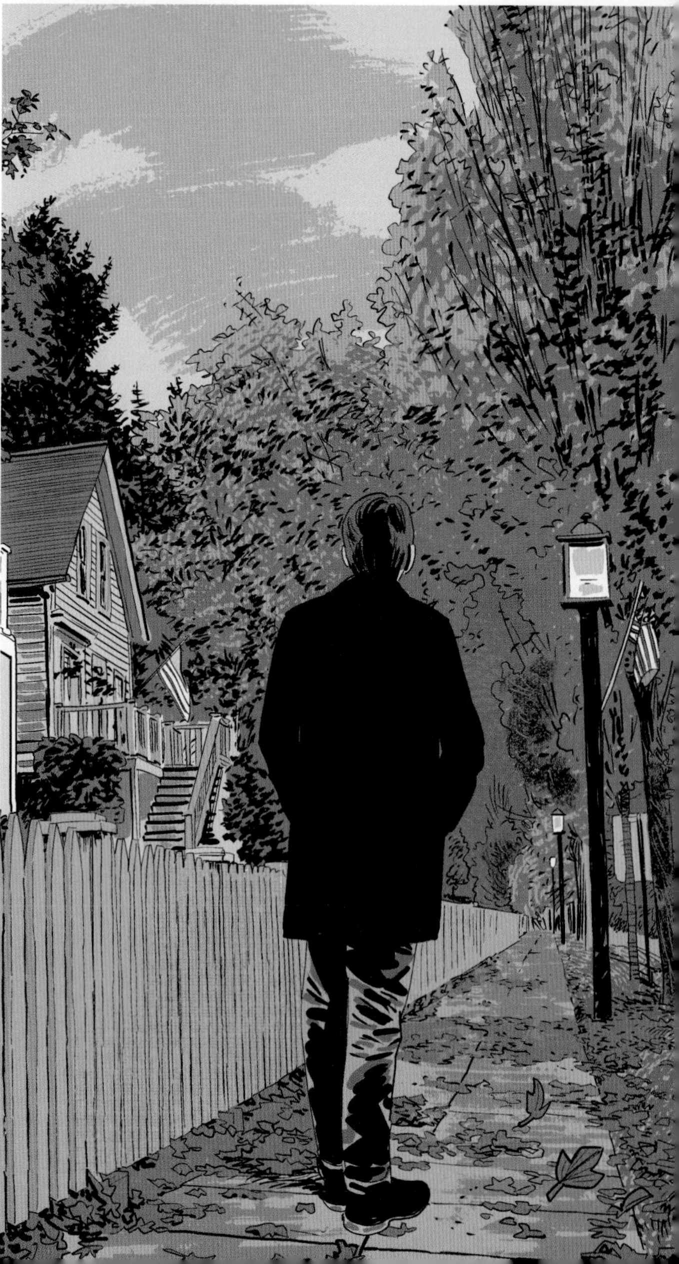

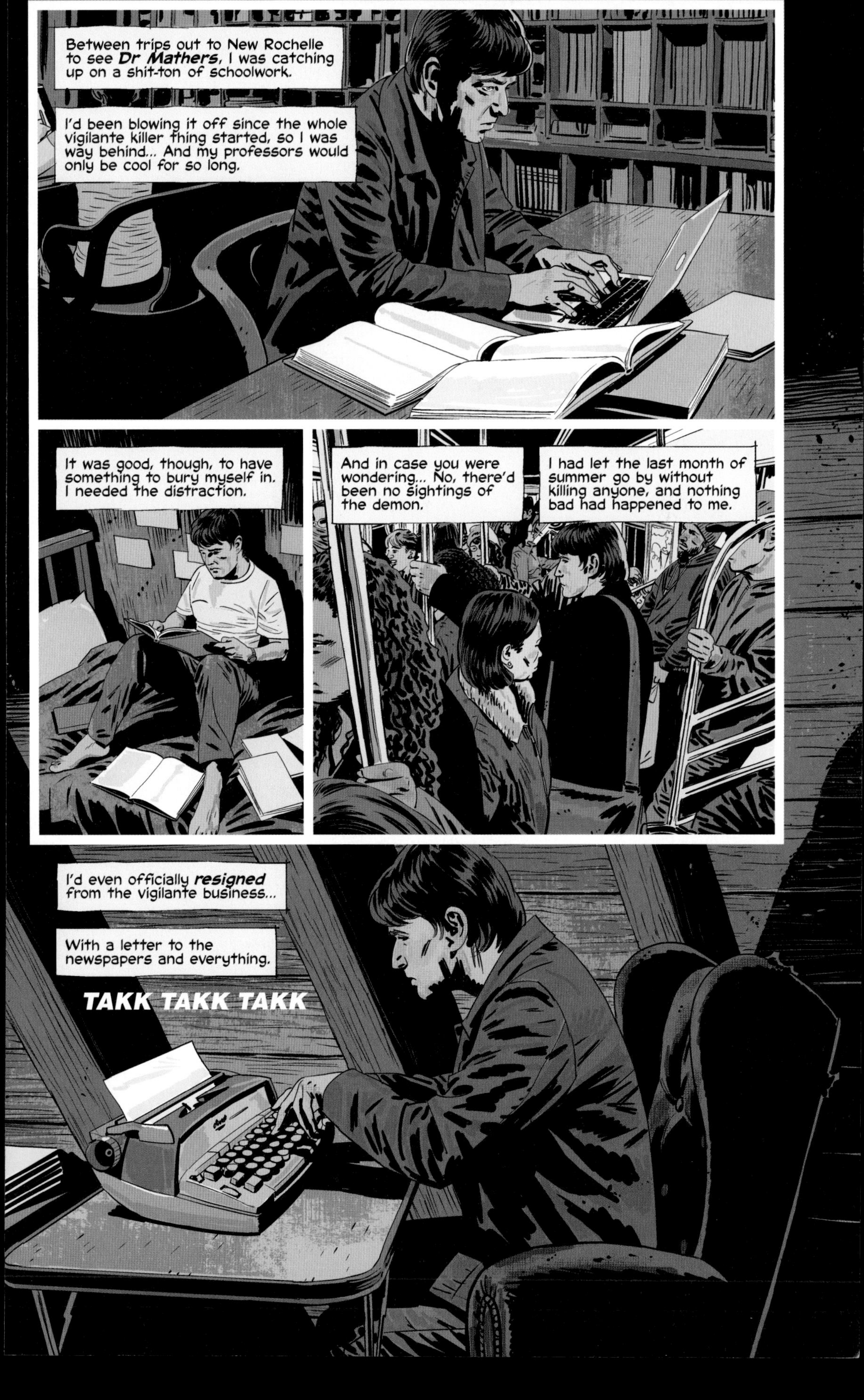
Between trips out to New Rochelle to see ***Dr Mathers***, I was catching up on a shit-ton of schoolwork.
I'd been blowing it off since the whole vigilante killer thing started, so I was way behind... And my professors would only be cool for so long.
It was good, though, to have something to bury myself in. I needed the distraction.
And in case you were wondering... No, there'd been no sightings of the demon.
I had let the last month of summer go by without killing anyone, and nothing bad had happened to me.
I'd even officially ***resigned*** from the vigilante business...
With a letter to the newspapers and everything.
TAKK TAKK TAKK

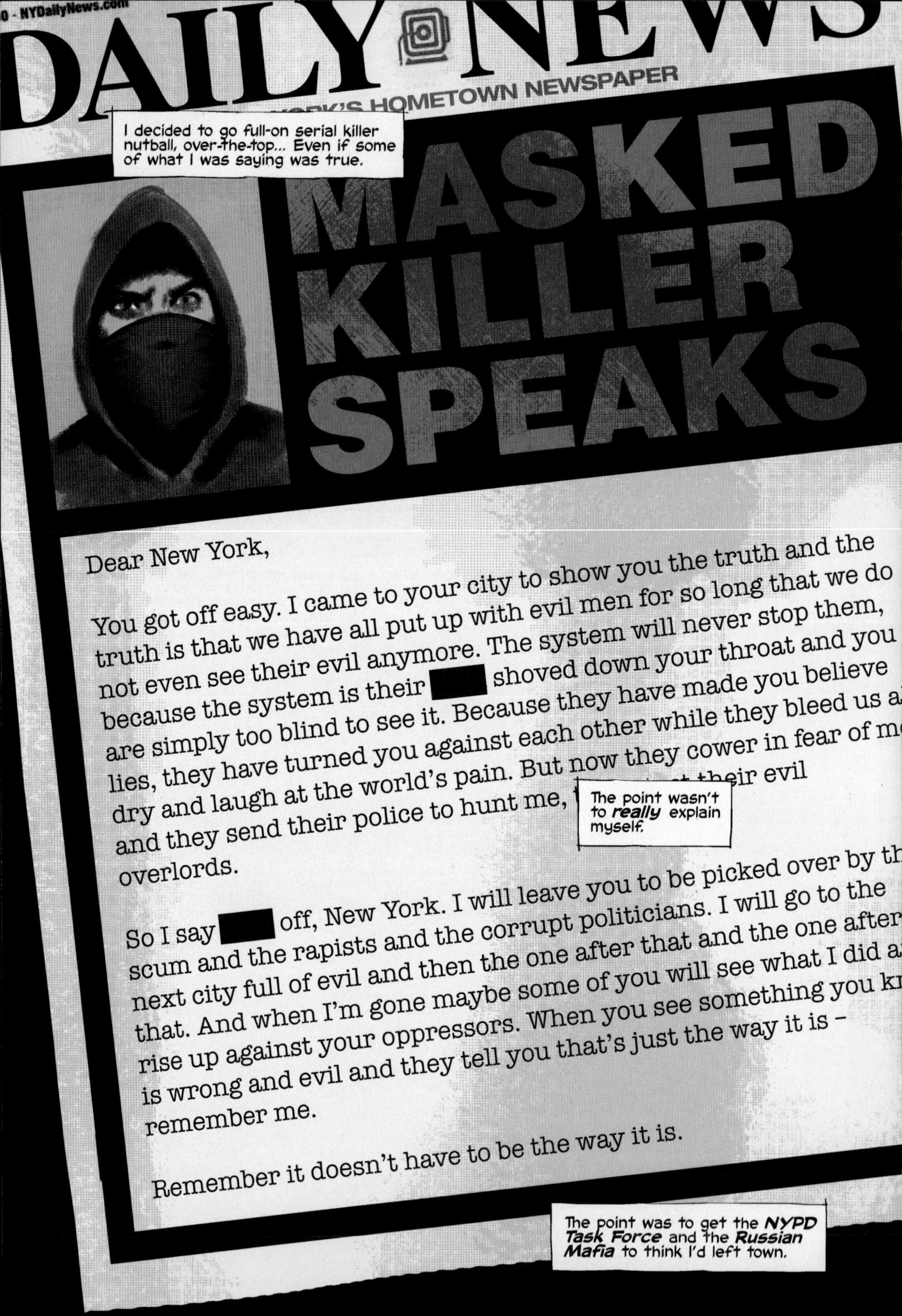
0 - NYDailyNews.com
DAILY NEWS
ORK'S HOMETOWN NEWSPAPER
I decided to go full-on serial killer nutball, over-the-top... Even if some of what I was saying was true.
MASKED KILLER SPEAKS
Dear New York,
You got off easy. I came to your city to show you the truth and the
truth is that we have all put up with evil men for so long that we do
not even see their evil anymore. The system will never stop them,
because the system is their [redacted] shoved down your throat and you
are simply too blind to see it. Because they have made you believe
lies, they have turned you against each other while they bleed us a
dry and laugh at the world's pain. But now they cower in fear of m
and they send their police to hunt me, their evil
overlords.
The point wasn't to *really* explain myself.
So I say [redacted] off, New York. I will leave you to be picked over by th
scum and the rapists and the corrupt politicians. I will go to the
next city full of evil and then the one after that and the one after
that. And when I'm gone maybe some of you will see what I did a
rise up against your oppressors. When you see something you kn
is wrong and evil and they tell you that's just the way it is –
remember me.
Remember it doesn't have to be the way it is.
The point was to get the *NYPD Task Force* and the *Russian Mafia* to think I'd left town.

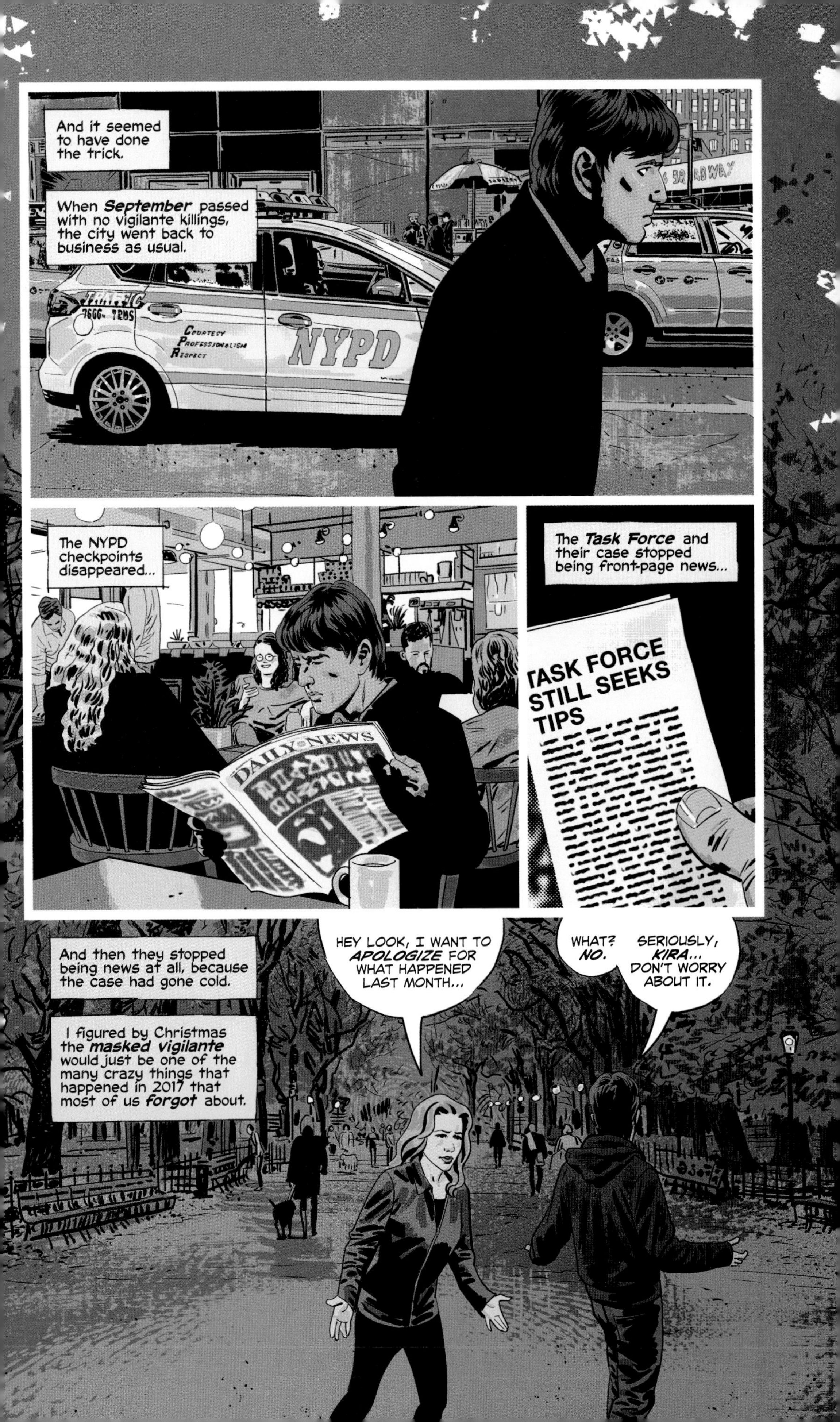
And it seemed to have done the trick.
When *September* passed with no vigilante killings, the city went back to business as usual.
NYPD
COURTESY PROFESSIONALISM RESPECT
The NYPD checkpoints disappeared...
DAILY NEWS
The *Task Force* and their case stopped being front-page news...
TASK FORCE STILL SEEKS TIPS
And then they stopped being news at all, because the case had gone cold.
I figured by Christmas the *masked vigilante* would just be one of the many crazy things that happened in 2017 that most of us *forgot* about.
HEY LOOK, I WANT TO *APOLOGIZE* FOR WHAT HAPPENED LAST MONTH...
WHAT? *NO.*
SERIOUSLY, *KIRA*... DON'T WORRY ABOUT IT.

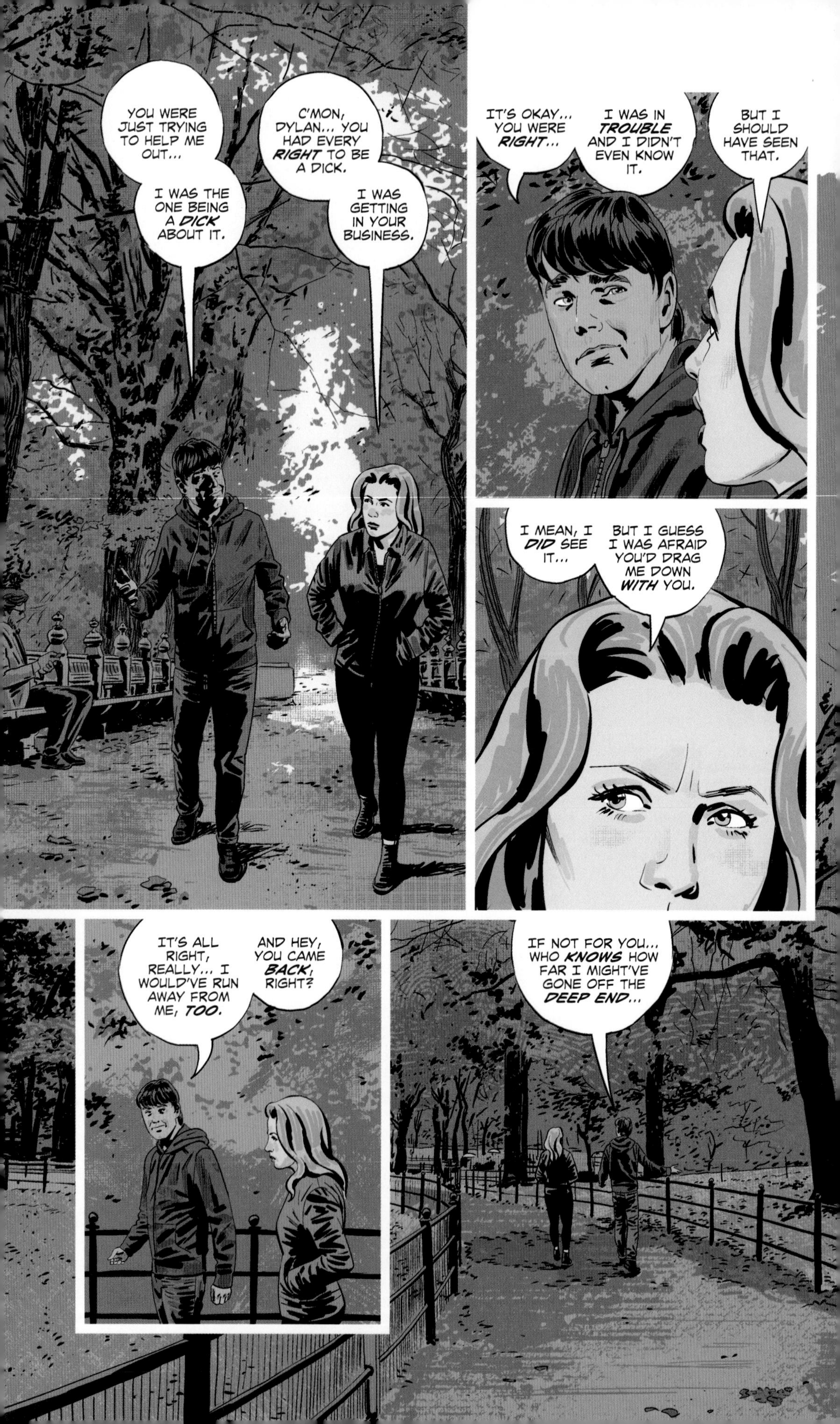
YOU WERE JUST TRYING TO HELP ME OUT...
I WAS THE ONE BEING A DICK ABOUT IT.
C'MON, DYLAN... YOU HAD EVERY RIGHT TO BE A DICK.
I WAS GETTING IN YOUR BUSINESS.
IT'S OKAY... YOU WERE RIGHT...
I WAS IN TROUBLE AND I DIDN'T EVEN KNOW IT.
BUT I SHOULD HAVE SEEN THAT.
I MEAN, I DID SEE IT...
BUT I GUESS I WAS AFRAID YOU'D DRAG ME DOWN WITH YOU.
IT'S ALL RIGHT, REALLY... I WOULD'VE RUN AWAY FROM ME, TOO.
AND HEY, YOU CAME BACK, RIGHT?
IF NOT FOR YOU... WHO KNOWS HOW FAR I MIGHT'VE GONE OFF THE DEEP END...

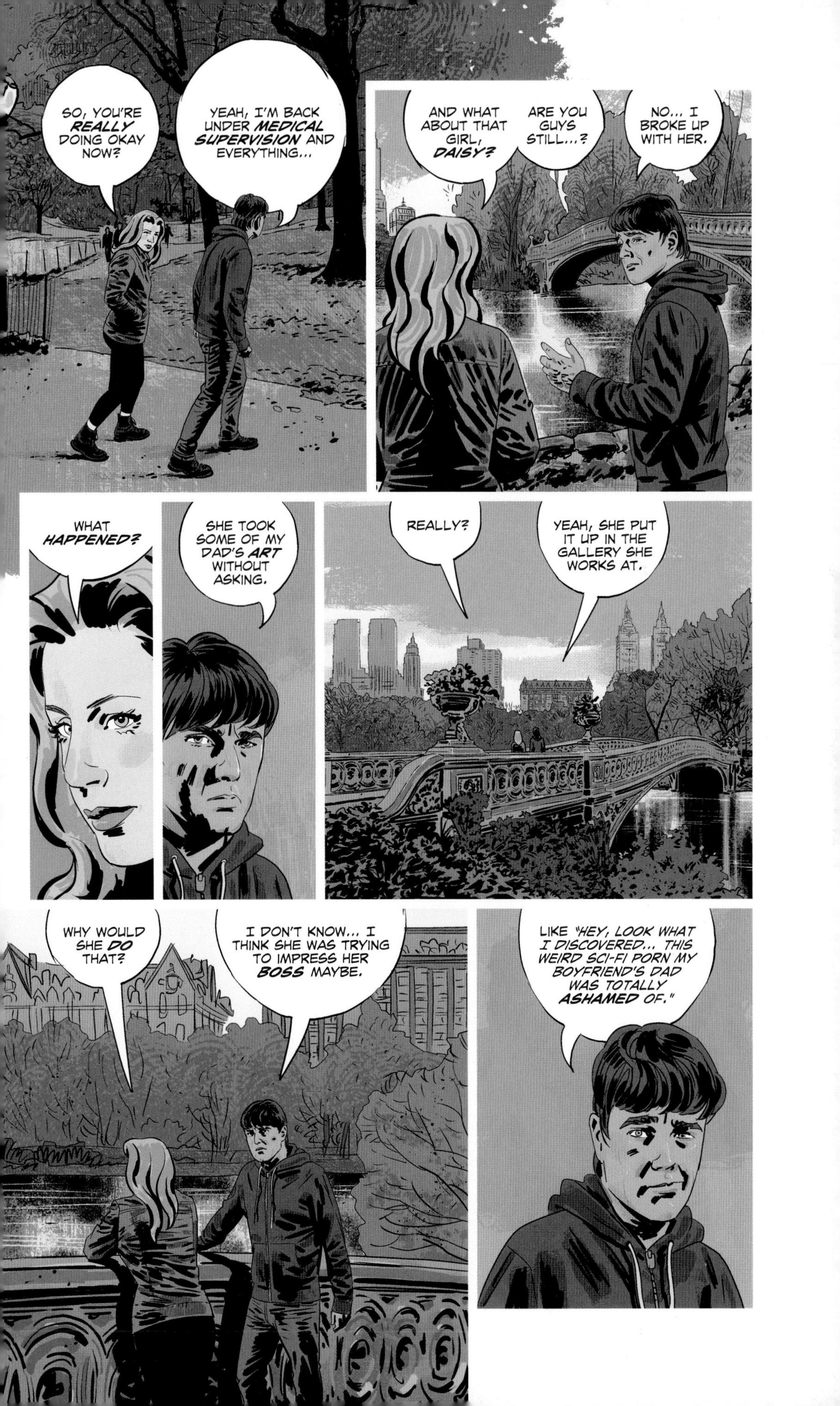
SO, YOU'RE *REALLY* DOING OKAY NOW?
YEAH, I'M BACK UNDER *MEDICAL SUPERVISION* AND EVERYTHING...
AND WHAT ABOUT THAT GIRL, *DAISY?*
ARE YOU GUYS STILL...?
NO... I BROKE UP WITH HER.
WHAT *HAPPENED?*
SHE TOOK SOME OF MY DAD'S *ART* WITHOUT ASKING.
REALLY?
YEAH, SHE PUT IT UP IN THE GALLERY SHE WORKS AT.
WHY WOULD SHE *DO* THAT?
I DON'T KNOW... I THINK SHE WAS TRYING TO IMPRESS HER *BOSS* MAYBE.
LIKE *"HEY, LOOK WHAT I DISCOVERED... THIS WEIRD SCI-FI PORN MY BOYFRIEND'S DAD WAS TOTALLY* ***ASHAMED*** *OF."*

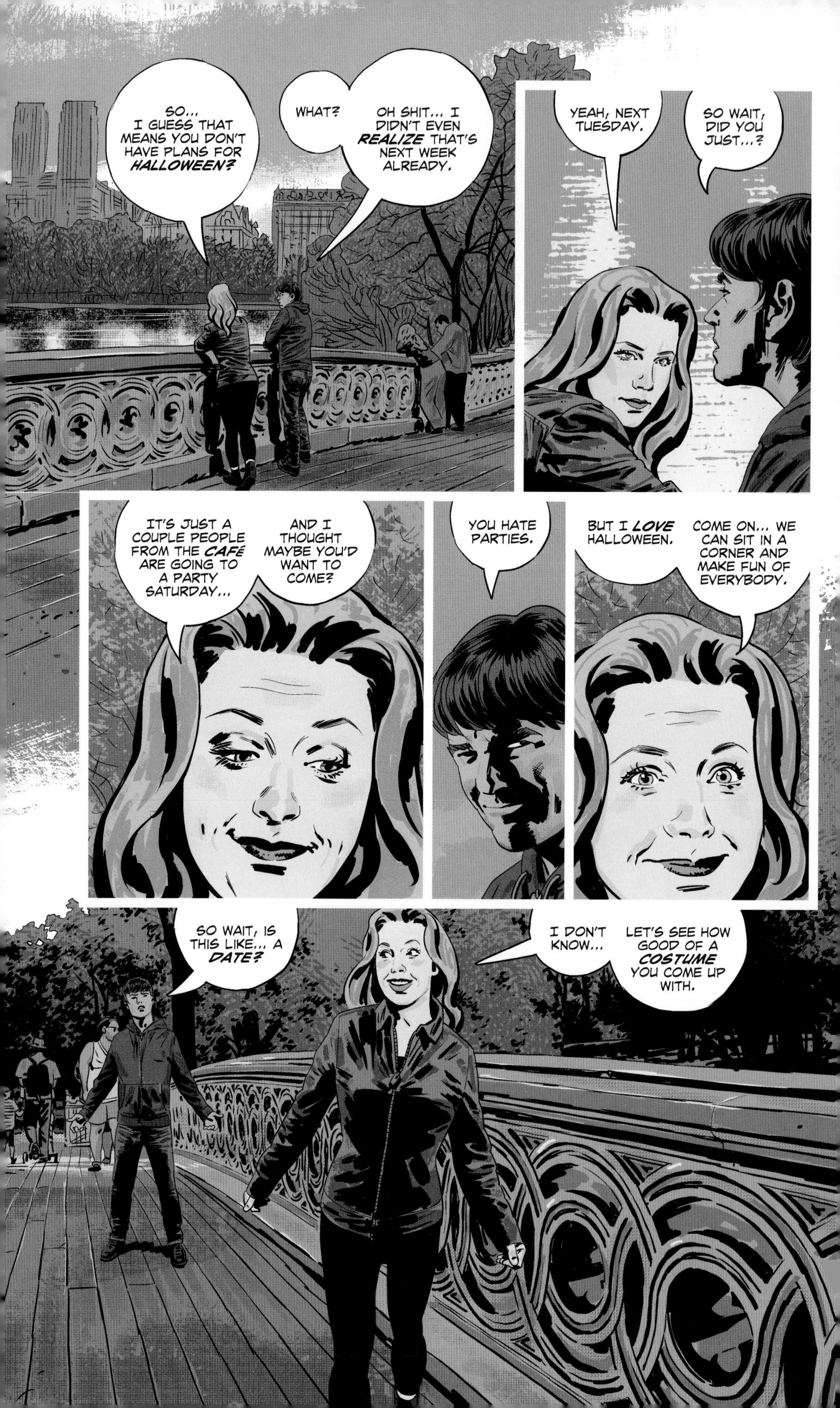

SO... I GUESS THAT MEANS YOU DON'T HAVE PLANS FOR *HALLOWEEN?*
WHAT?
OH SHIT... I DIDN'T EVEN *REALIZE* THAT'S NEXT WEEK ALREADY.
YEAH, NEXT TUESDAY.
SO WAIT, DID YOU JUST...?
IT'S JUST A COUPLE PEOPLE FROM THE *CAFÉ* ARE GOING TO A PARTY SATURDAY...
AND I THOUGHT MAYBE YOU'D WANT TO COME?
YOU HATE PARTIES.
BUT I *LOVE* HALLOWEEN.
COME ON... WE CAN SIT IN A CORNER AND MAKE FUN OF EVERYBODY.
SO WAIT, IS THIS LIKE... A *DATE?*
I DON'T KNOW...
LET'S SEE HOW GOOD OF A *COSTUME* YOU COME UP WITH.

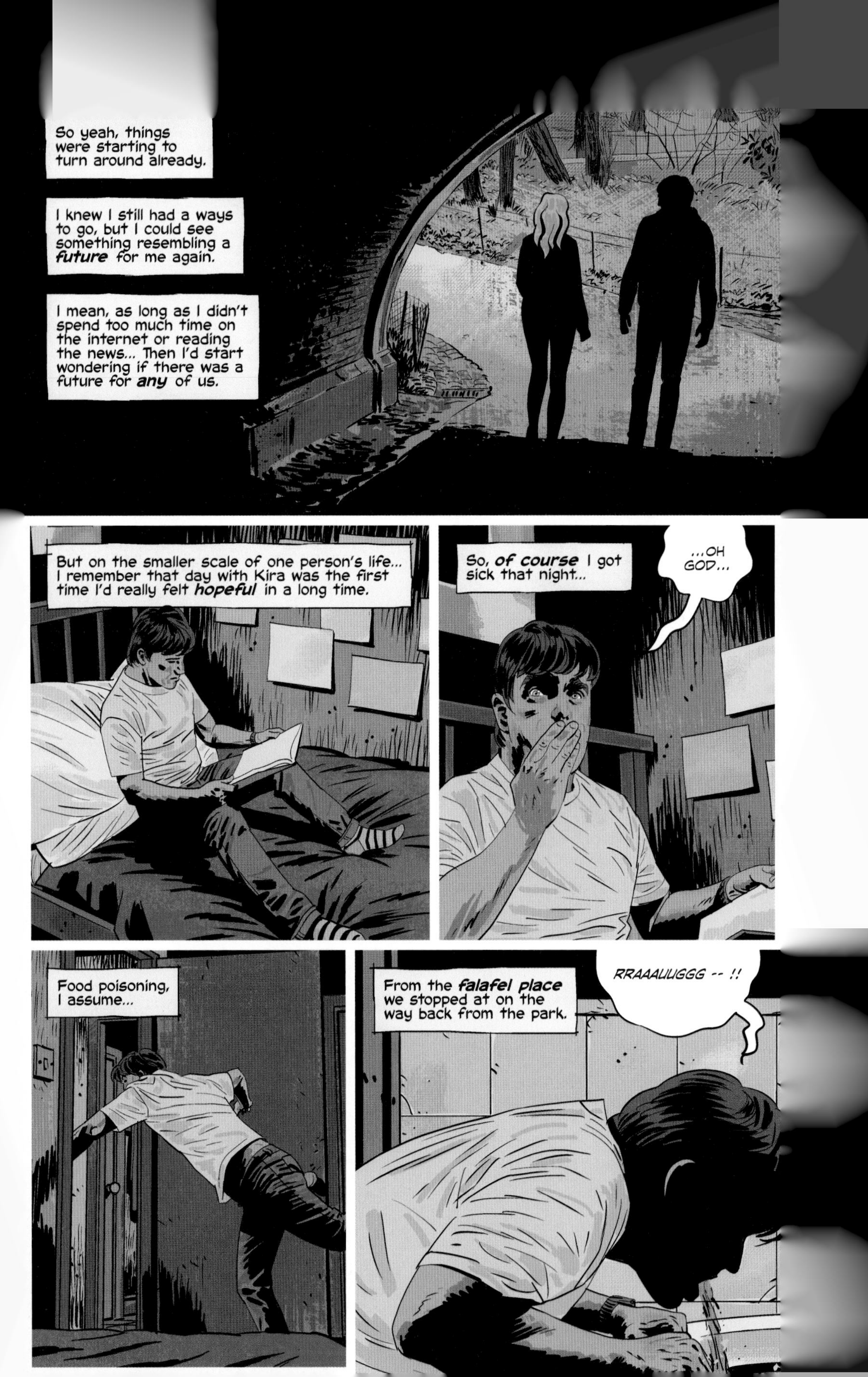

So yeah, things were starting to turn around already.
I knew I still had a ways to go, but I could see something resembling a *future* for me again.
I mean, as long as I didn't spend too much time on the internet or reading the news... Then I'd start wondering if there was a future for *any* of us.
But on the smaller scale of one person's life... I remember that day with Kira was the first time I'd really felt *hopeful* in a long time.
So, *of course* I got sick that night...
...OH GOD...
Food poisoning, I assume...
From the *falafel place* we stopped at on the way back from the park.
RRAAAUUGGG -- !!

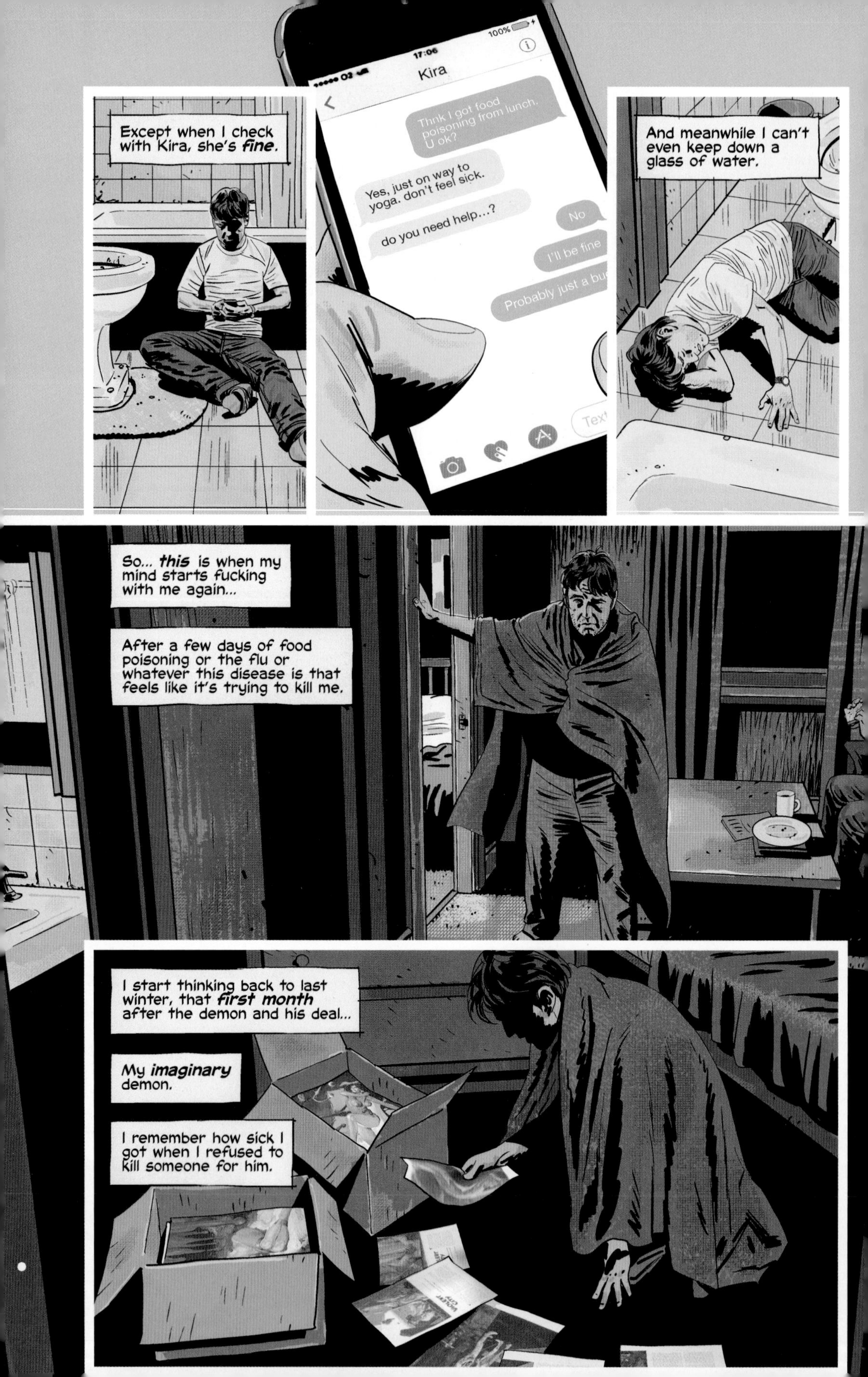
Except when I check with Kira, she's *fine*.
100%
17:06
Kira
Thnk I got food poisoning from lunch. U ok?
Yes, just on way to yoga. don't feel sick.
do you need help...?
No
I'll be fine
Probably just a bu
And meanwhile I can't even keep down a glass of water.
So... *this* is when my mind starts fucking with me again...
After a few days of food poisoning or the flu or whatever this disease is that feels like it's trying to kill me.
I start thinking back to last winter, that *first month* after the demon and his deal...
My *imaginary* demon.
I remember how sick I got when I refused to kill someone for him.

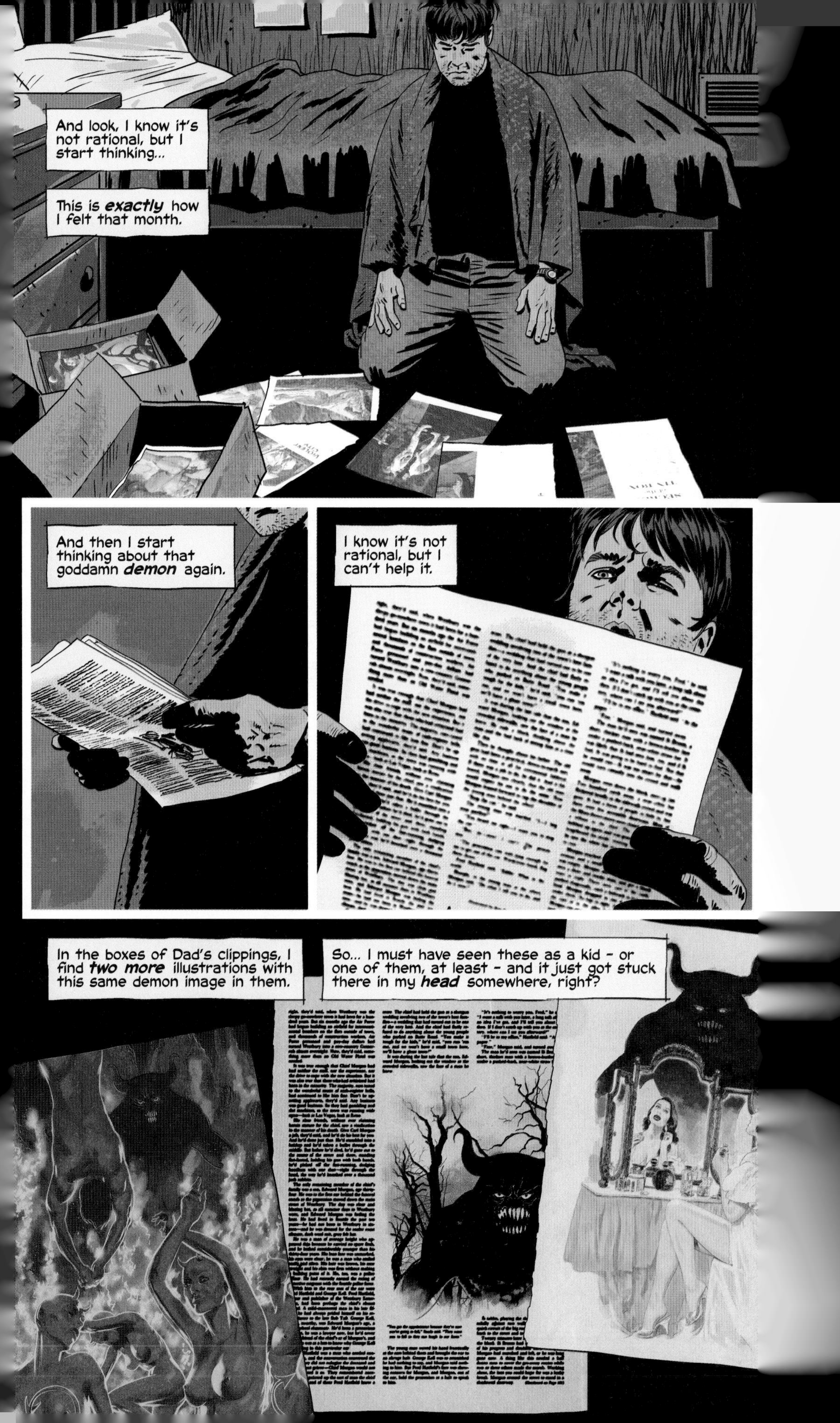

And look, I know it's not rational, but I start thinking...
This is *exactly* how I felt that month.
And then I start thinking about that goddamn *demon* again.
I know it's not rational, but I can't help it.
In the boxes of Dad's clippings, I find *two more* illustrations with this same demon image in them.
So... I must have seen these as a kid - or one of them, at least - and it just got stuck there in my *head* somewhere, right?

Here's the thing, though... You don't ***forget*** stuff that gets stuck in your head as a kid. That's the whole point of the phrase "stuck in your head."

I have ***tons*** of vivid memories from my childhood. Too many, honestly.

And I have at least a dozen of Dad's more salacious paintings burned so deeply into my mental retina that I'll be seeing them in my grave...

So why do I have ***no memory*** of these drawings?

And why did Dad paint this image over and over again?

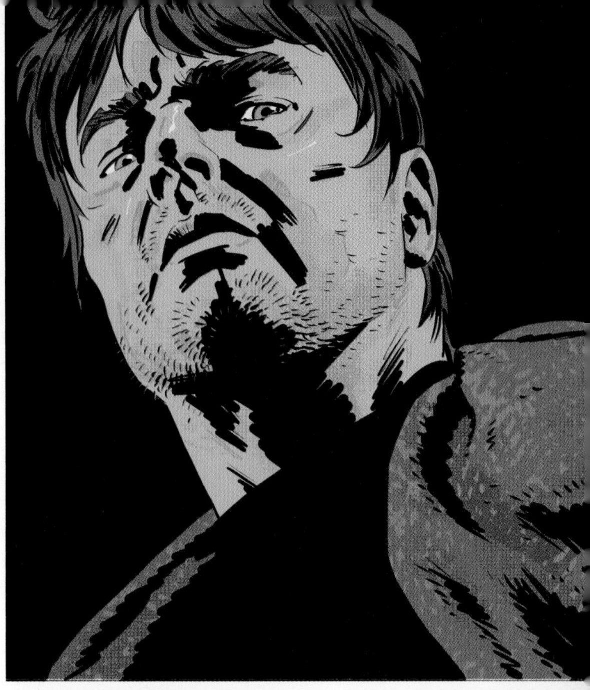

This is how I allowed myself the smallest amount of leeway that maybe I wasn't actually crazy all those months.

Maybe there really was a demon and maybe, just maybe, my dad had seen this ***same*** demon...?

You can see how that might make a certain amount of sense if you hadn't been able to keep down food or water for a few days, right?

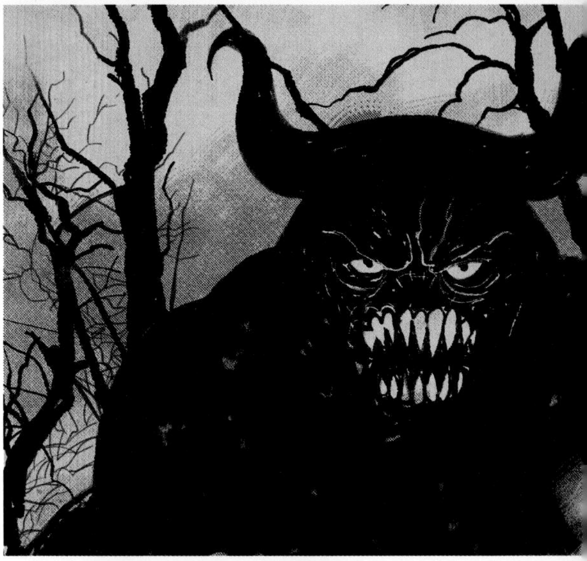

By the time I passed out that night, I'd even figured out why this demon – if it maybe, possibly existed – had left me alone in September.

Because I had killed ***two people*** in August.

I got extra credit for the ***friend*** I accidently shot in the back.

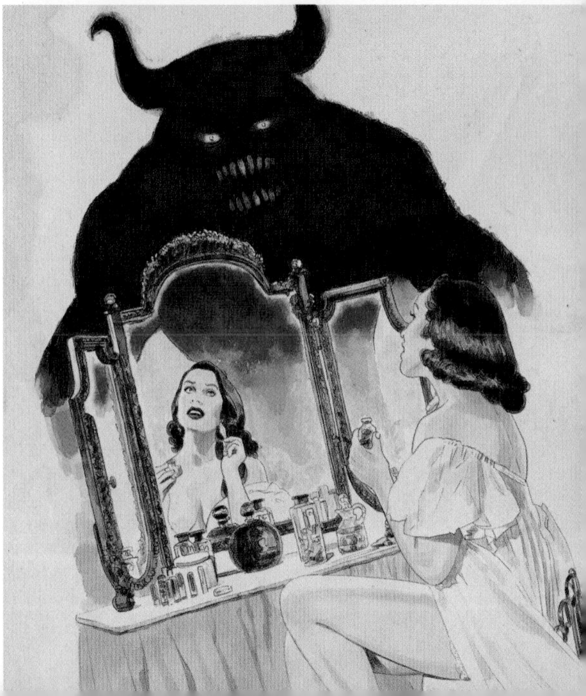

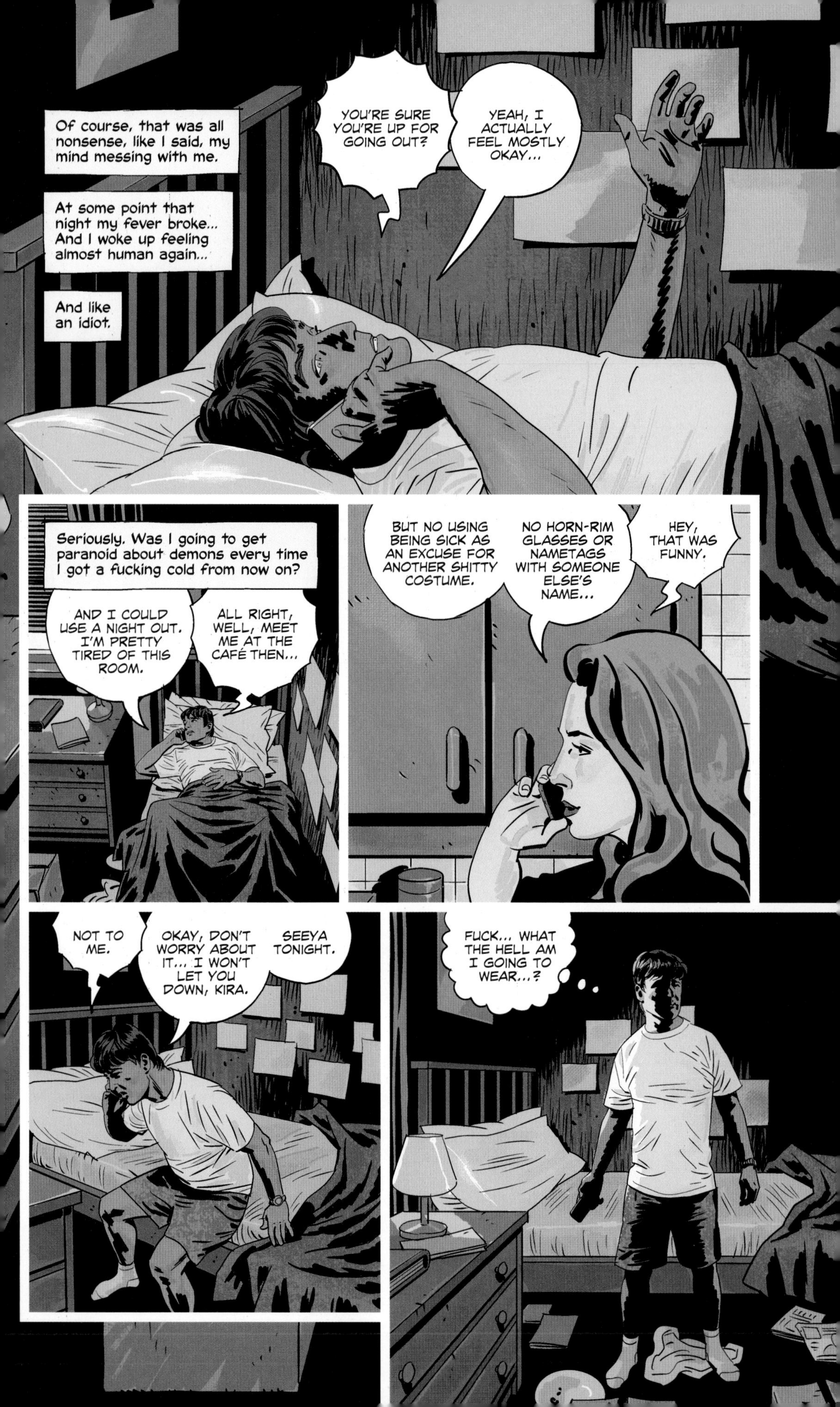

Of course, that was all nonsense, like I said, my mind messing with me.
At some point that night my fever broke... And I woke up feeling almost human again...
And like an idiot.
YOU'RE SURE YOU'RE UP FOR GOING OUT?
YEAH, I ACTUALLY FEEL MOSTLY OKAY...
Seriously. Was I going to get paranoid about demons every time I got a fucking cold from now on?
AND I COULD USE A NIGHT OUT. I'M PRETTY TIRED OF THIS ROOM.
ALL RIGHT, WELL, MEET ME AT THE CAFÉ THEN...
BUT NO USING BEING SICK AS AN EXCUSE FOR ANOTHER SHITTY COSTUME.
NO HORN-RIM GLASSES OR NAMETAGS WITH SOMEONE ELSE'S NAME...
HEY, THAT WAS FUNNY.
NOT TO ME.
OKAY, DON'T WORRY ABOUT IT... I WON'T LET YOU DOWN, KIRA.
SEEYA TONIGHT.
FUCK... WHAT THE HELL AM I GOING TO WEAR...?

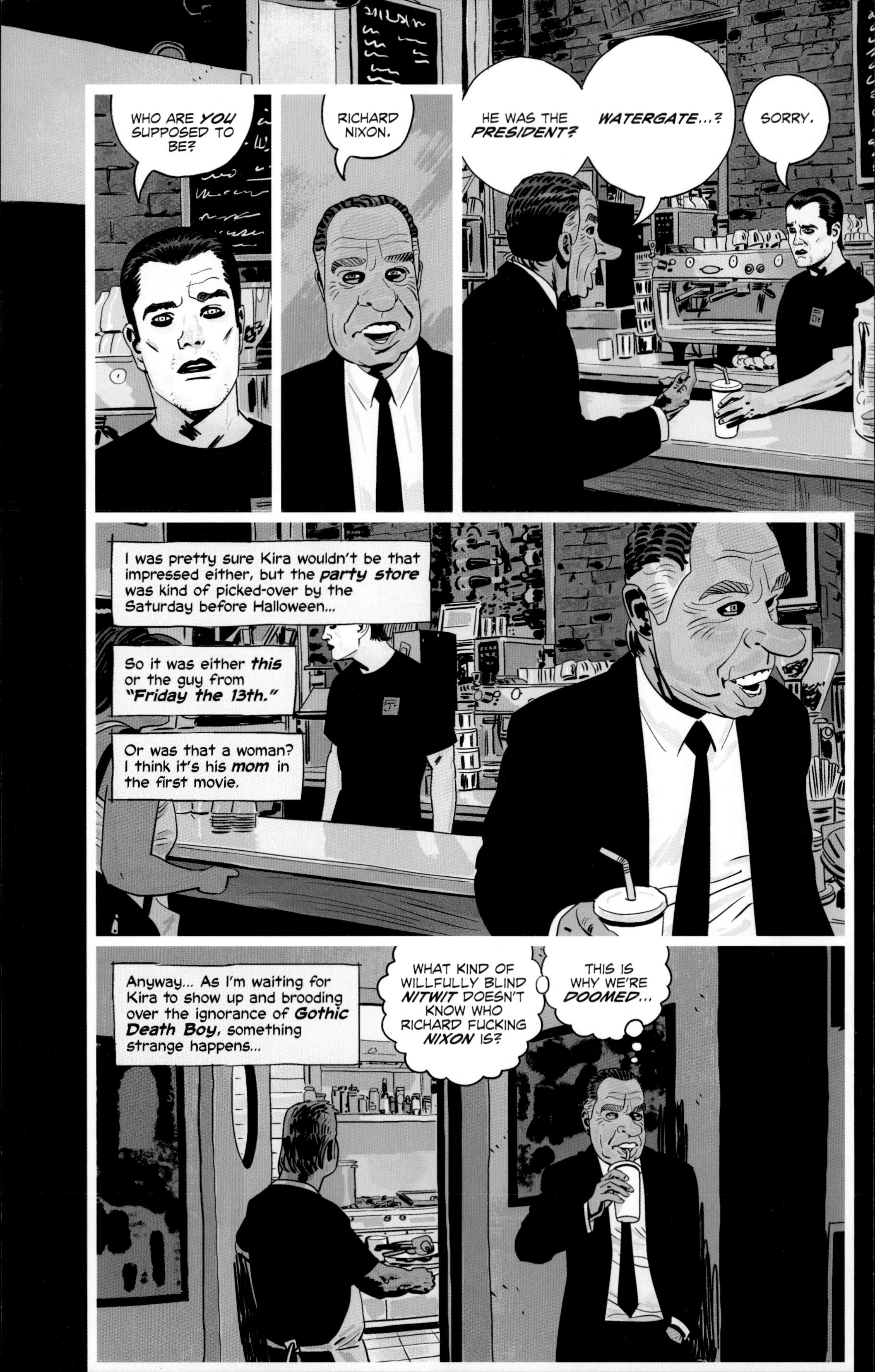

WHO ARE YOU SUPPOSED TO BE?
RICHARD NIXON.
HE WAS THE PRESIDENT?
WATERGATE...?
SORRY.
I was pretty sure Kira wouldn't be that impressed either, but the party store was kind of picked-over by the Saturday before Halloween...
So it was either this or the guy from "Friday the 13th."
Or was that a woman? I think it's his mom in the first movie.
Anyway... As I'm waiting for Kira to show up and brooding over the ignorance of Gothic Death Boy, something strange happens...
WHAT KIND OF WILLFULLY BLIND NITWIT DOESN'T KNOW WHO RICHARD FUCKING NIXON IS?
THIS IS WHY WE'RE DOOMED...

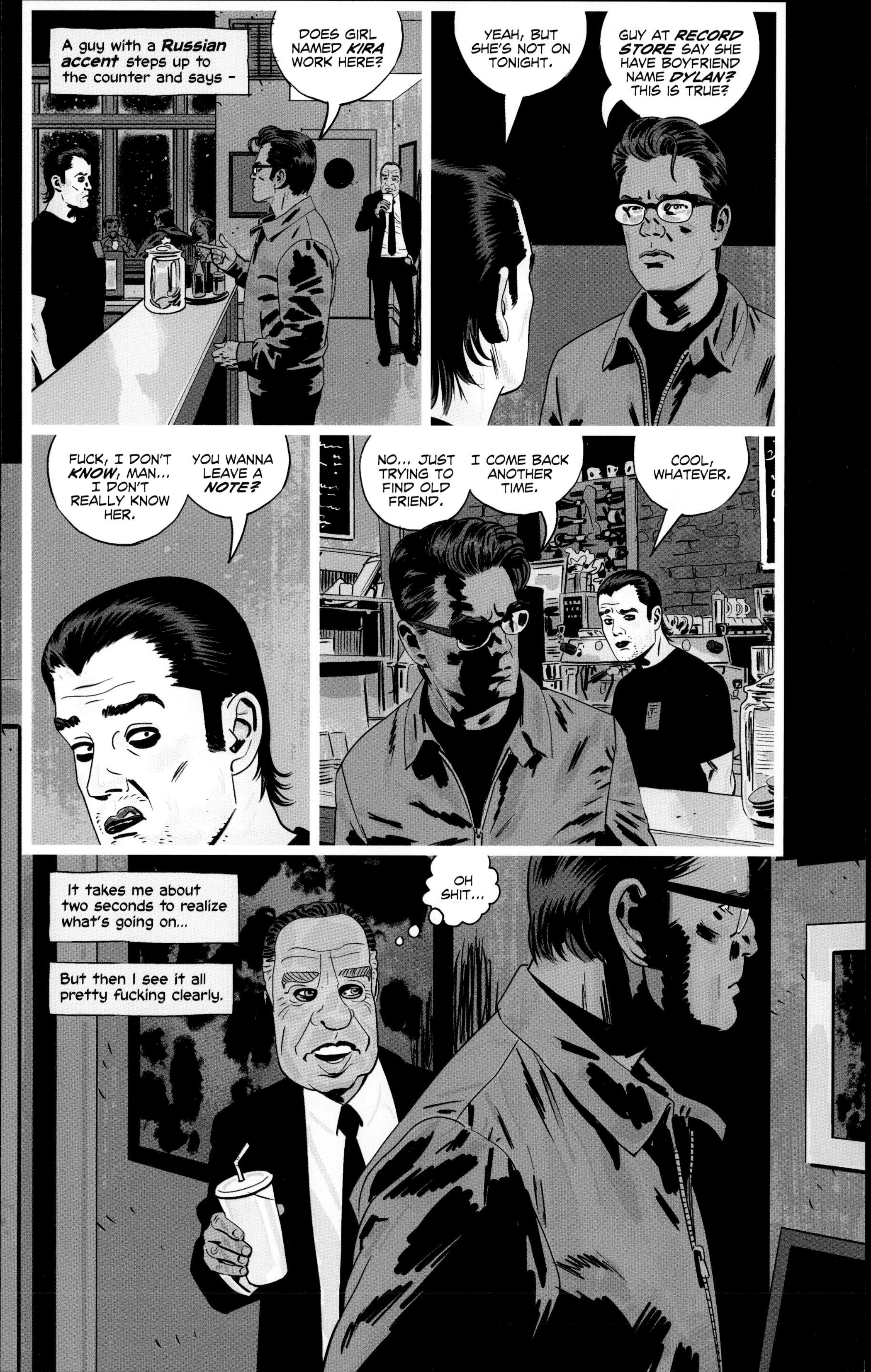

A guy with a **Russian accent** steps up to the counter and says -
DOES GIRL NAMED ***KIRA*** WORK HERE?
YEAH, BUT SHE'S NOT ON TONIGHT.
GUY AT ***RECORD STORE*** SAY SHE HAVE BOYFRIEND NAME ***DYLAN?*** THIS IS TRUE?
FUCK, I DON'T ***KNOW***, MAN... I DON'T REALLY KNOW HER.
YOU WANNA LEAVE A ***NOTE?***
NO... JUST TRYING TO FIND OLD FRIEND.
I COME BACK ANOTHER TIME.
COOL, WHATEVER.
It takes me about two seconds to realize what's going on...
But then I see it all pretty fucking clearly.
OH SHIT...

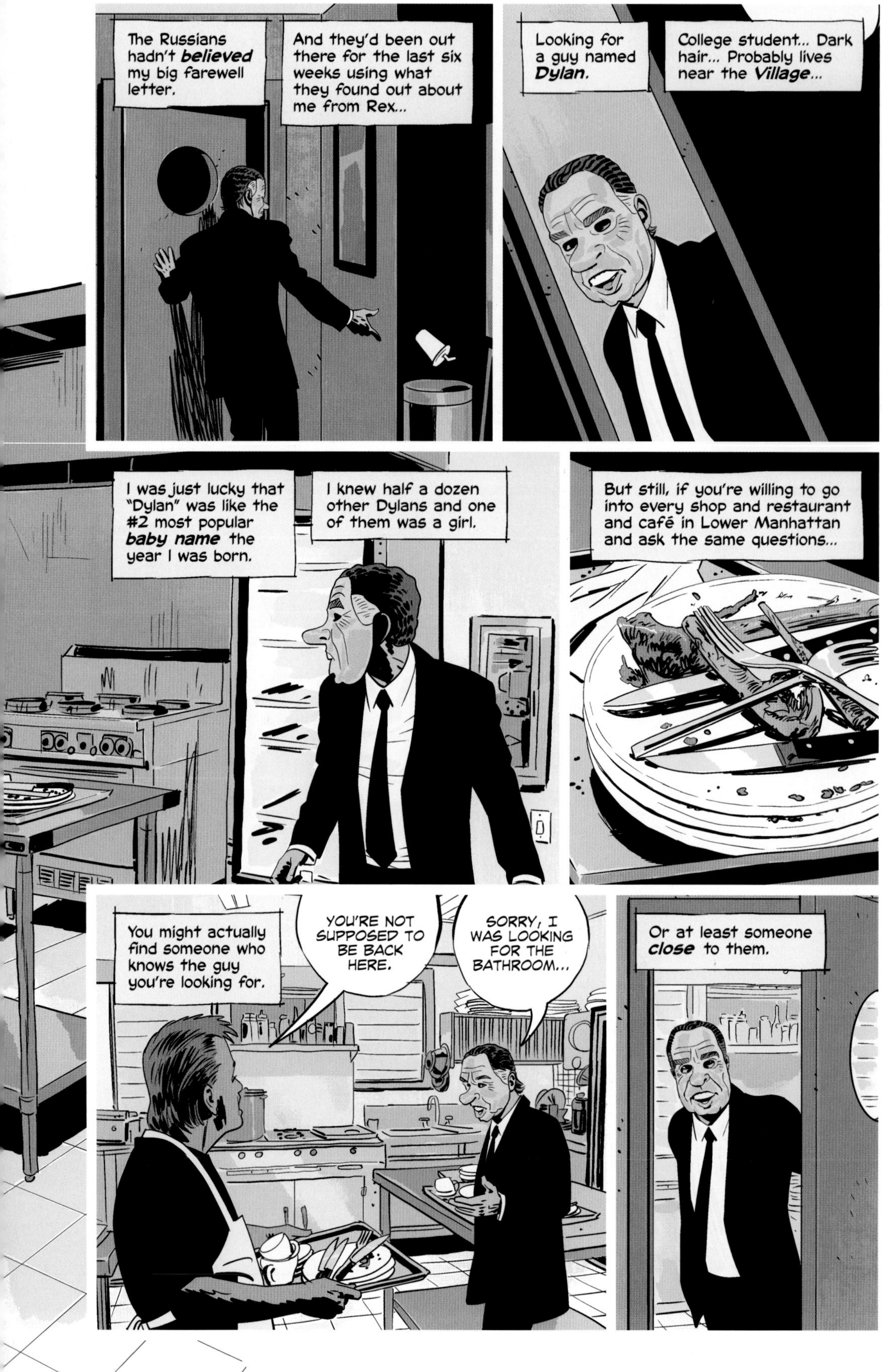

The Russians hadn't *believed* my big farewell letter.
And they'd been out there for the last six weeks using what they found out about me from Rex...
Looking for a guy named *Dylan.*
College student... Dark hair... Probably lives near the *Village*...
I was just lucky that "Dylan" was like the #2 most popular *baby name* the year I was born.
I knew half a dozen other Dylans and one of them was a girl.
But still, if you're willing to go into every shop and restaurant and café in Lower Manhattan and ask the same questions...
You might actually find someone who knows the guy you're looking for.
YOU'RE NOT SUPPOSED TO BE BACK HERE.
SORRY, I WAS LOOKING FOR THE BATHROOM...
Or at least someone *close* to them.

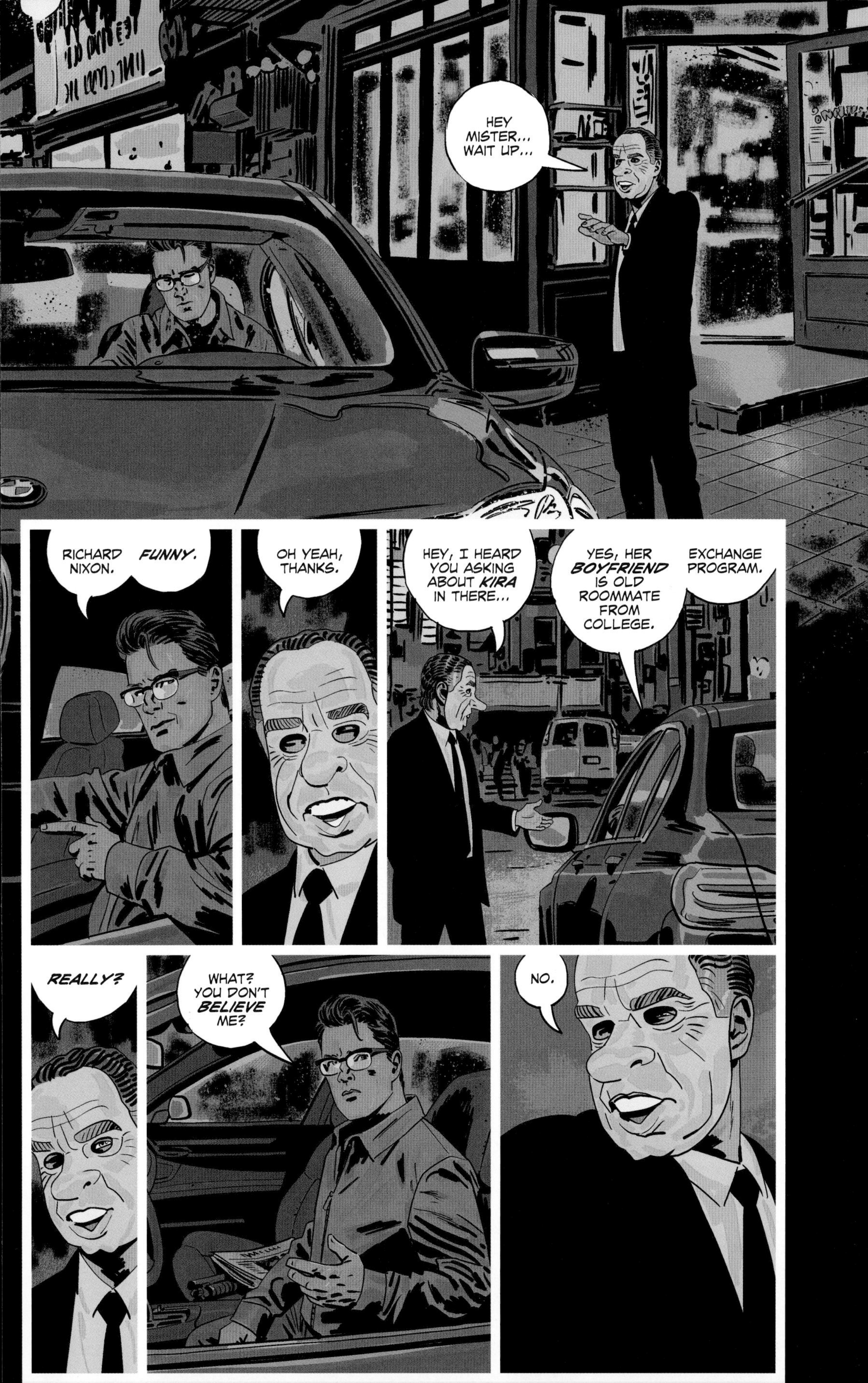
HEY MISTER... WAIT UP...
RICHARD NIXON.
FUNNY.
OH YEAH, THANKS.
HEY, I HEARD YOU ASKING ABOUT KIRA IN THERE...
YES, HER BOYFRIEND IS OLD ROOMMATE FROM COLLEGE.
EXCHANGE PROGRAM.
REALLY?
WHAT? YOU DON'T BELIEVE ME?
NO.

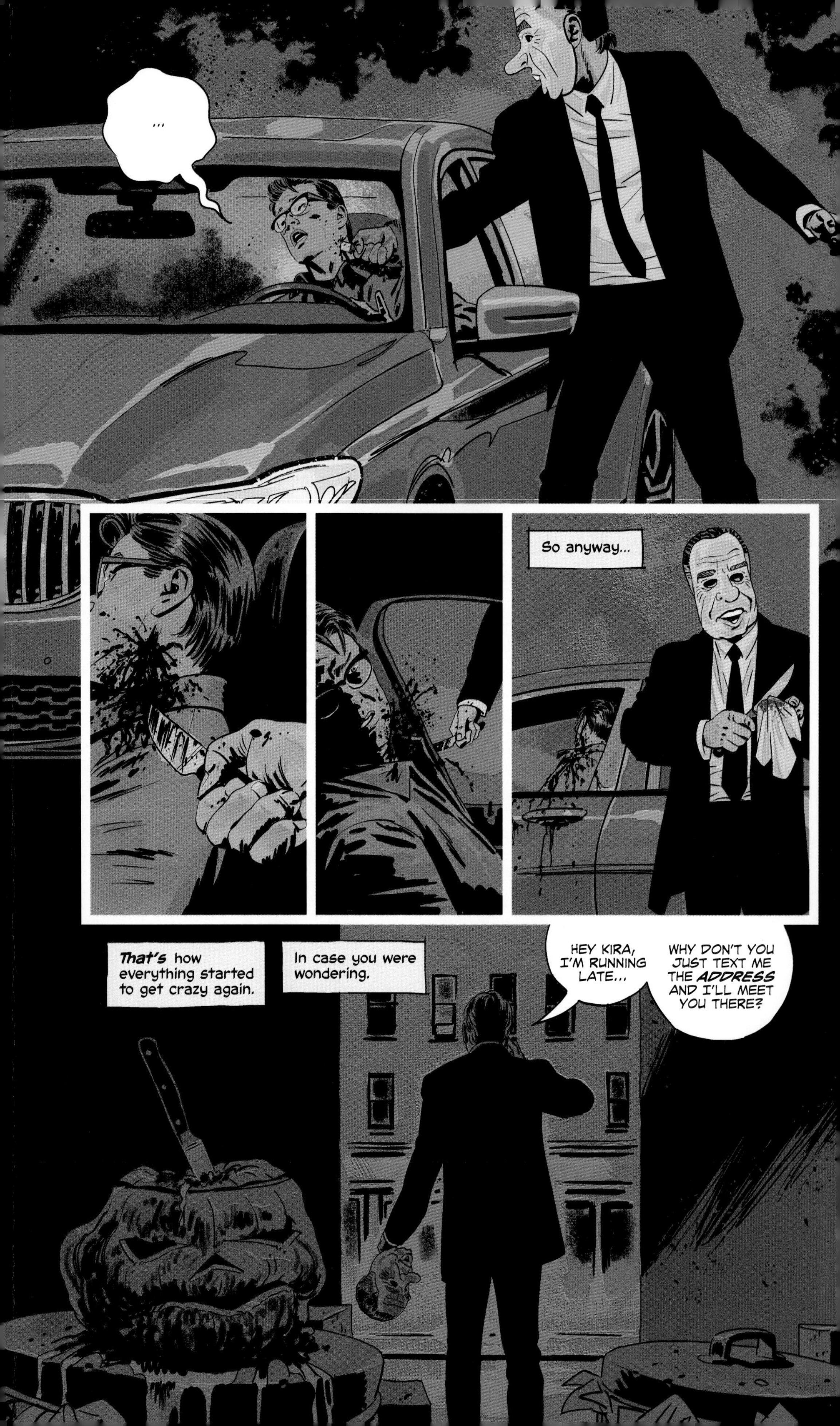
...
So anyway...
That's how everything started to get crazy again.
In case you were wondering.
HEY KIRA, I'M RUNNING LATE...
WHY DON'T YOU JUST TEXT ME THE ***ADDRESS*** AND I'LL MEET YOU THERE?

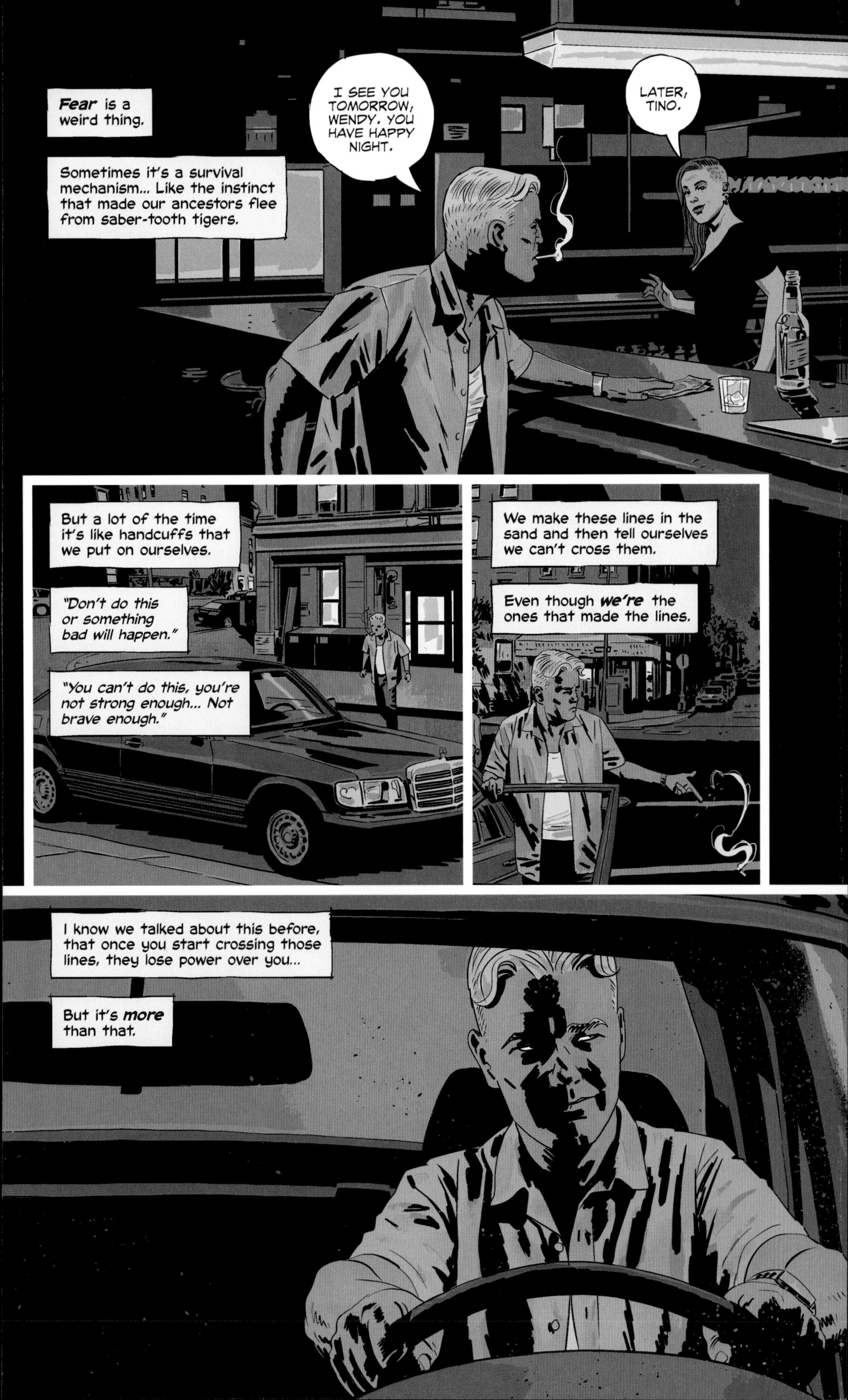
Fear is a weird thing.
Sometimes it's a survival mechanism... Like the instinct that made our ancestors flee from saber-tooth tigers.
I SEE YOU TOMORROW, WENDY. YOU HAVE HAPPY NIGHT.
LATER, TINO.
But a lot of the time it's like handcuffs that we put on ourselves.
"Don't do this or something bad will happen."
"You can't do this, you're not strong enough... Not brave enough."
We make these lines in the sand and then tell ourselves we can't cross them.
Even though we're the ones that made the lines.
I know we talked about this before, that once you start crossing those lines, they lose power over you...
But it's more than that.

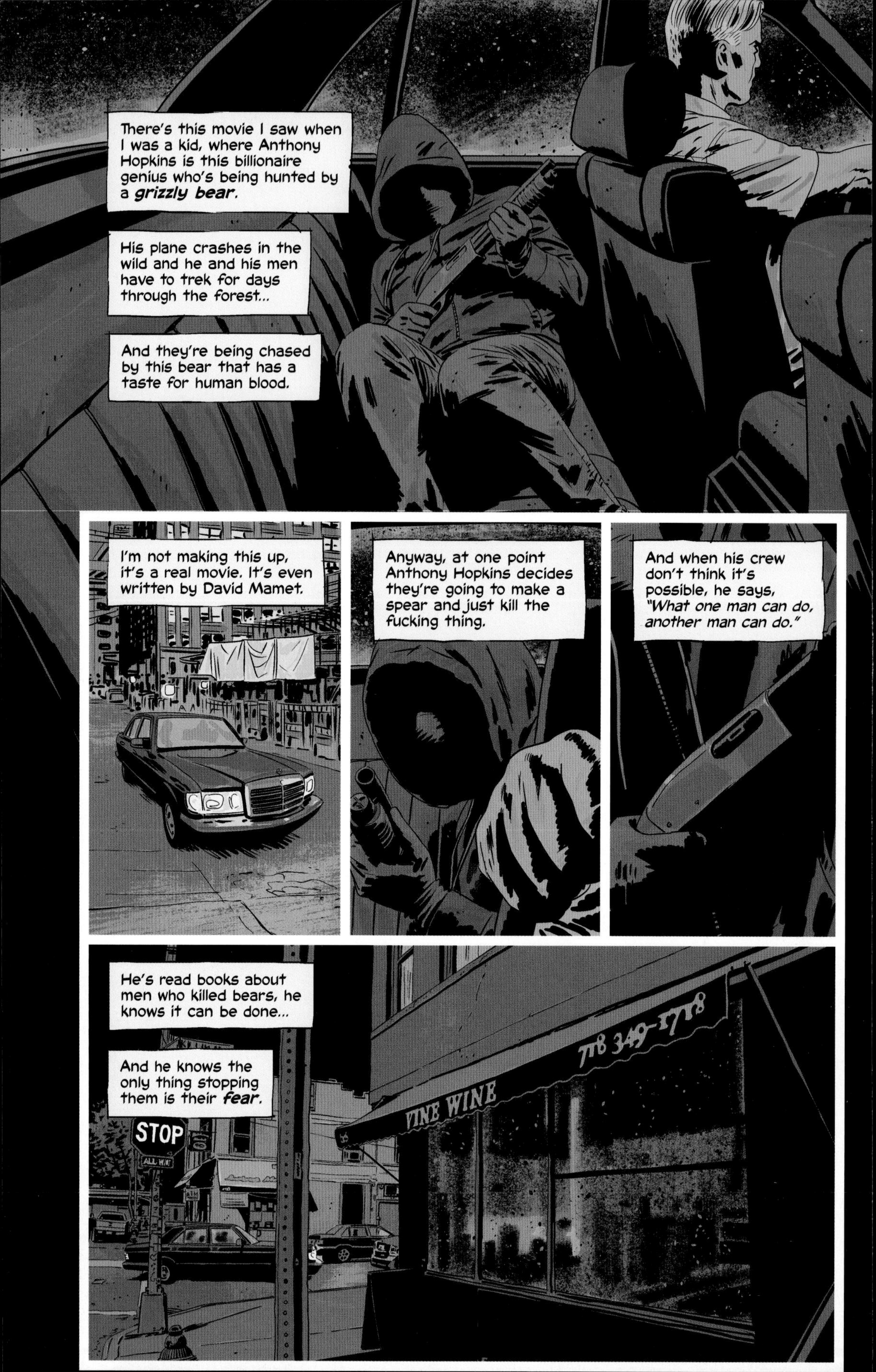
There's this movie I saw when I was a kid, where Anthony Hopkins is this billionaire genius who's being hunted by a *grizzly bear*.
His plane crashes in the wild and he and his men have to trek for days through the forest...
And they're being chased by this bear that has a taste for human blood.
I'm not making this up, it's a real movie. It's even written by David Mamet.
Anyway, at one point Anthony Hopkins decides they're going to make a spear and just kill the fucking thing.
And when his crew don't think it's possible, he says, *"What one man can do, another man can do."*
He's read books about men who killed bears, he knows it can be done...
And he knows the only thing stopping them is their *fear*.
STOP
778 349-1788
VINE WINE

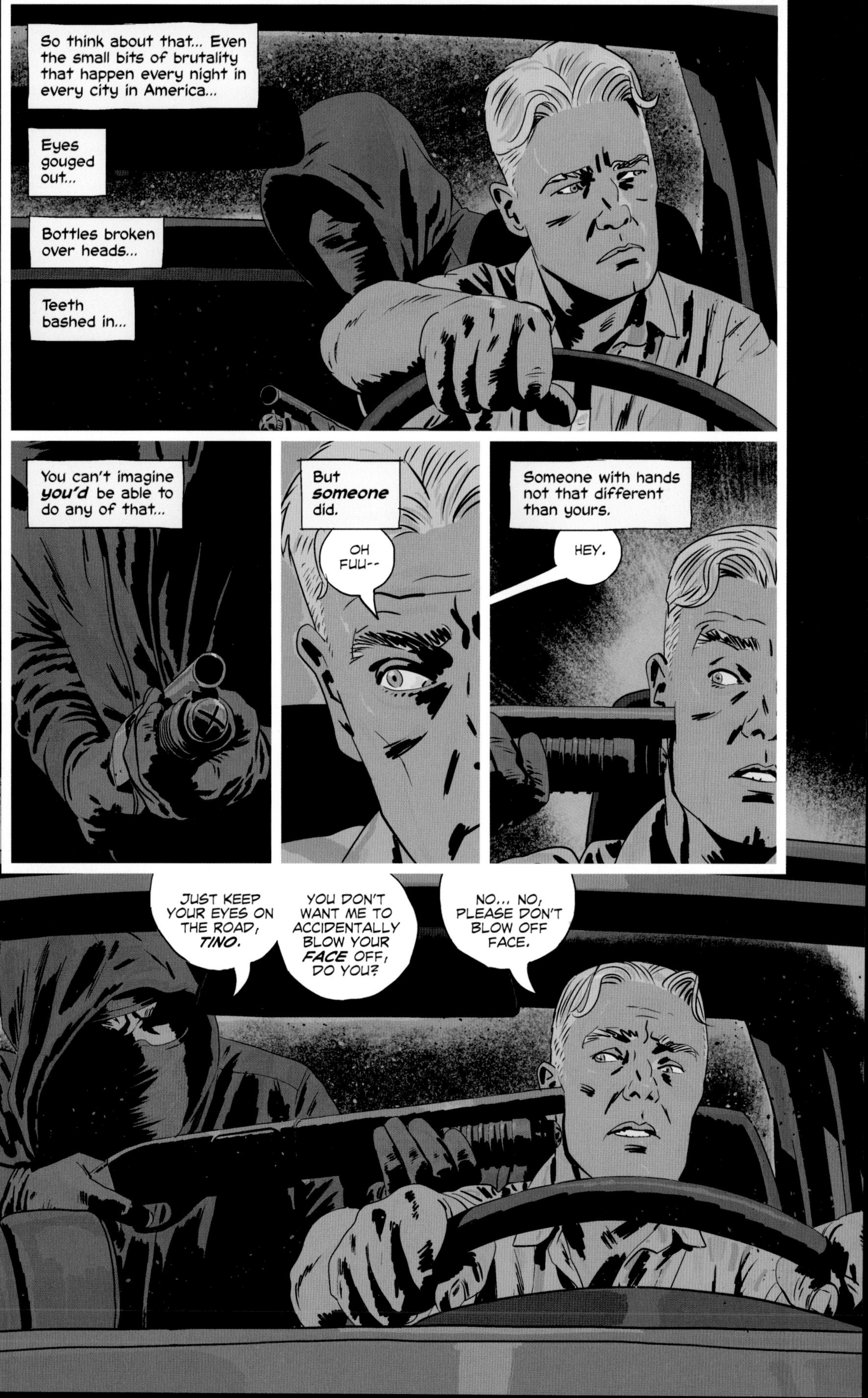
So think about that... Even the small bits of brutality that happen every night in every city in America...
Eyes gouged out...
Bottles broken over heads...
Teeth bashed in...
You can't imagine *you'd* be able to do any of that...
But *someone* did.
OH FUU--
Someone with hands not that different than yours.
HEY.
JUST KEEP YOUR EYES ON THE ROAD, *TINO.*
YOU DON'T WANT ME TO ACCIDENTALLY BLOW YOUR *FACE* OFF, DO YOU?
NO... NO, PLEASE DON'T BLOW OFF FACE.

Okay, wait... Hold on.

Before we get to that part, let me tell you how the ***Halloween party*** went.

And obviously, it went better than expected.

I mean, this is just two friends who might be more than ***"just"*** friends sleeping in their clothes even though they used to have sex...

But it feels like a lot more than that.

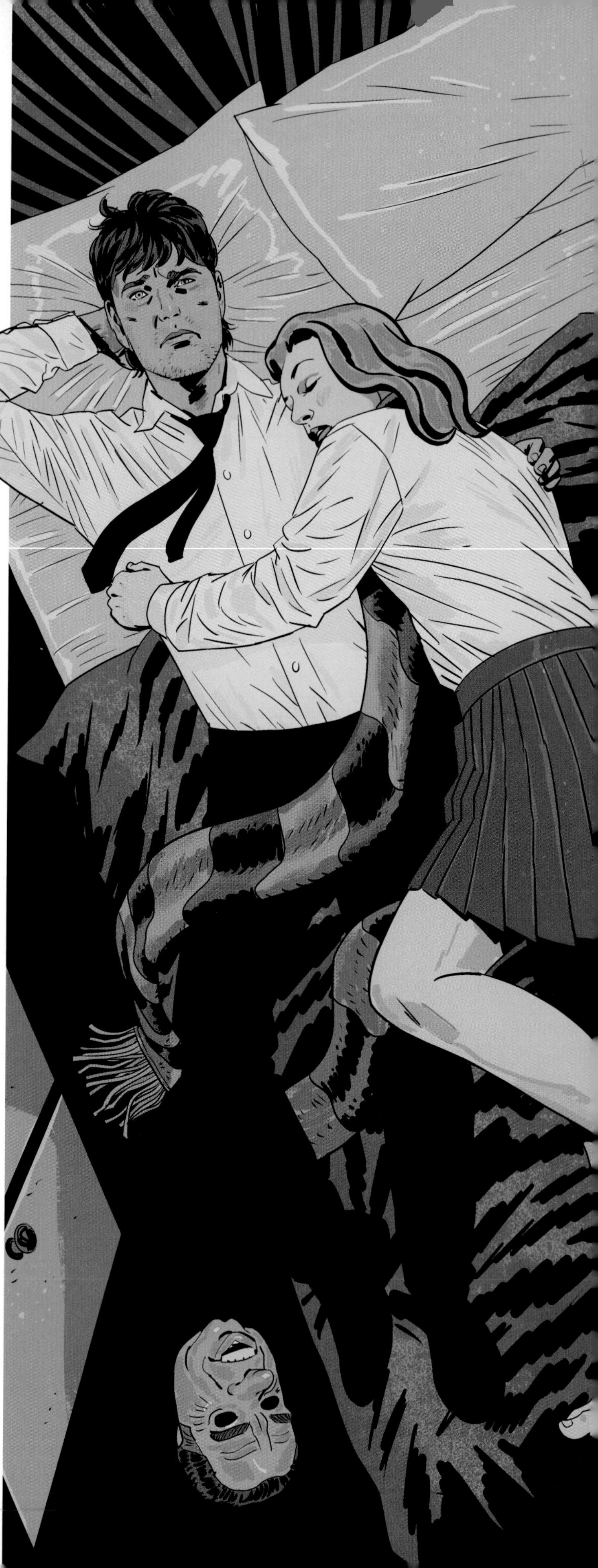

Everything about Kira was like that now... more full of soul, more vibrant...

Ever since I had killed that guy to protect her.

And I know what that sounds like, but I don't mean it like some kind of fucked-up ***"man-pain"*** thing...

Like *"how dare they go after my woman"* or some garbage like that.

I mean, maybe that ***did*** get to me on some ***primal*** level... But I'm not talking about that caveman shit...

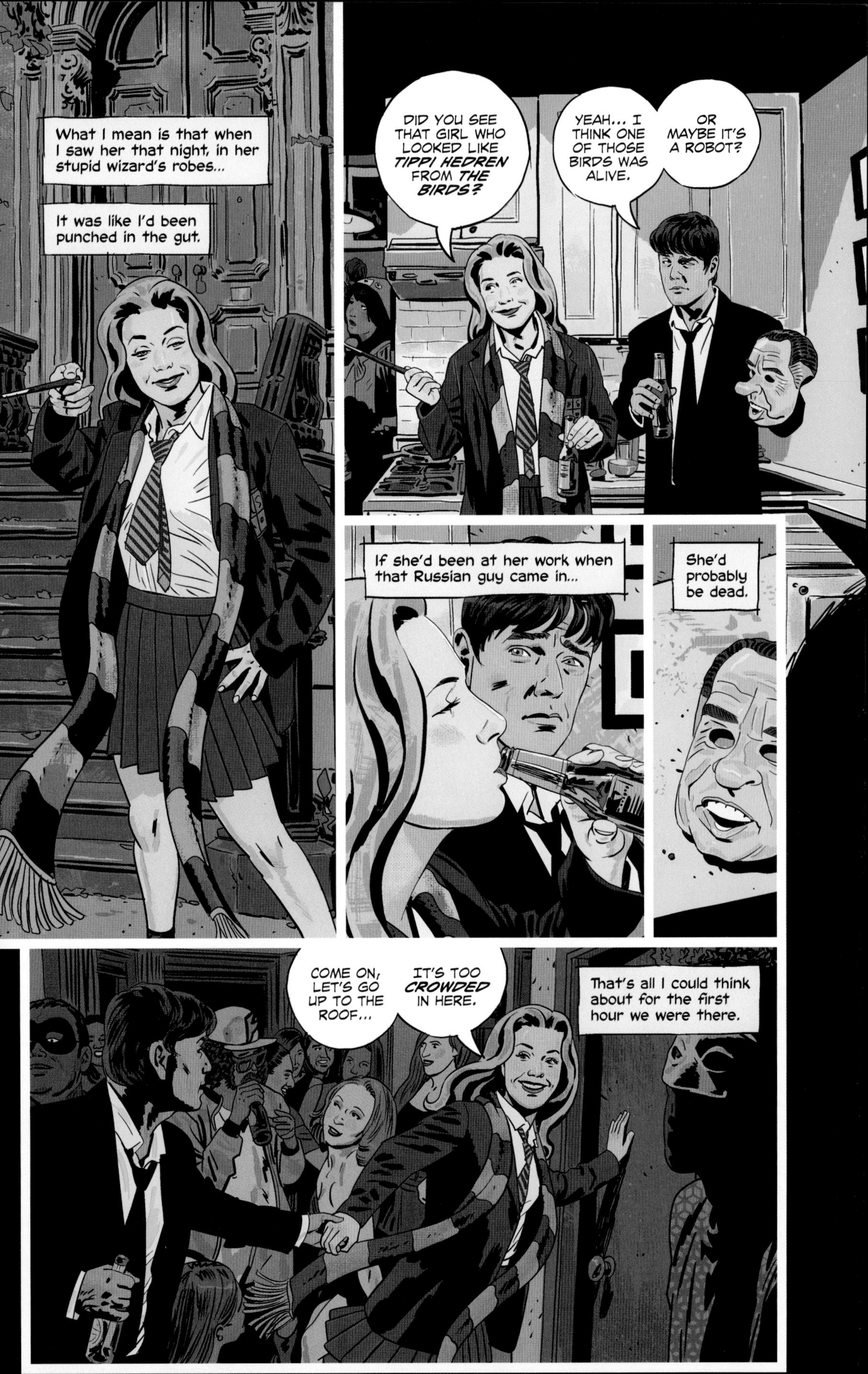
What I mean is that when I saw her that night, in her stupid wizard's robes...
It was like I'd been punched in the gut.
DID YOU SEE THAT GIRL WHO LOOKED LIKE TIPPI HEDREN FROM THE BIRDS?
YEAH... I THINK ONE OF THOSE BIRDS WAS ALIVE.
OR MAYBE IT'S A ROBOT?
If she'd been at her work when that Russian guy came in...
She'd probably be dead.
COME ON, LET'S GO UP TO THE ROOF...
IT'S TOO CROWDED IN HERE.
That's all I could think about for the first hour we were there.

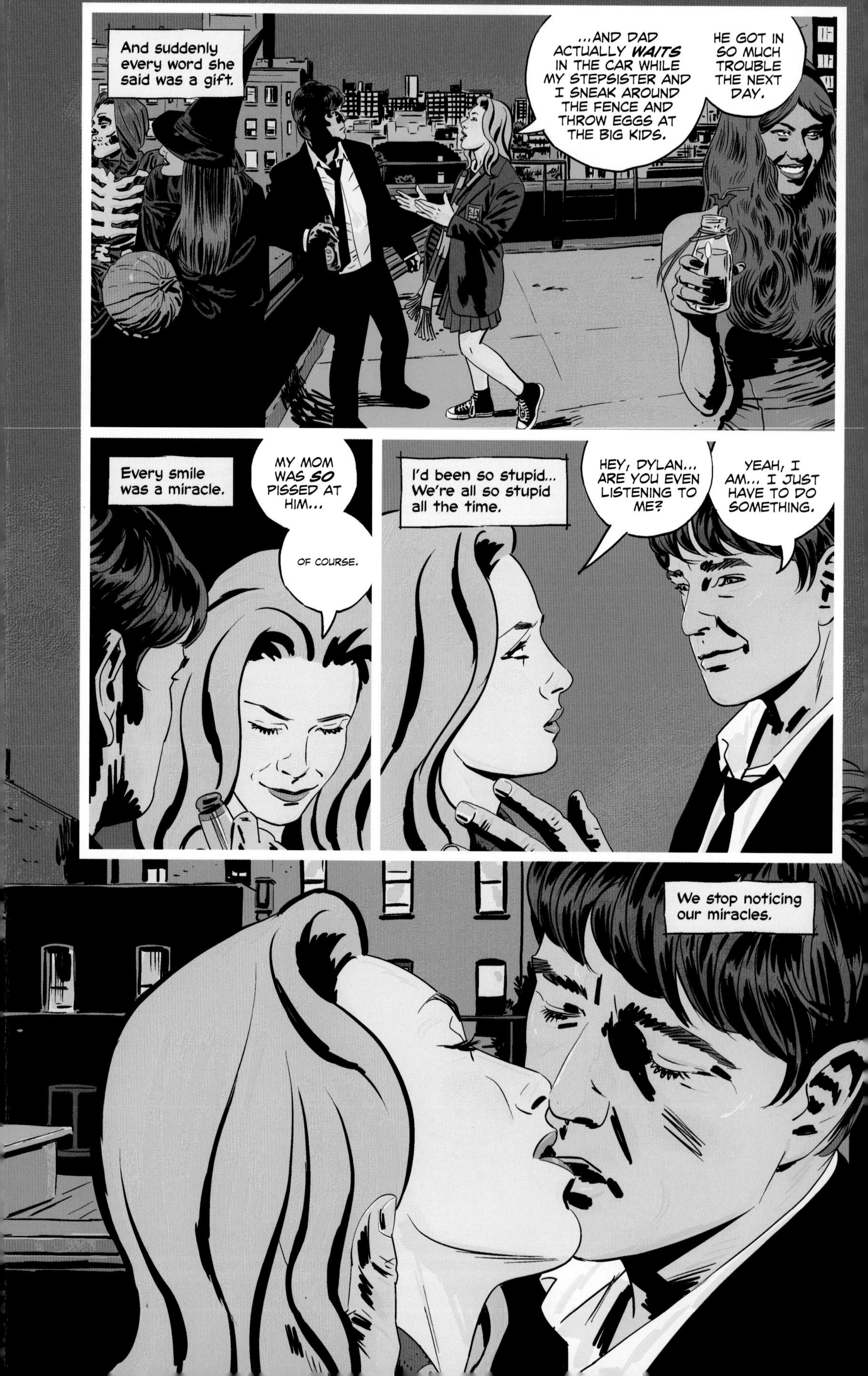
And suddenly every word she said was a gift.
...AND DAD ACTUALLY WAITS IN THE CAR WHILE MY STEPSISTER AND I SNEAK AROUND THE FENCE AND THROW EGGS AT THE BIG KIDS.
HE GOT IN SO MUCH TROUBLE THE NEXT DAY.
Every smile was a miracle.
MY MOM WAS SO PISSED AT HIM...
OF COURSE.
I'd been so stupid... We're all so stupid all the time.
HEY, DYLAN... ARE YOU EVEN LISTENING TO ME?
YEAH, I AM... I JUST HAVE TO DO SOMETHING.
We stop noticing our miracles.

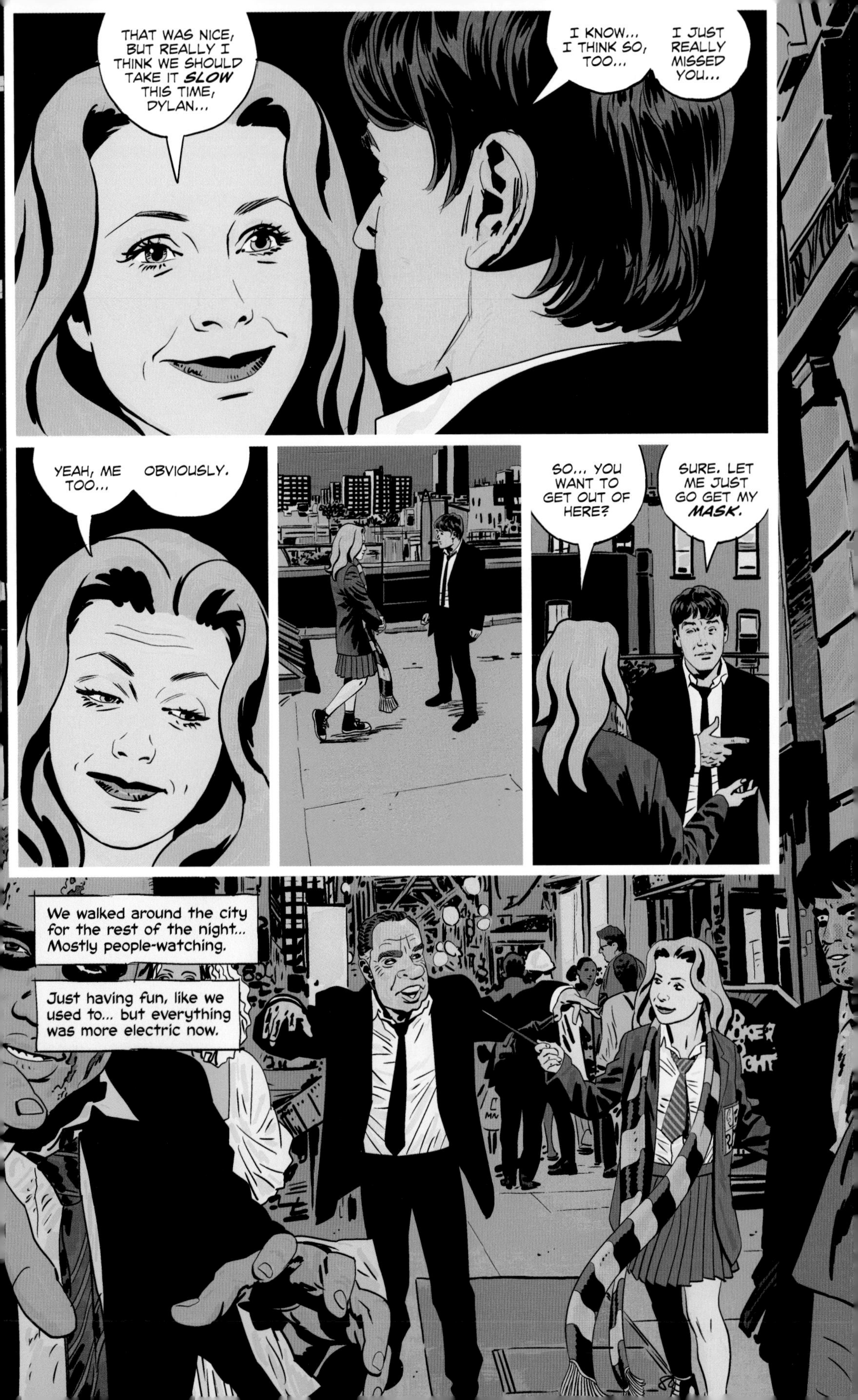
THAT WAS NICE, BUT REALLY I THINK WE SHOULD TAKE IT SLOW THIS TIME, DYLAN...
I KNOW... I THINK SO, TOO...
I JUST REALLY MISSED YOU...
YEAH, ME TOO...
OBVIOUSLY.
SO... YOU WANT TO GET OUT OF HERE?
SURE. LET ME JUST GO GET MY MASK.
We walked around the city for the rest of the night... Mostly people-watching.
Just having fun, like we used to... but everything was more electric now.

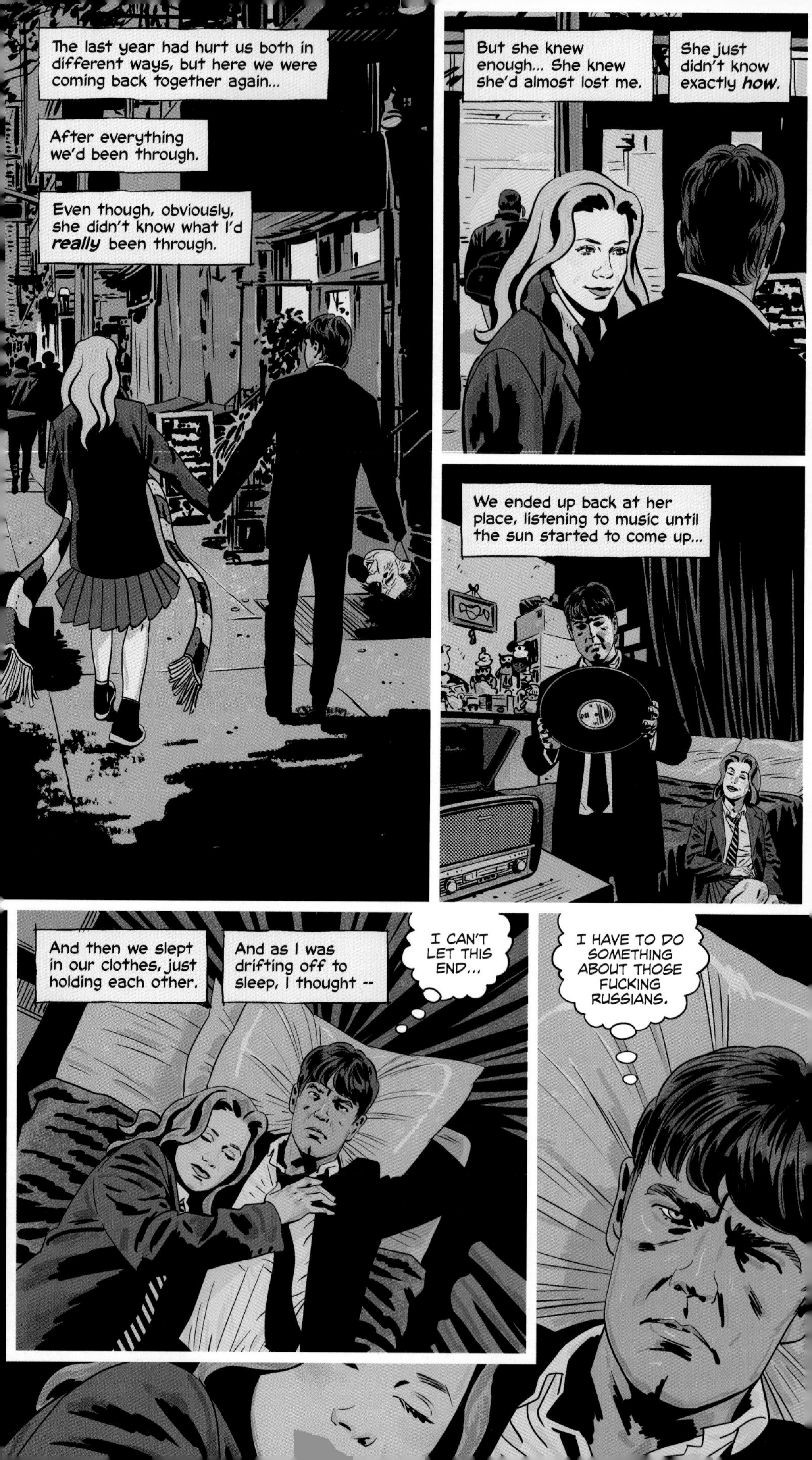
The last year had hurt us both in different ways, but here we were coming back together again...
After everything we'd been through.
Even though, obviously, she didn't know what I'd ***really*** been through.
But she knew enough... She knew she'd almost lost me.
She just didn't know exactly ***how***.
We ended up back at her place, listening to music until the sun started to come up...
And then we slept in our clothes, just holding each other.
And as I was drifting off to sleep, I thought --
I CAN'T LET THIS END...
I HAVE TO DO SOMETHING ABOUT THOSE FUCKING RUSSIANS.

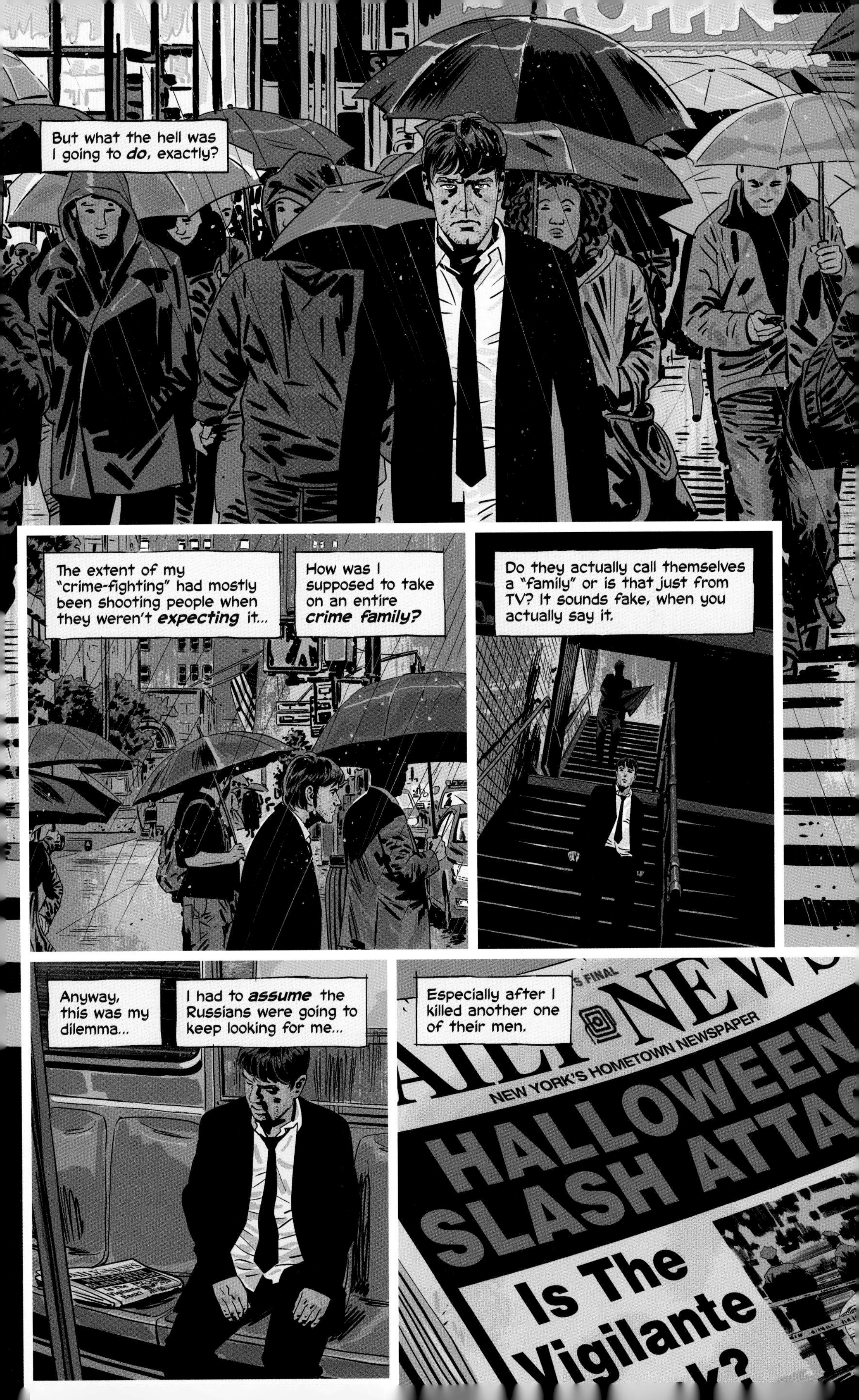
But what the hell was I going to *do*, exactly?
The extent of my "crime-fighting" had mostly been shooting people when they weren't *expecting* it...
How was I supposed to take on an entire *crime family?*
Do they actually call themselves a "family" or is that just from TV? It sounds fake, when you actually say it.
Anyway, this was my dilemma...
I had to *assume* the Russians were going to keep looking for me...
Especially after I killed another one of their men.
NEW YORK'S HOMETOWN NEWSPAPER
HALLOWEEN
SLASH ATTA
Is The
Vigilante

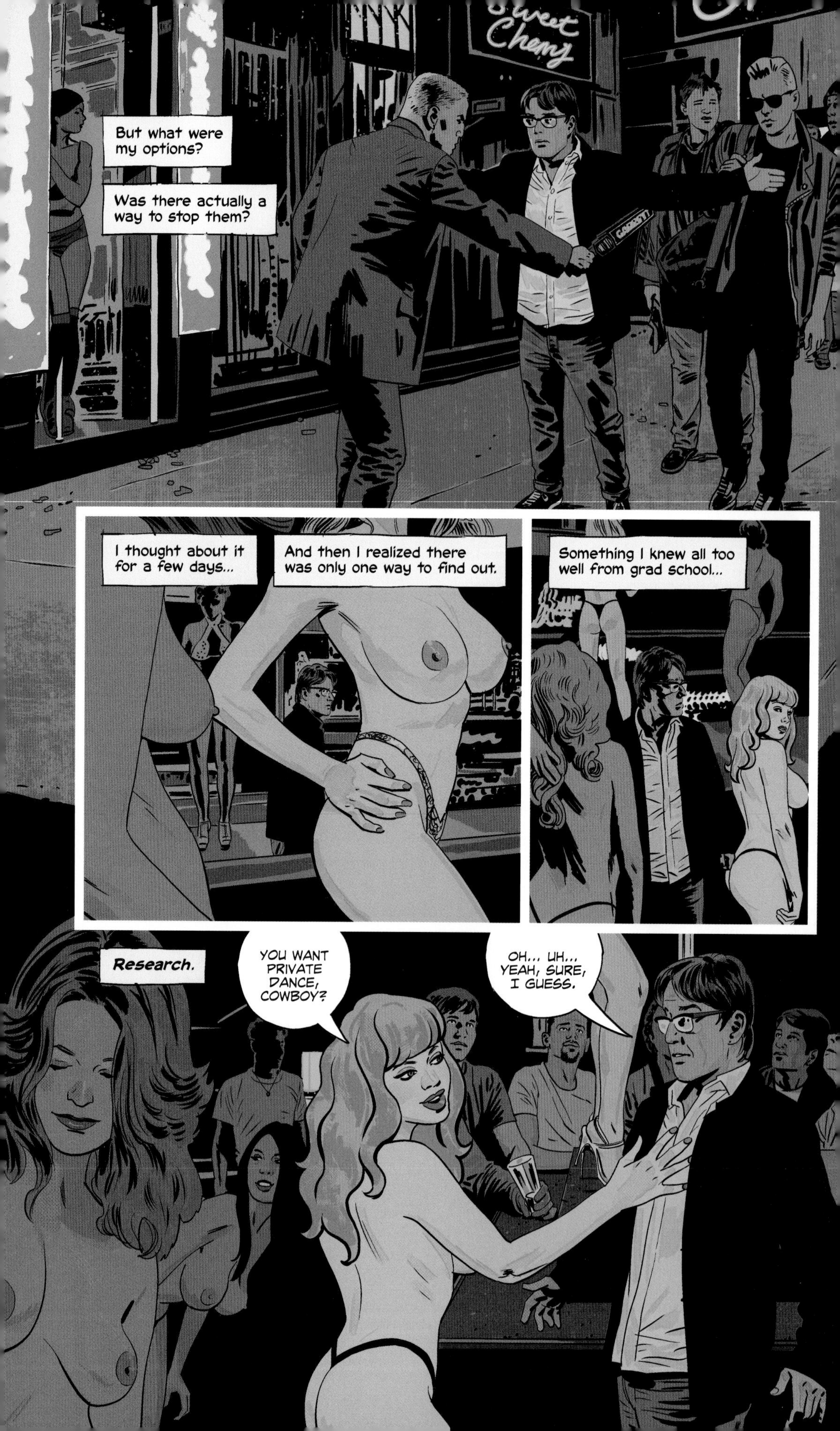
But what were my options?
Was there actually a way to stop them?
I thought about it for a few days...
And then I realized there was only one way to find out.
Something I knew all too well from grad school...
Research.
YOU WANT PRIVATE DANCE, COWBOY?
OH... UH... YEAH, SURE, I GUESS.

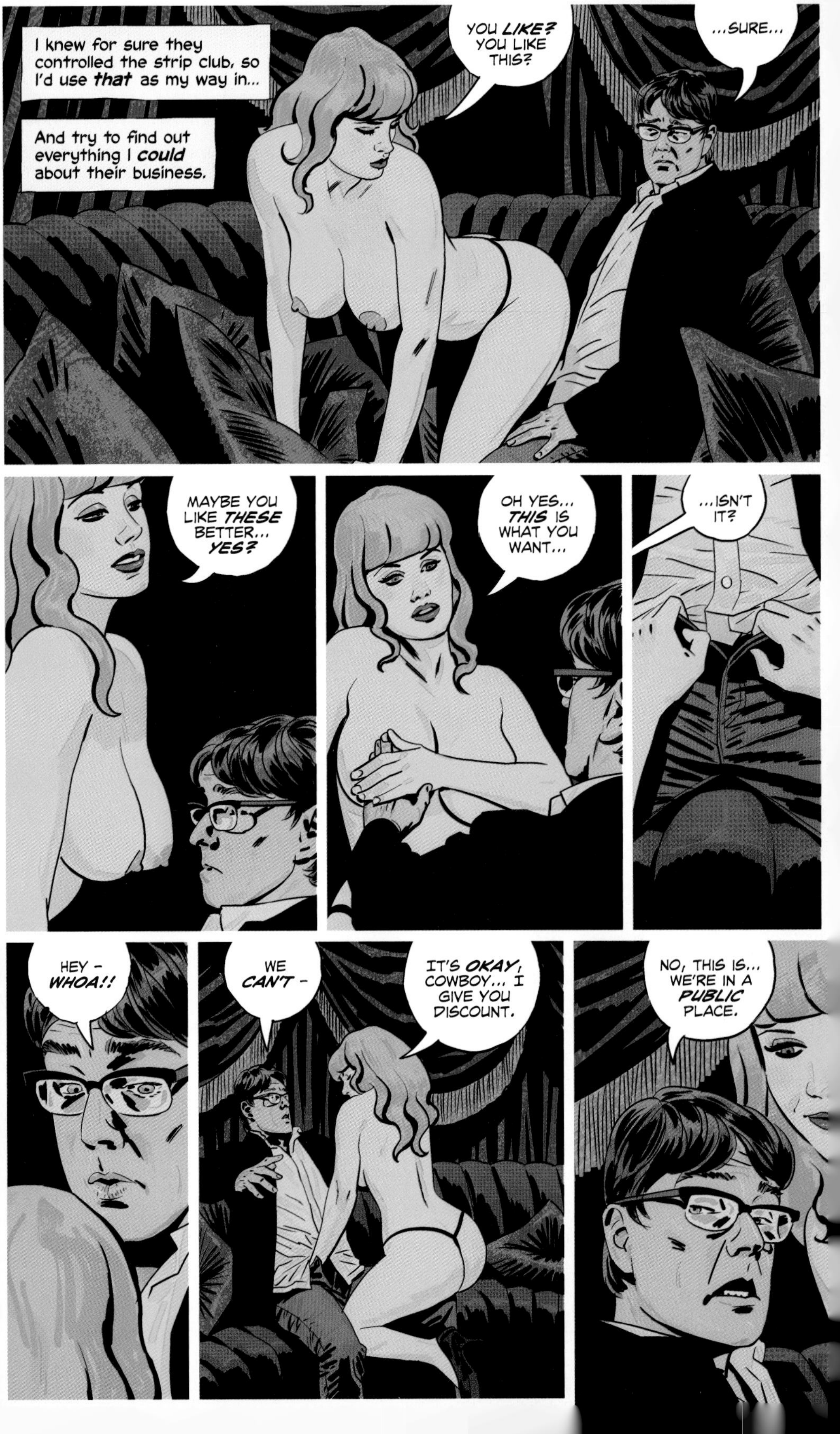
I knew for sure they controlled the strip club, so I'd use *that* as my way in...
And try to find out everything I *could* about their business.
YOU *LIKE?* YOU LIKE THIS?
...SURE...
MAYBE YOU LIKE *THESE* BETTER... *YES?*
OH YES... *THIS* IS WHAT YOU WANT...
...ISN'T IT?
HEY - *WHOA!!*
WE *CAN'T* -
IT'S *OKAY,* COWBOY... I GIVE YOU DISCOUNT.
NO, THIS IS... WE'RE IN A *PUBLIC* PLACE.

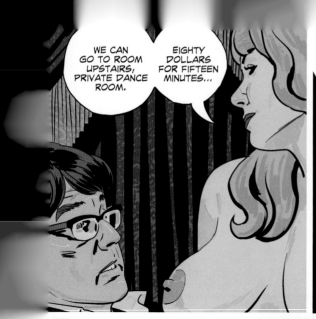

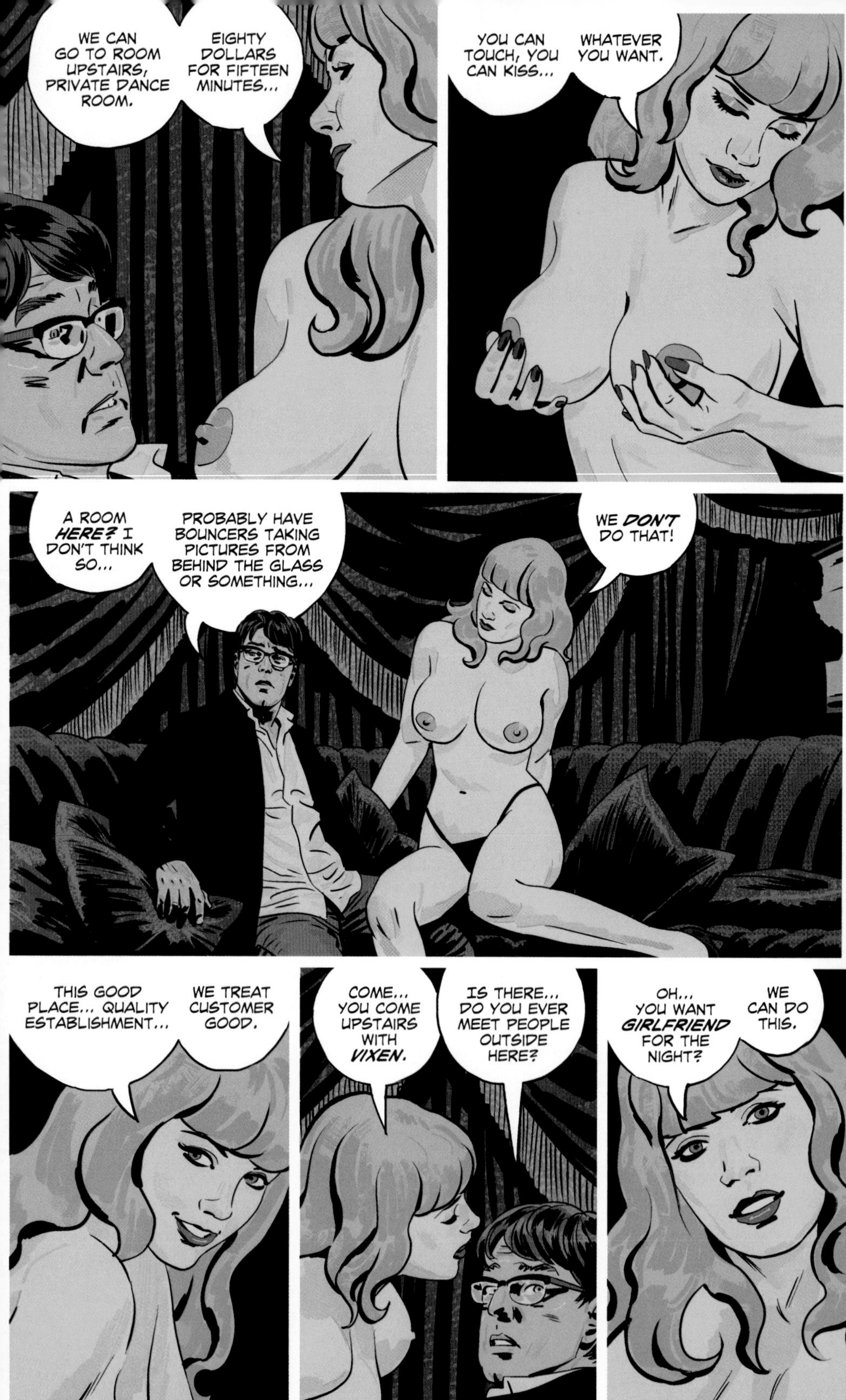
WE CAN GO TO ROOM UPSTAIRS, PRIVATE DANCE ROOM.
EIGHTY DOLLARS FOR FIFTEEN MINUTES...
YOU CAN TOUCH, YOU CAN KISS...
WHATEVER YOU WANT.
A ROOM *HERE?* I DON'T THINK SO...
PROBABLY HAVE BOUNCERS TAKING PICTURES FROM BEHIND THE GLASS OR SOMETHING...
WE *DON'T* DO THAT!
THIS GOOD PLACE... QUALITY ESTABLISHMENT...
WE TREAT CUSTOMER GOOD.
COME... YOU COME UPSTAIRS WITH *VIXEN.*
IS THERE... DO YOU EVER MEET PEOPLE OUTSIDE HERE?
OH... YOU WANT *GIRLFRIEND* FOR THE NIGHT?
WE CAN DO THIS.

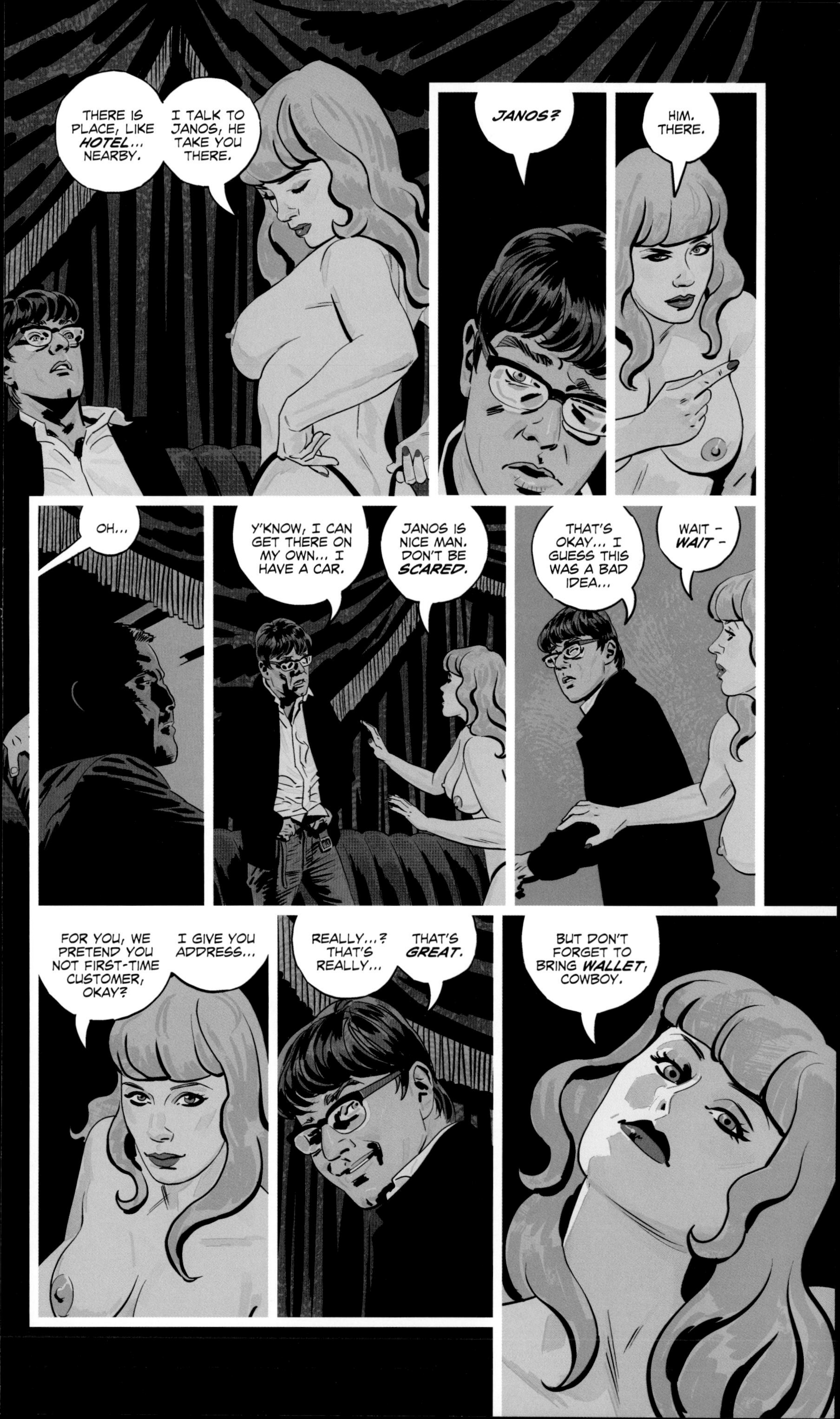
THERE IS PLACE, LIKE HOTEL... NEARBY.
I TALK TO JANOS, HE TAKE YOU THERE.
JANOS?
HIM. THERE.
OH...
Y'KNOW, I CAN GET THERE ON MY OWN... I HAVE A CAR.
JANOS IS NICE MAN. DON'T BE SCARED.
THAT'S OKAY... I GUESS THIS WAS A BAD IDEA...
WAIT - WAIT -
FOR YOU, WE PRETEND YOU NOT FIRST-TIME CUSTOMER, OKAY?
I GIVE YOU ADDRESS...
REALLY...? THAT'S REALLY...
THAT'S GREAT.
BUT DON'T FORGET TO BRING WALLET, COWBOY.

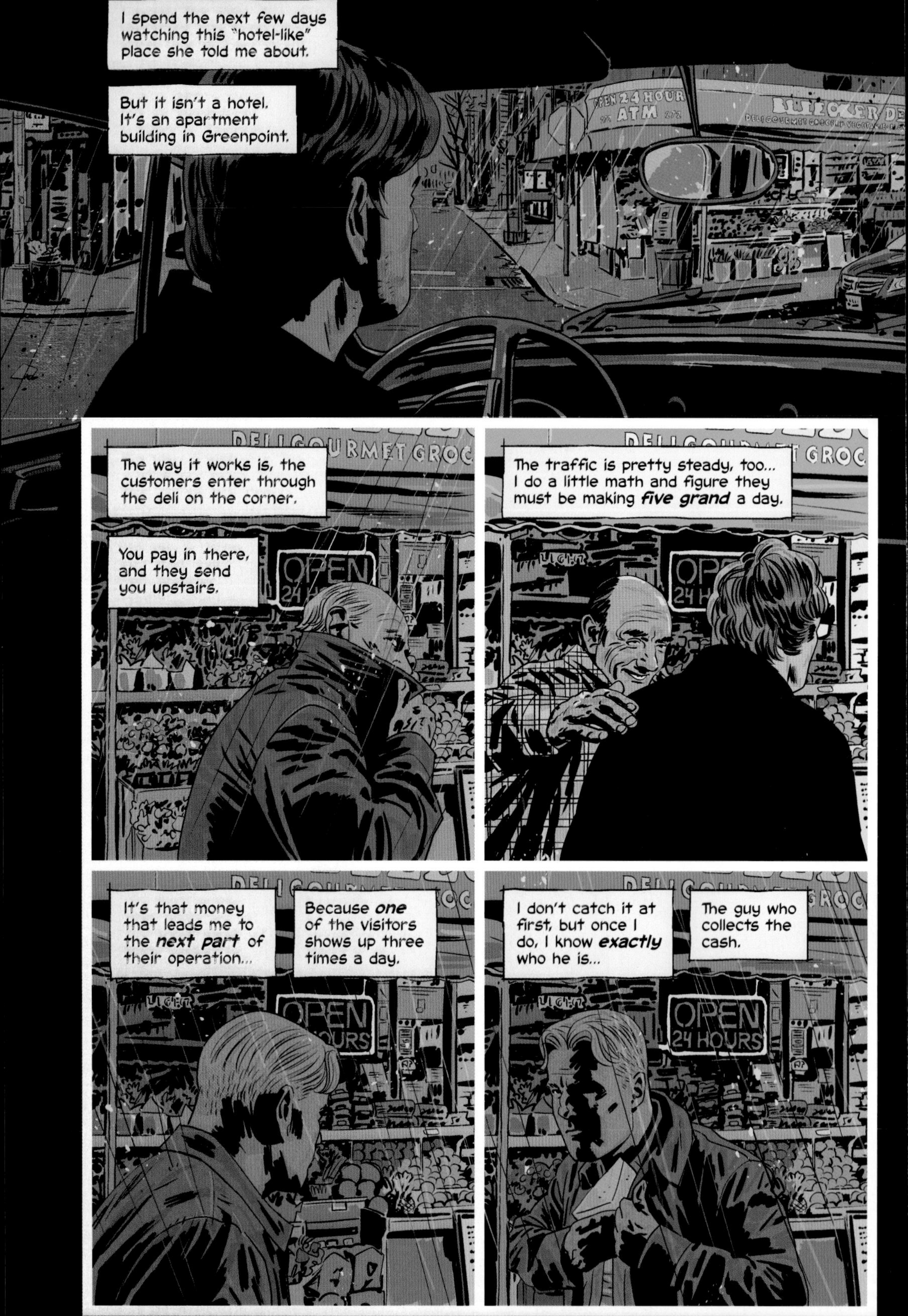
I spend the next few days watching this "hotel-like" place she told me about.
But it isn't a hotel. It's an apartment building in Greenpoint.
OPEN 24 HOUR
ATM
The way it works is, the customers enter through the deli on the corner.
You pay in there, and they send you upstairs.
The traffic is pretty steady, too... I do a little math and figure they must be making *five grand* a day.
It's that money that leads me to the *next part* of their operation...
Because *one* of the visitors shows up three times a day.
I don't catch it at first, but once I do, I know *exactly* who he is...
The guy who collects the cash.
OPEN 24 HOURS

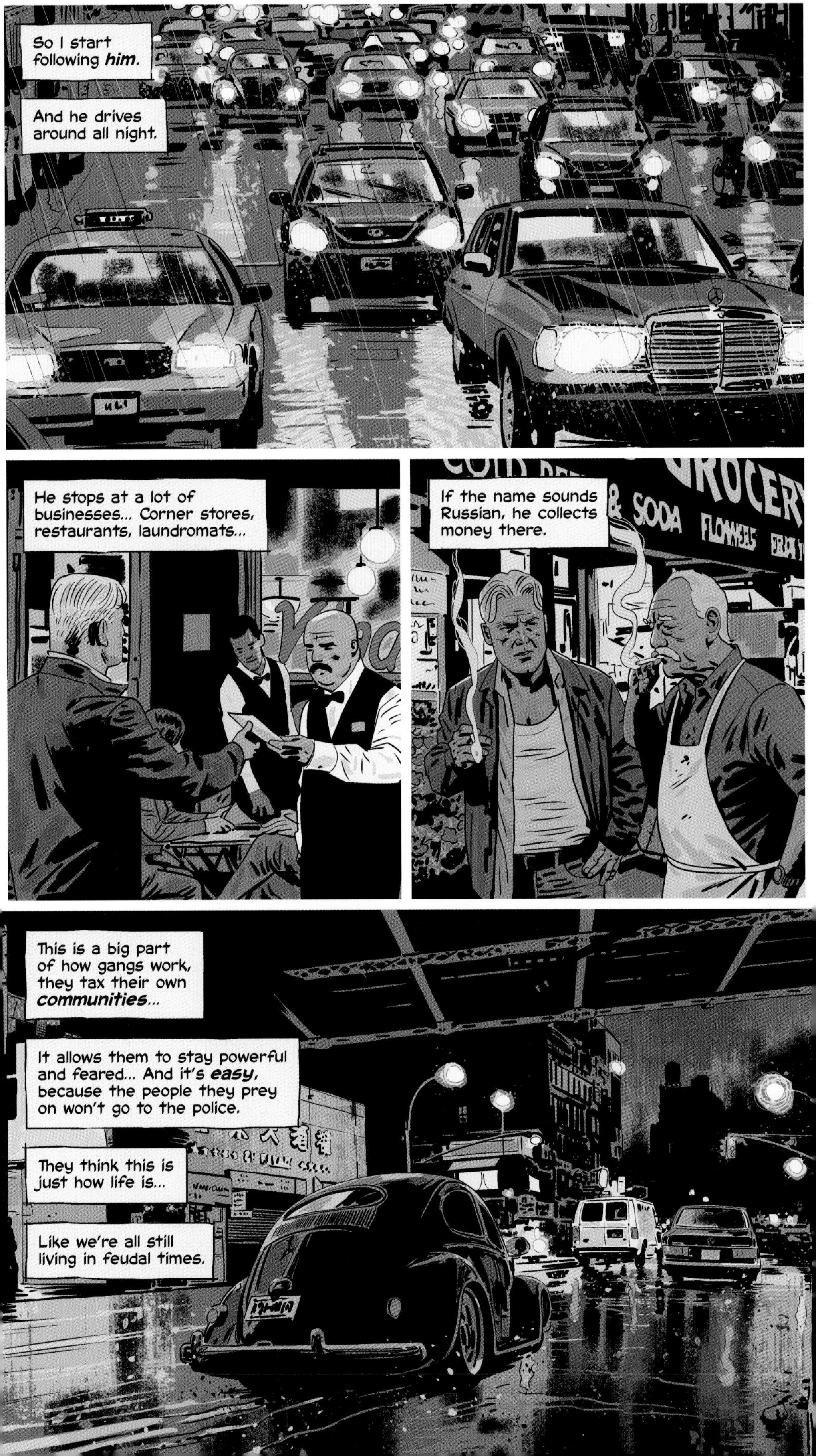

So I start following ***him***.
And he drives around all night.
He stops at a lot of businesses... Corner stores, restaurants, laundromats...
If the name sounds Russian, he collects money there.
& SODA
This is a big part of how gangs work, they tax their own ***communities***...
It allows them to stay powerful and feared... And it's ***easy***, because the people they prey on won't go to the police.
They think this is just how life is...
Like we're all still living in feudal times.

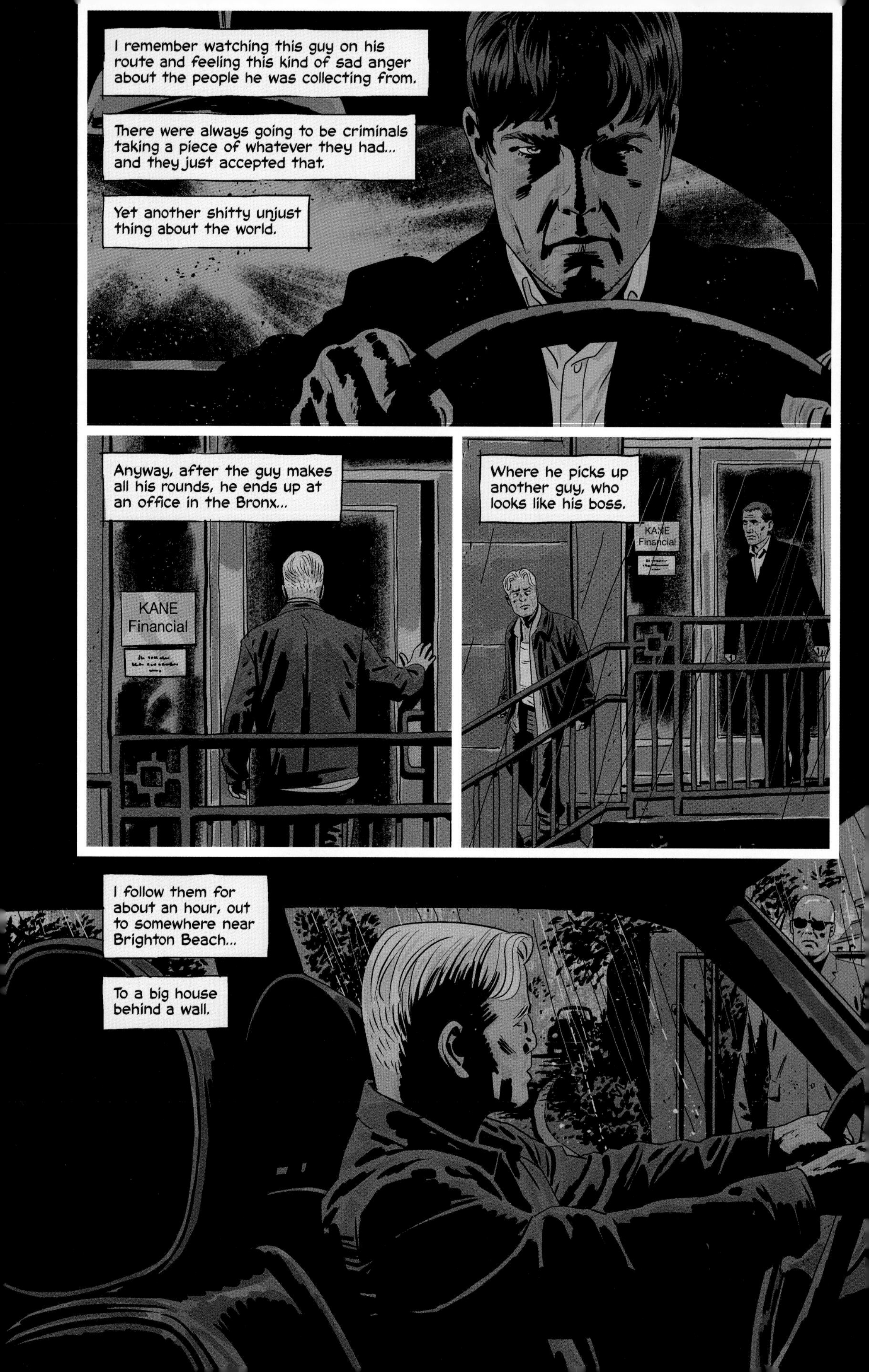

I remember watching this guy on his route and feeling this kind of sad anger about the people he was collecting from.
There were always going to be criminals taking a piece of whatever they had... and they just accepted that.
Yet another shitty unjust thing about the world.
Anyway, after the guy makes all his rounds, he ends up at an office in the Bronx...
KANE Financial
Where he picks up another guy, who looks like his boss.
KANE Financial
I follow them for about an hour, out to somewhere near Brighton Beach...
To a big house behind a wall.

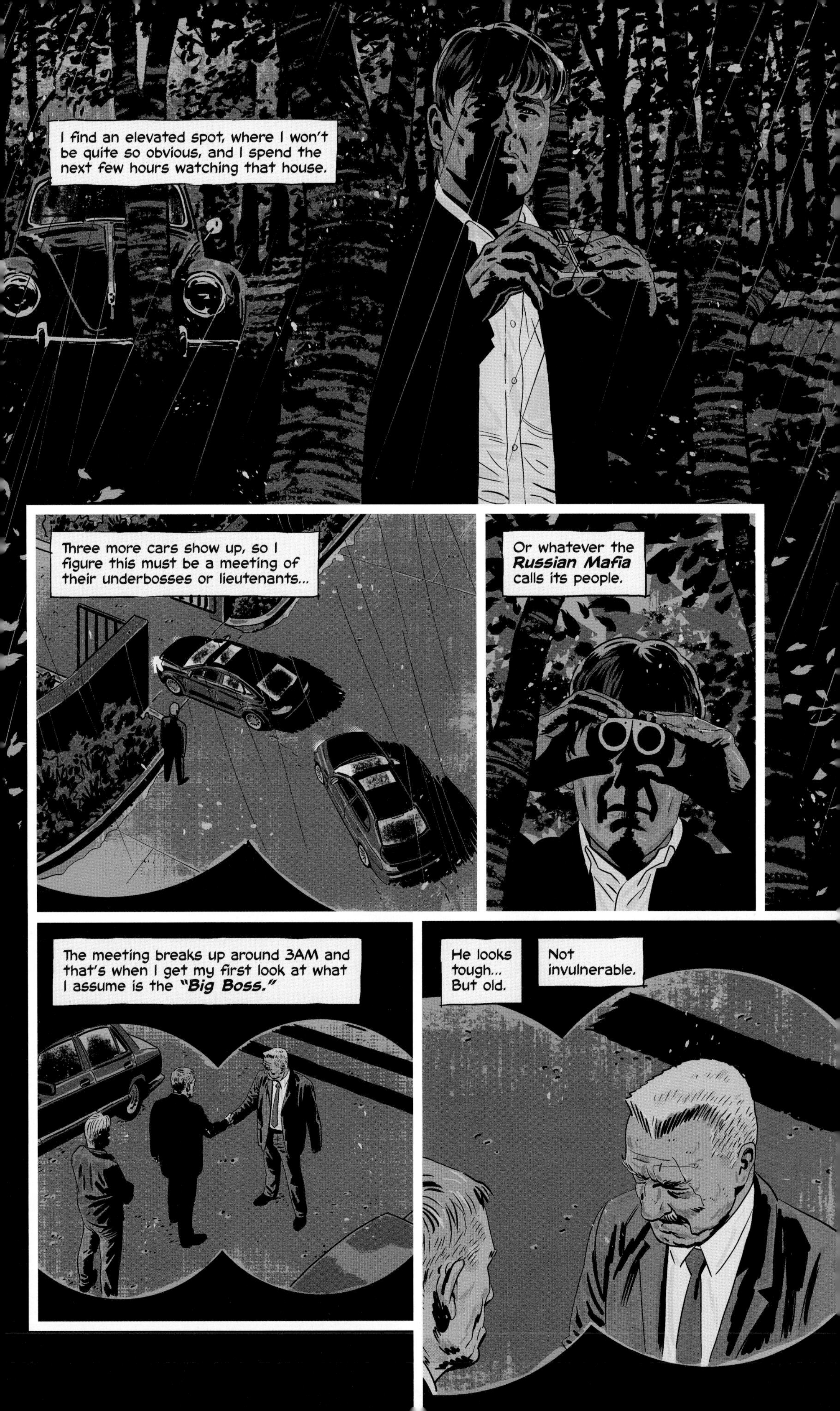

I find an elevated spot, where I won't be quite so obvious, and I spend the next few hours watching that house.
Three more cars show up, so I figure this must be a meeting of their underbosses or lieutenants...
Or whatever the *Russian Mafia* calls its people.
The meeting breaks up around 3AM and that's when I get my first look at what I assume is the *"Big Boss."*
He looks tough... But old.
Not invulnerable.

From that point on, I was hatching a plan.

One that was a bit crazy, even for me...

But I was ***one man*** going up against a couple dozen, so crazy would probably be my only advantage.

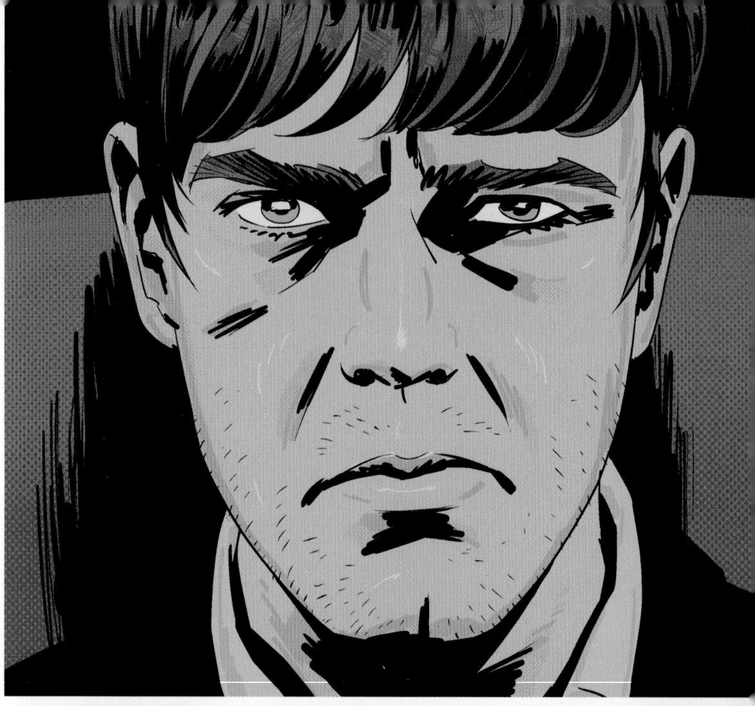

Still, before I could put ***any*** plan into action, I had to find out some things...

Like how close they were to finding me.

And if that guy I stabbed had told ***anyone else*** about Kira before he came into the café that night.

I also needed to find the ***weak spots*** in their operation ...

They were sloppy and confident, so I was sure there would be a few to choose from.

And I had a pretty good idea who could provide me with all this information.

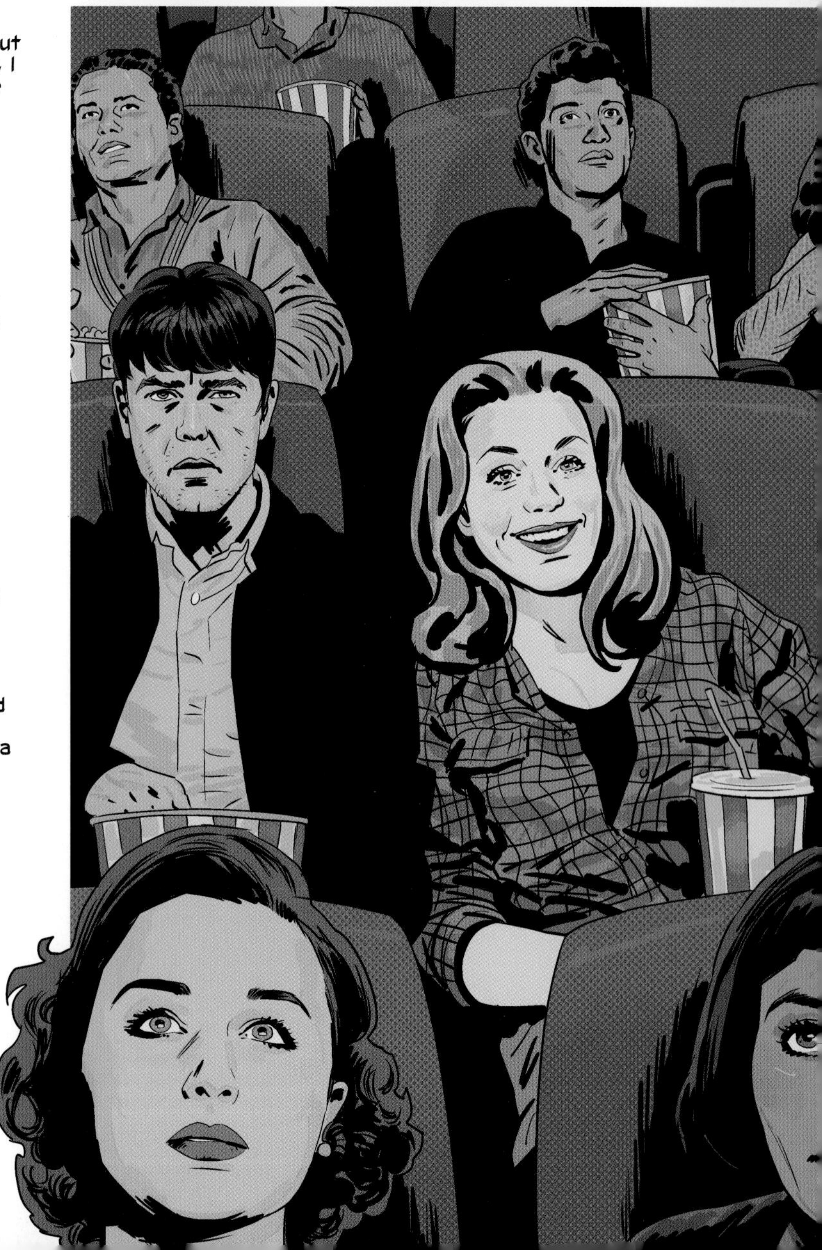

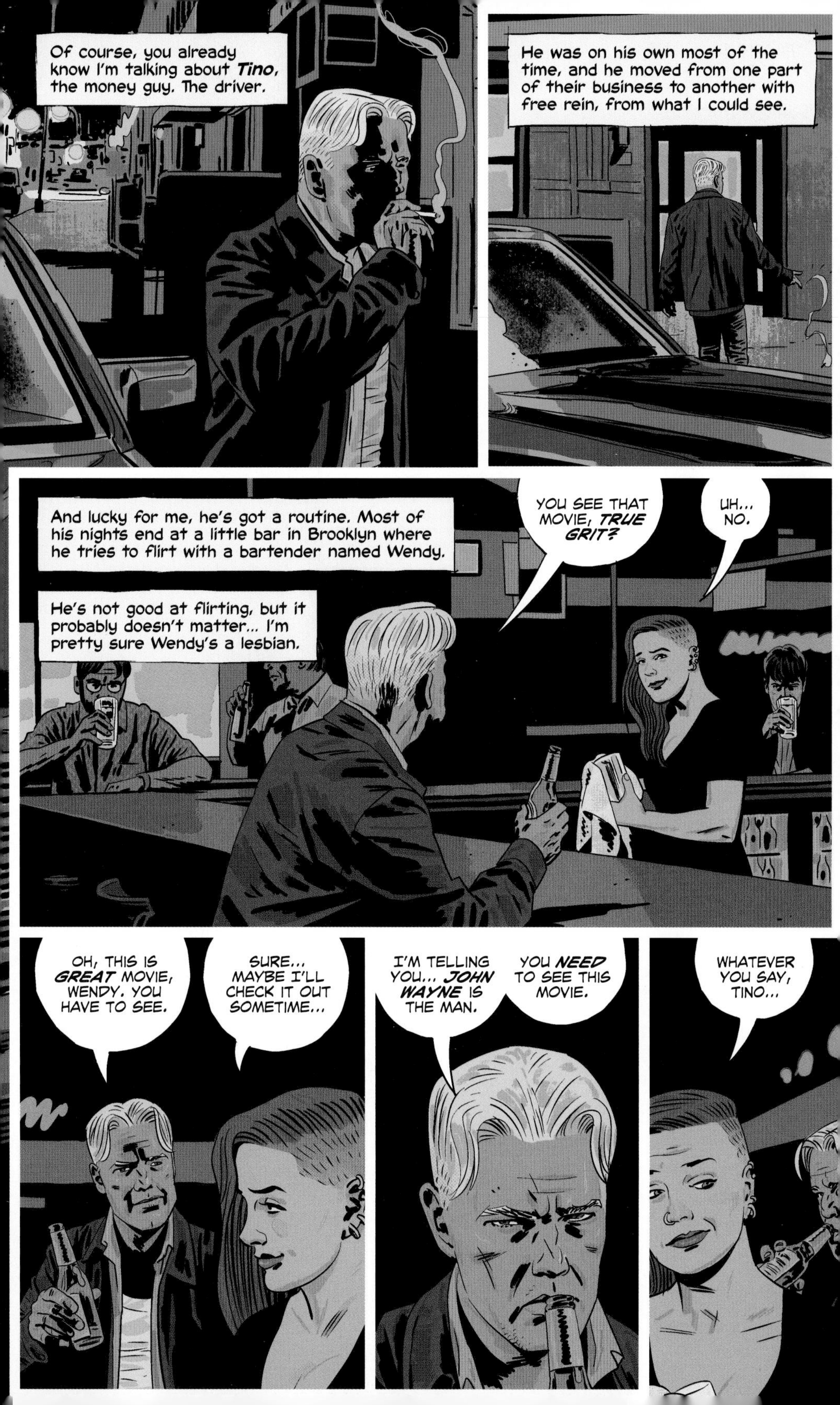

Of course, you already know I'm talking about *Tino*, the money guy. The driver.
He was on his own most of the time, and he moved from one part of their business to another with free rein, from what I could see.
And lucky for me, he's got a routine. Most of his nights end at a little bar in Brooklyn where he tries to flirt with a bartender named Wendy.
He's not good at flirting, but it probably doesn't matter... I'm pretty sure Wendy's a lesbian.
YOU SEE THAT MOVIE, *TRUE GRIT?*
UH... NO.
OH, THIS IS *GREAT* MOVIE, WENDY. YOU HAVE TO SEE.
SURE... MAYBE I'LL CHECK IT OUT SOMETIME...
I'M TELLING YOU... *JOHN WAYNE* IS THE MAN.
YOU *NEED* TO SEE THIS MOVIE.
WHATEVER YOU SAY, TINO...

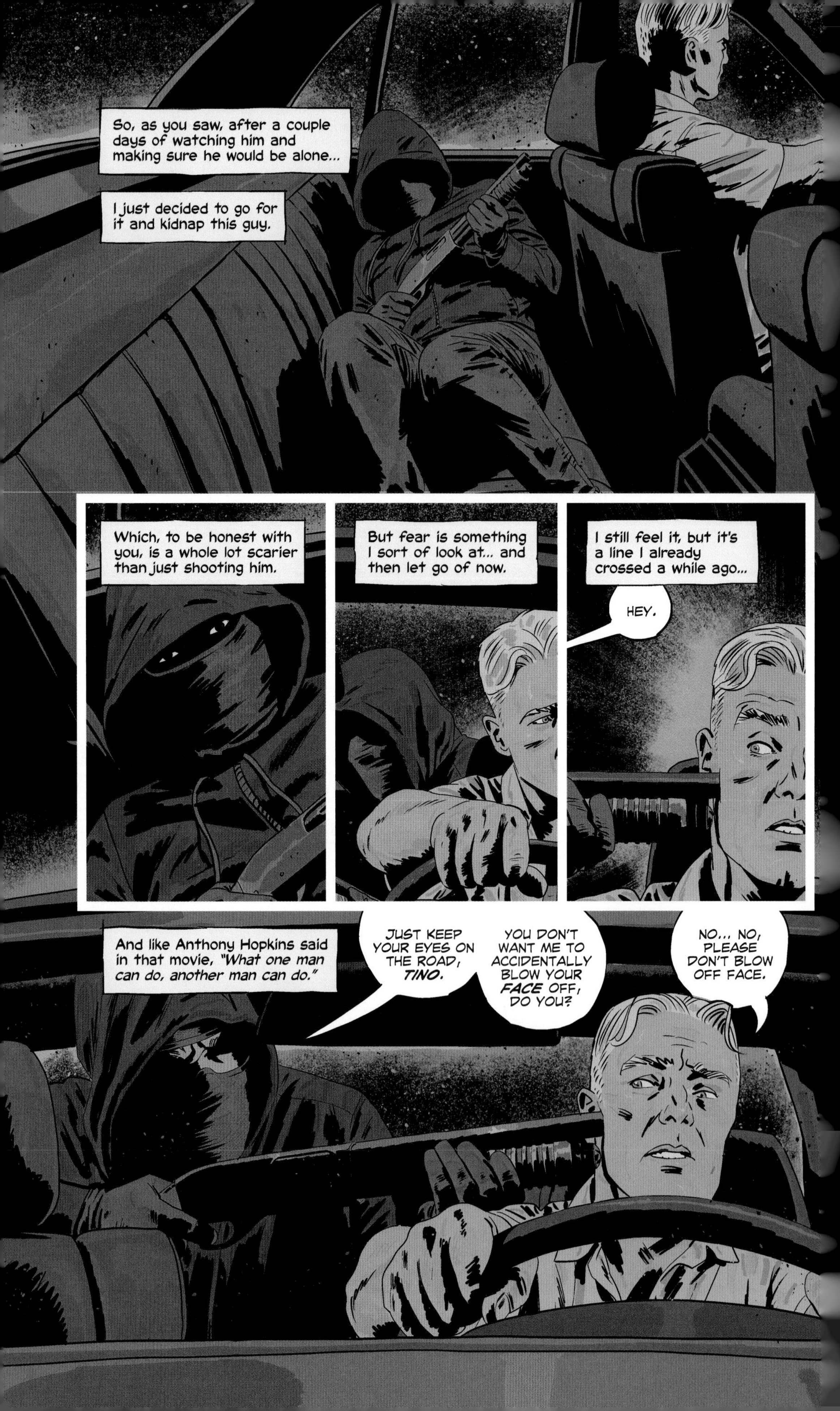
So, as you saw, after a couple days of watching him and making sure he would be alone...
I just decided to go for it and kidnap this guy.
Which, to be honest with you, is a whole lot scarier than just shooting him.
But fear is something I sort of look at... and then let go of now.
I still feel it, but it's a line I already crossed a while ago...
HEY.
And like Anthony Hopkins said in that movie, *"What one man can do, another man can do."*
JUST KEEP YOUR EYES ON THE ROAD, *TINO.*
YOU DON'T WANT ME TO ACCIDENTALLY BLOW YOUR *FACE* OFF, DO YOU?
NO... NO, PLEASE DON'T BLOW OFF FACE.

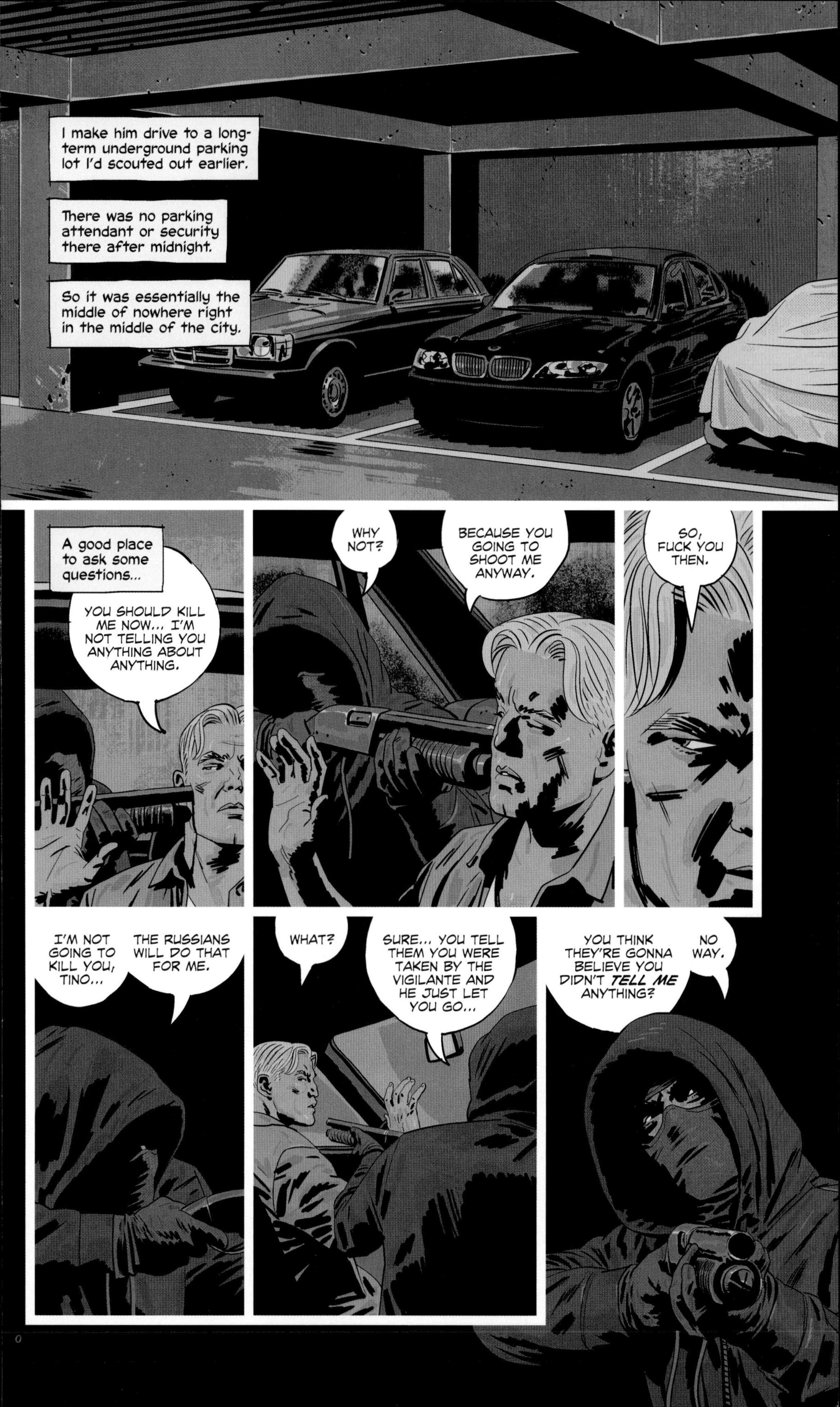
I make him drive to a long-term underground parking lot I'd scouted out earlier.
There was no parking attendant or security there after midnight.
So it was essentially the middle of nowhere right in the middle of the city.
A good place to ask some questions...
YOU SHOULD KILL ME NOW... I'M NOT TELLING YOU ANYTHING ABOUT ANYTHING.
WHY NOT?
BECAUSE YOU GOING TO SHOOT ME ANYWAY.
SO, FUCK YOU THEN.
I'M NOT GOING TO KILL YOU, TINO...
THE RUSSIANS WILL DO THAT FOR ME.
WHAT?
SURE... YOU TELL THEM YOU WERE TAKEN BY THE VIGILANTE AND HE JUST LET YOU GO...
YOU THINK THEY'RE GONNA BELIEVE YOU DIDN'T *TELL ME* ANYTHING?
NO WAY.

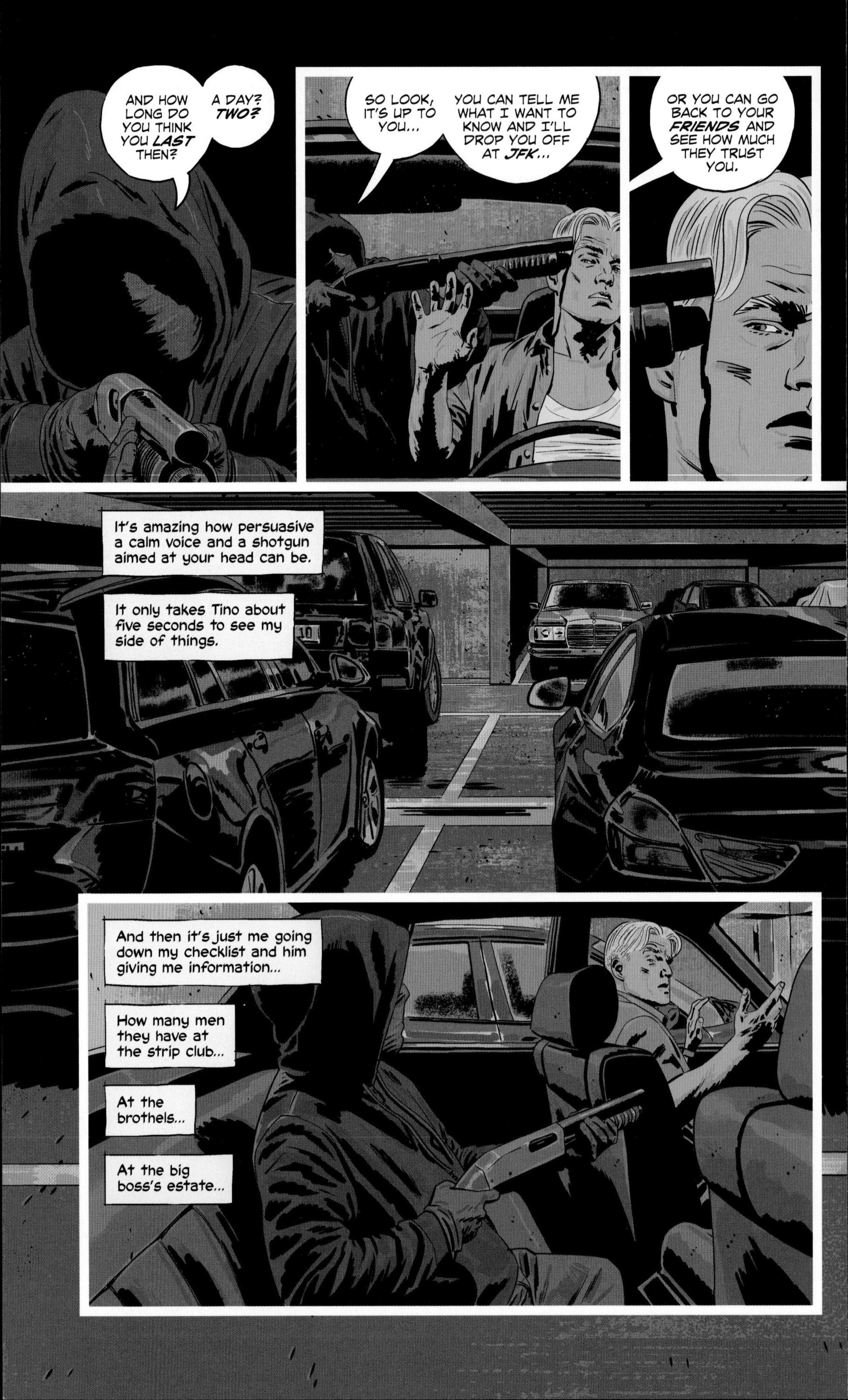
AND HOW LONG DO YOU THINK YOU *LAST* THEN?
A DAY? *TWO?*
SO LOOK, IT'S UP TO YOU...
YOU CAN TELL ME WHAT I WANT TO KNOW AND I'LL DROP YOU OFF AT *JFK*...
OR YOU CAN GO BACK TO YOUR *FRIENDS* AND SEE HOW MUCH THEY TRUST YOU.
It's amazing how persuasive a calm voice and a shotgun aimed at your head can be.
It only takes Tino about five seconds to see my side of things.
And then it's just me going down my checklist and him giving me information...
How many men they have at the strip club...
At the brothels...
At the big boss's estate...

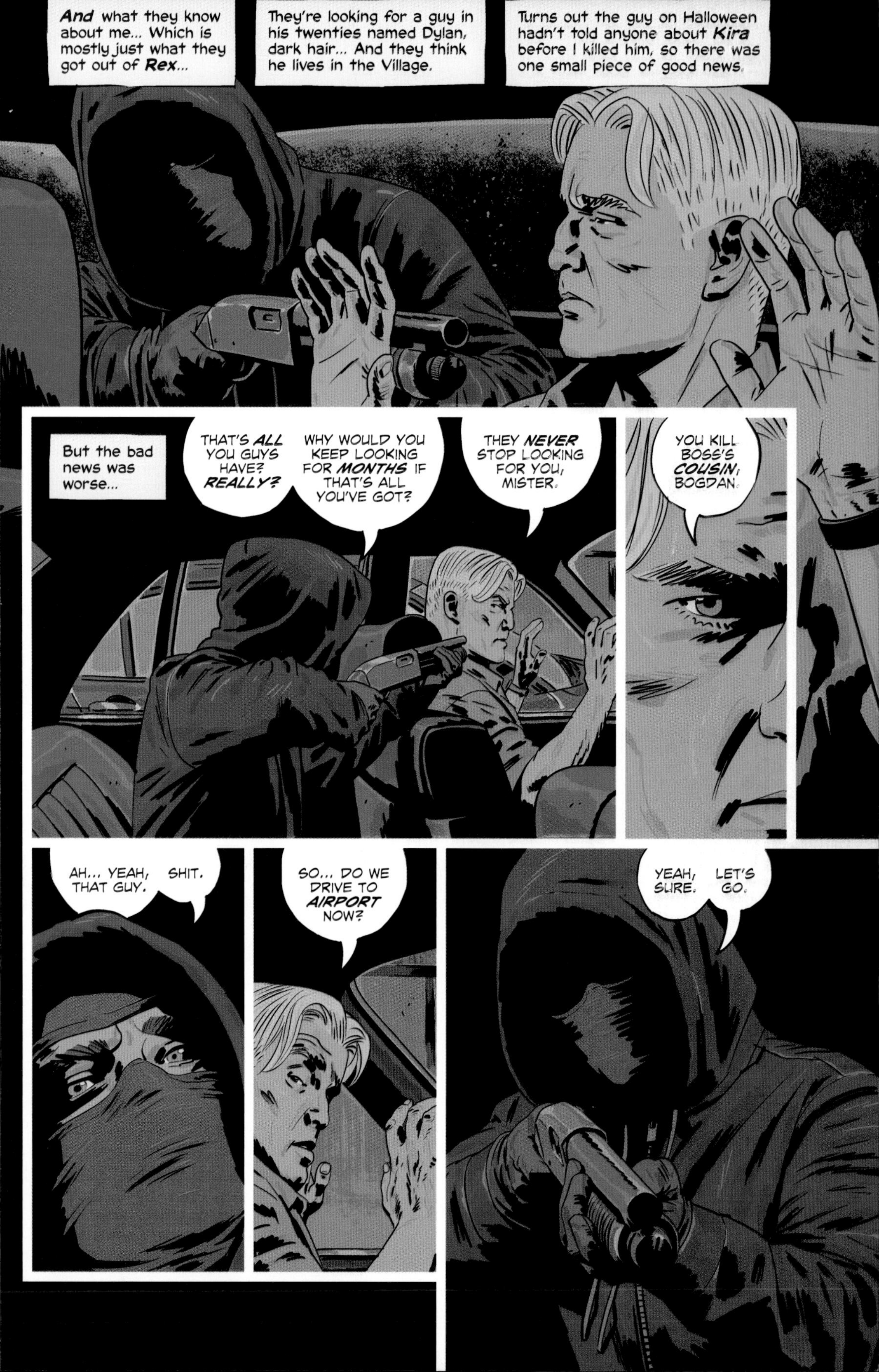
And what they know about me... Which is mostly just what they got out of Rex...
They're looking for a guy in his twenties named Dylan, dark hair... And they think he lives in the Village.
Turns out the guy on Halloween hadn't told anyone about Kira before I killed him, so there was one small piece of good news.
But the bad news was worse...
THAT'S ALL YOU GUYS HAVE? REALLY?
WHY WOULD YOU KEEP LOOKING FOR MONTHS IF THAT'S ALL YOU'VE GOT?
THEY NEVER STOP LOOKING FOR YOU, MISTER.
YOU KILL BOSS'S COUSIN, BOGDAN.
AH... YEAH, THAT GUY.
SHIT.
SO... DO WE DRIVE TO AIRPORT NOW?
YEAH, SURE.
LET'S GO.

I fire the shotgun as he turns away.

The noise is deafening inside the car, but up on the street you probably couldn't even hear it.

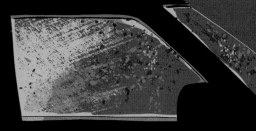

I didn't want to kill him.

But obviously I couldn't trust him to just run and never look back.

And I had to make sure they didn't see me coming.

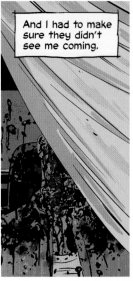

Because I had a plan now.

If the big boss wasn't going to give up on *hunting* me...

...Then I was just going to have to go after the big boss.

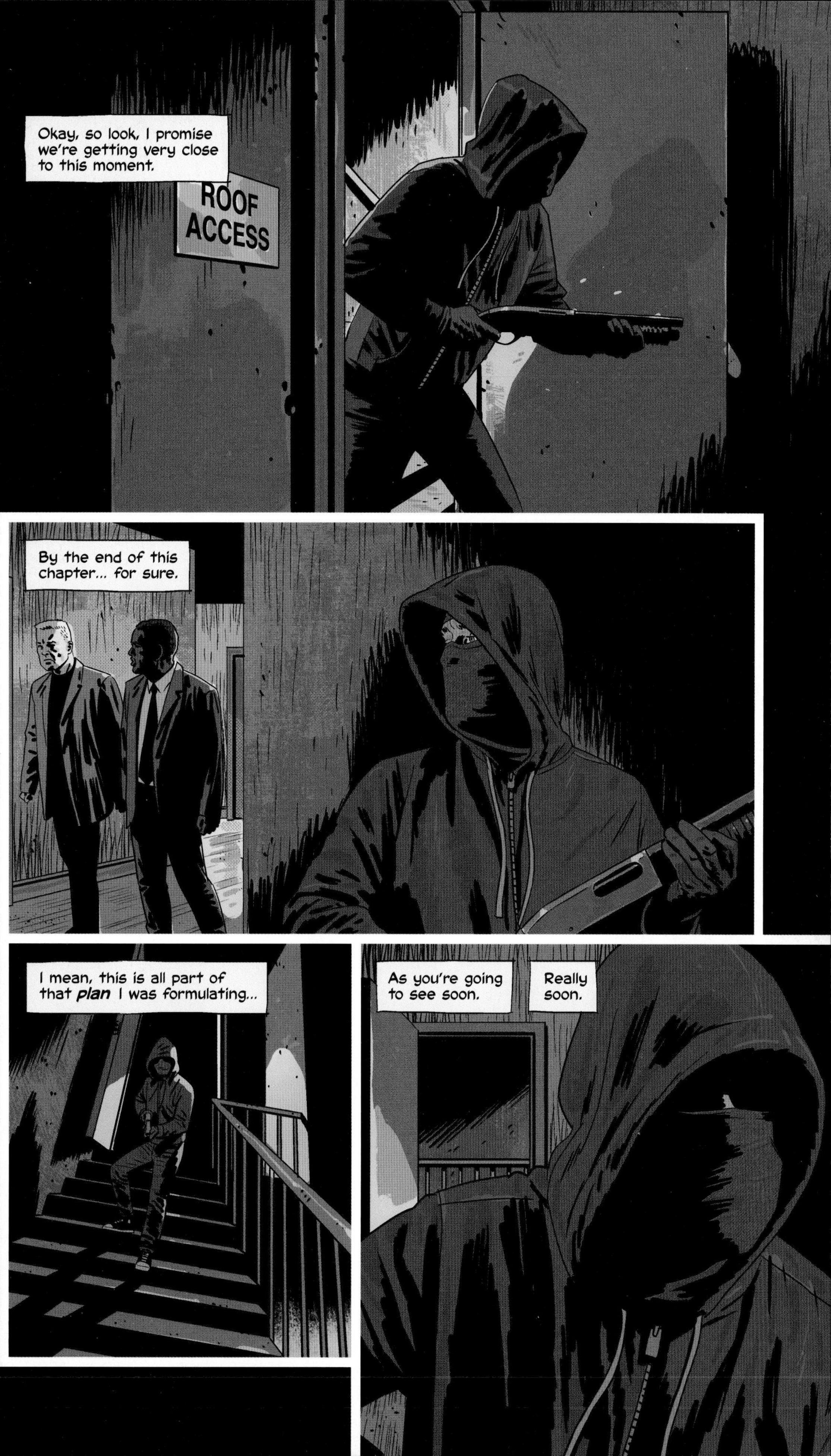

Okay, so look, I promise we're getting very close to this moment.
ROOF ACCESS
By the end of this chapter... for sure.
I mean, this is all part of that *plan* I was formulating...
As you're going to see soon.
Really soon.

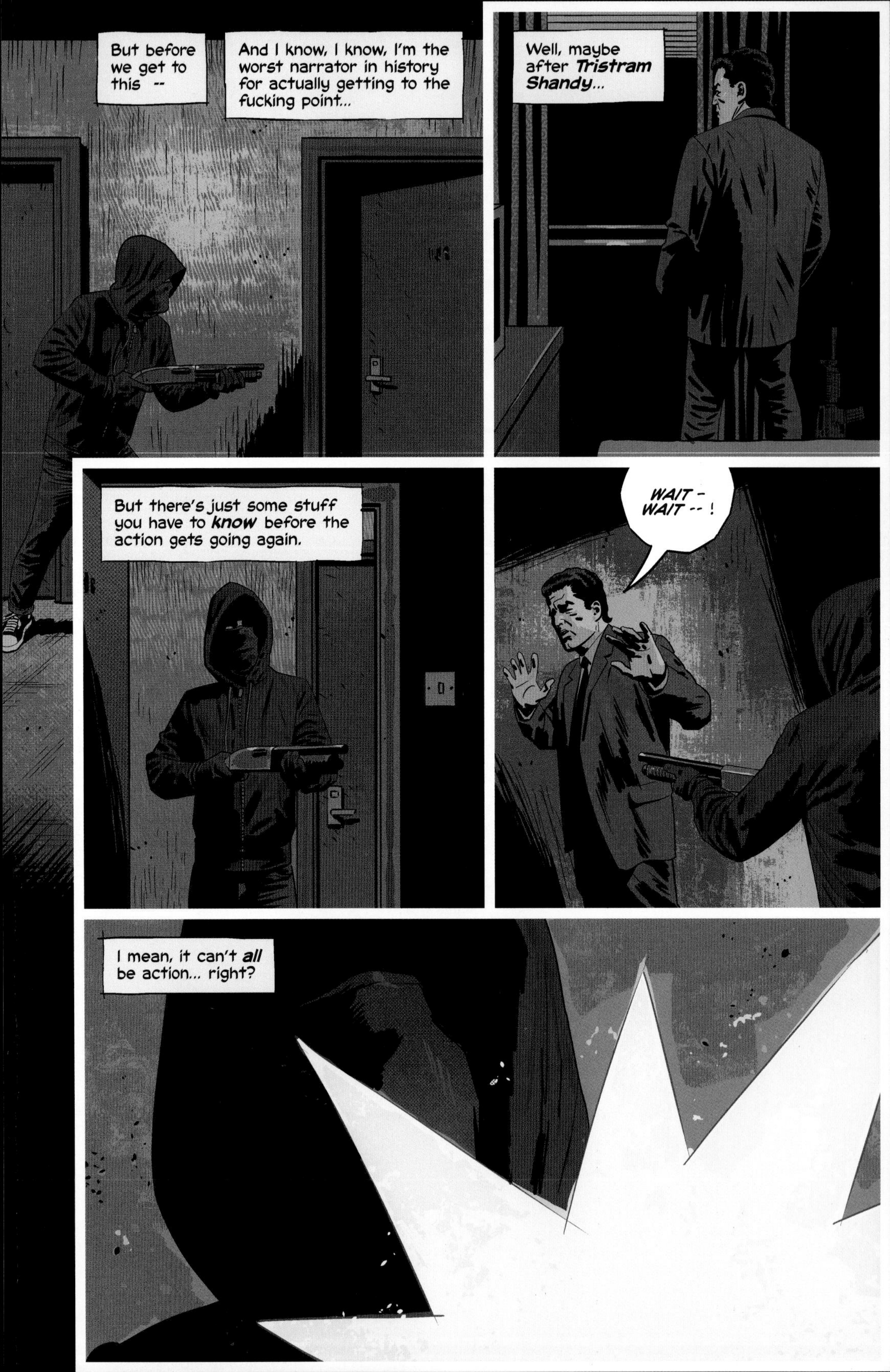
But before we get to this --
And I know, I know, I'm the worst narrator in history for actually getting to the fucking point...
Well, maybe after *Tristram Shandy*...
But there's just some stuff you have to ***know*** before the action gets going again.
WAIT - WAIT -- !
I mean, it can't ***all*** be action... right?

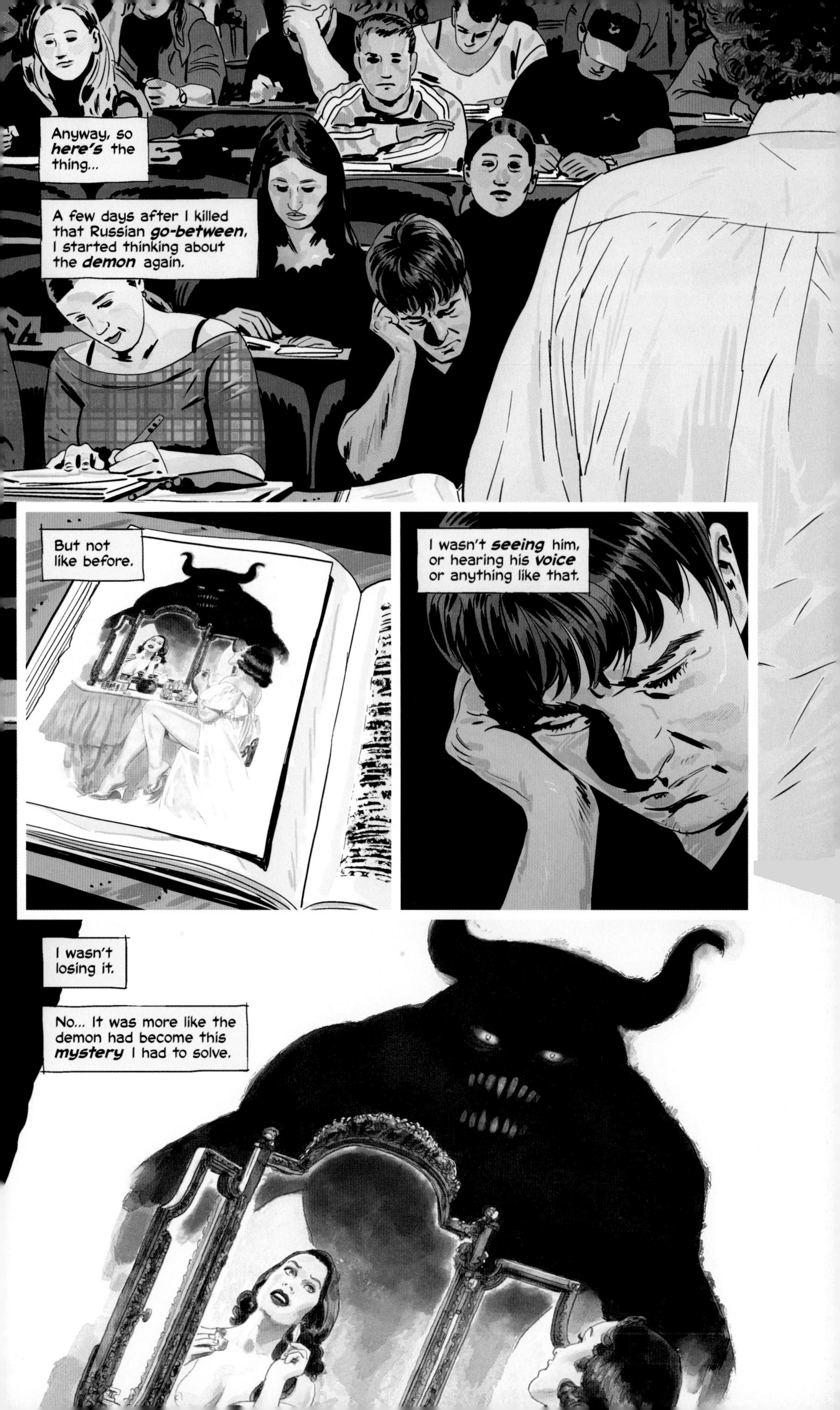
Anyway, so **here's** the thing...
A few days after I killed that Russian **go-between**, I started thinking about the **demon** again.
But not like before.
I wasn't **seeing** him, or hearing his **voice** or anything like that.
I wasn't losing it.
No... It was more like the demon had become this **mystery** I had to solve.

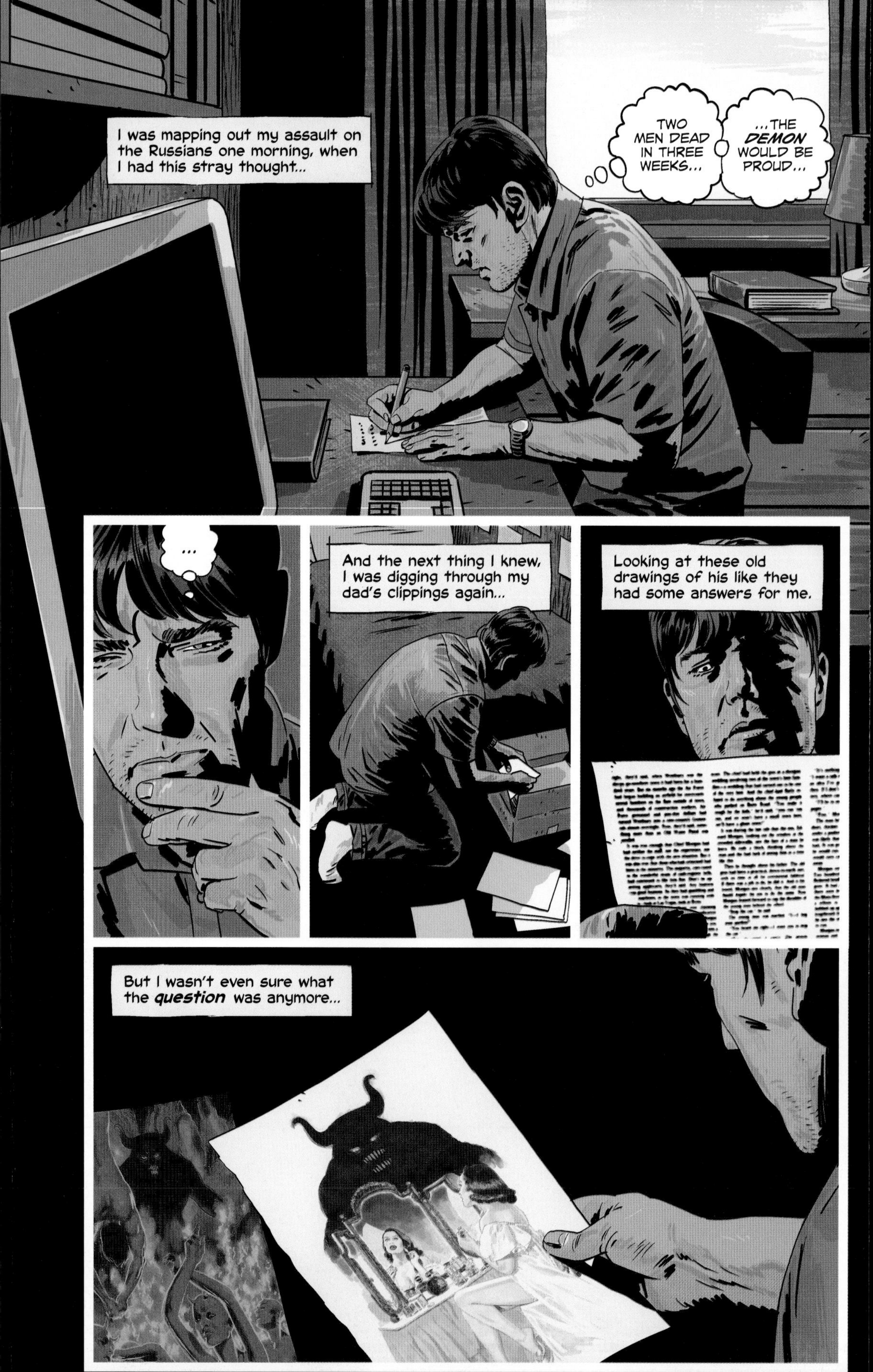
I was mapping out my assault on the Russians one morning, when I had this stray thought...
TWO MEN DEAD IN THREE WEEKS...
...THE *DEMON* WOULD BE PROUD...
...
And the next thing I knew, I was digging through my dad's clippings again...
Looking at these old drawings of his like they had some answers for me.
But I wasn't even sure what the *question* was anymore...

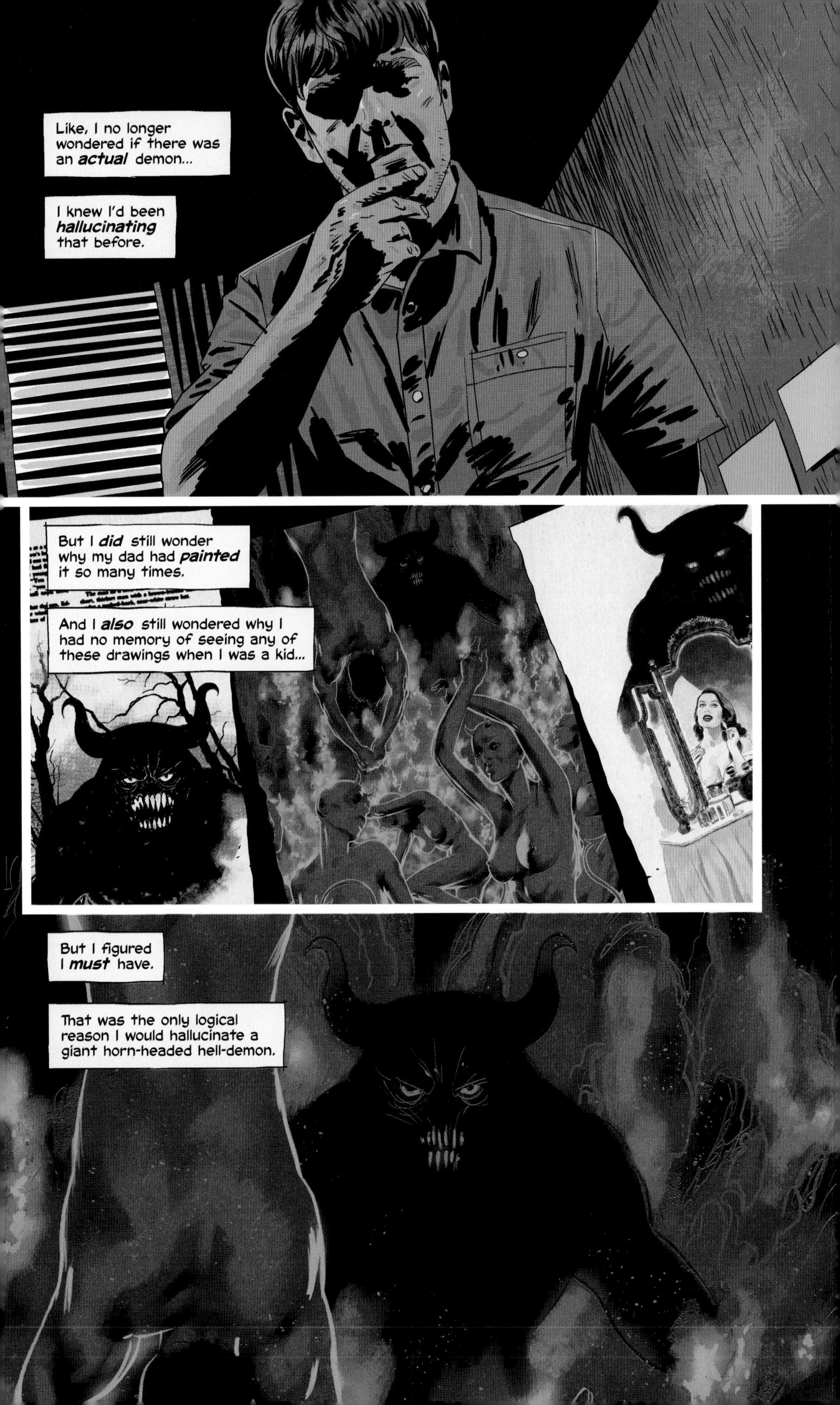
Like, I no longer wondered if there was an actual demon...
I knew I'd been hallucinating that before.
But I did still wonder why my dad had painted it so many times.
And I also still wondered why I had no memory of seeing any of these drawings when I was a kid...
But I figured I must have.
That was the only logical reason I would hallucinate a giant horn-headed hell-demon.

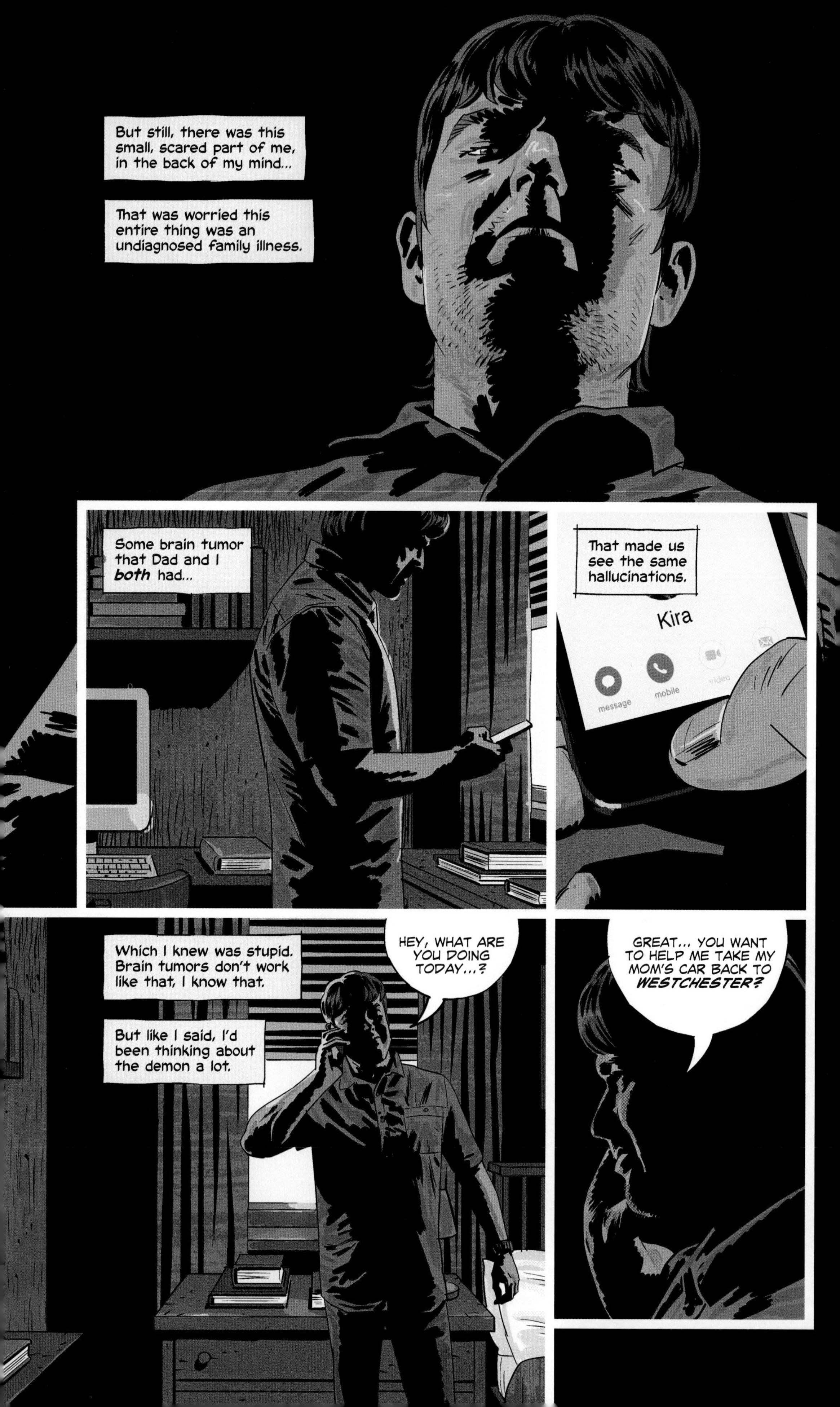

But still, there was this small, scared part of me, in the back of my mind...
That was worried this entire thing was an undiagnosed family illness.
Some brain tumor that Dad and I *both* had...
That made us see the same hallucinations.
Kira
message
mobile
video
Which I knew was stupid. Brain tumors don't work like that, I know that.
But like I said, I'd been thinking about the demon a lot.
HEY, WHAT ARE YOU DOING TODAY...?
GREAT... YOU WANT TO HELP ME TAKE MY MOM'S CAR BACK TO ***WESTCHESTER?***

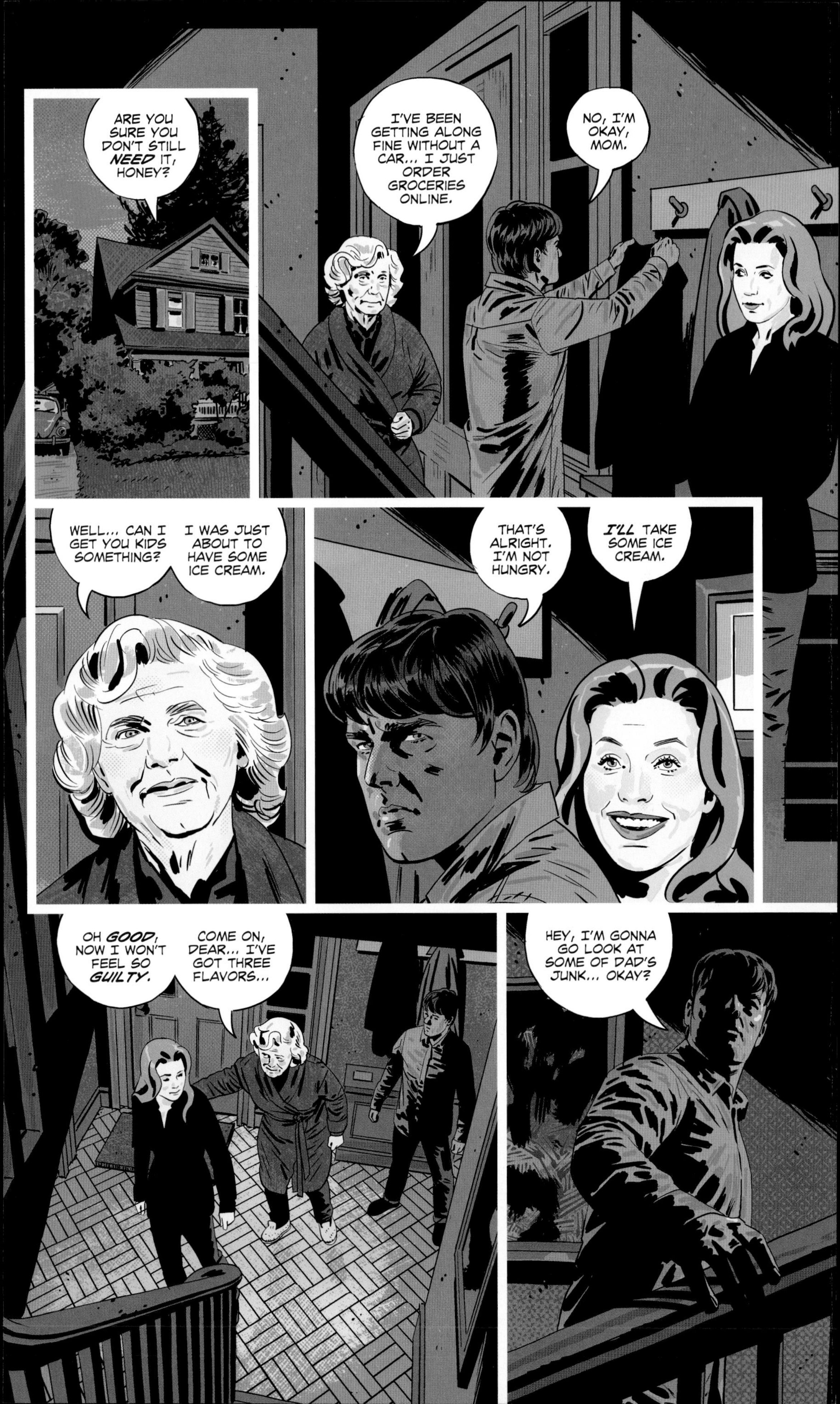
ARE YOU SURE YOU DON'T STILL NEED IT, HONEY?
I'VE BEEN GETTING ALONG FINE WITHOUT A CAR... I JUST ORDER GROCERIES ONLINE.
NO, I'M OKAY, MOM.
WELL... CAN I GET YOU KIDS SOMETHING?
I WAS JUST ABOUT TO HAVE SOME ICE CREAM.
THAT'S ALRIGHT. I'M NOT HUNGRY.
I'LL TAKE SOME ICE CREAM.
OH GOOD, NOW I WON'T FEEL SO GUILTY.
COME ON, DEAR... I'VE GOT THREE FLAVORS...
HEY, I'M GONNA GO LOOK AT SOME OF DAD'S JUNK... OKAY?

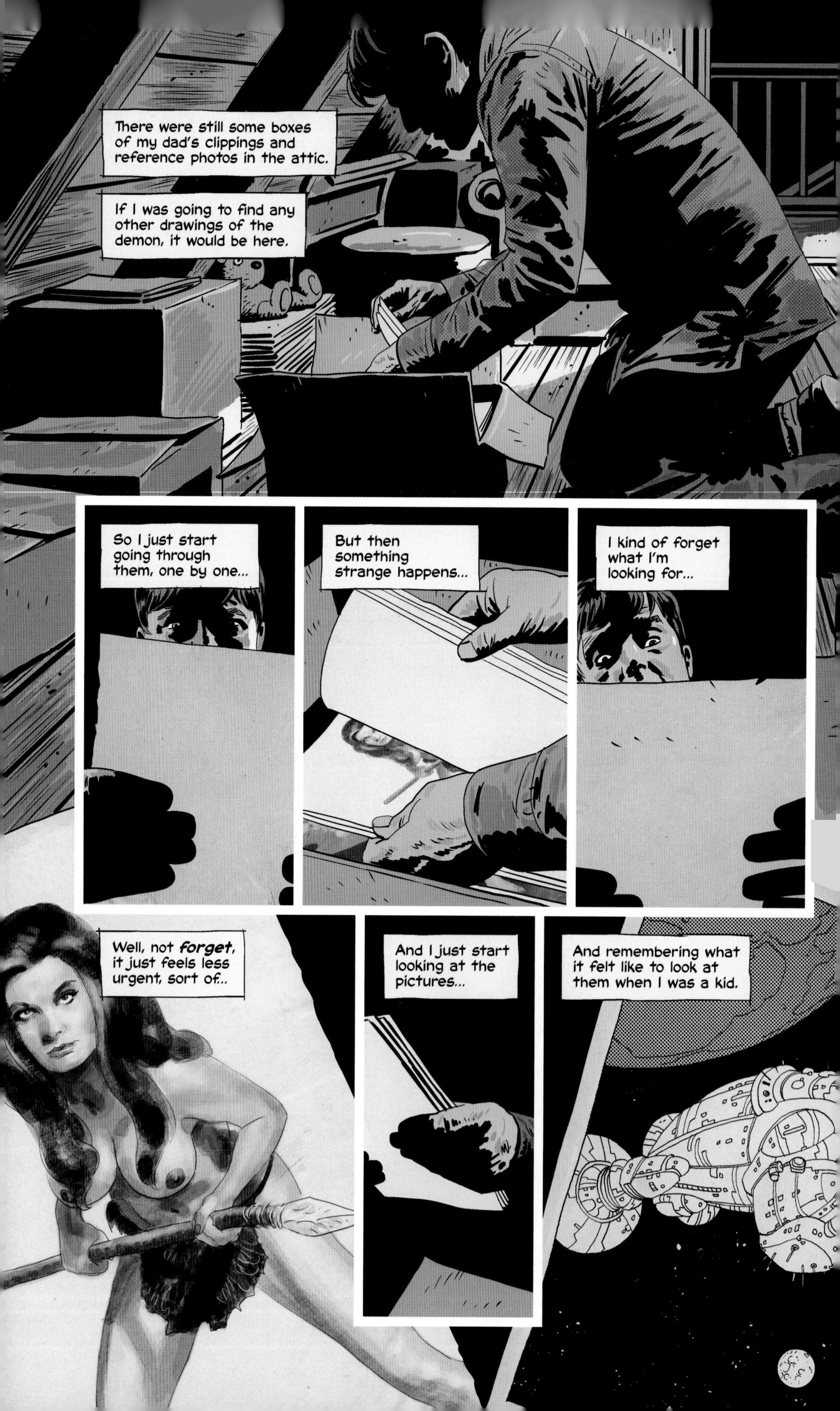
There were still some boxes of my dad's clippings and reference photos in the attic.
If I was going to find any other drawings of the demon, it would be here.
So I just start going through them, one by one...
But then something strange happens...
I kind of forget what I'm looking for...
Well, not *forget*, it just feels less urgent, sort of...
And I just start looking at the pictures...
And remembering what it felt like to look at them when I was a kid.

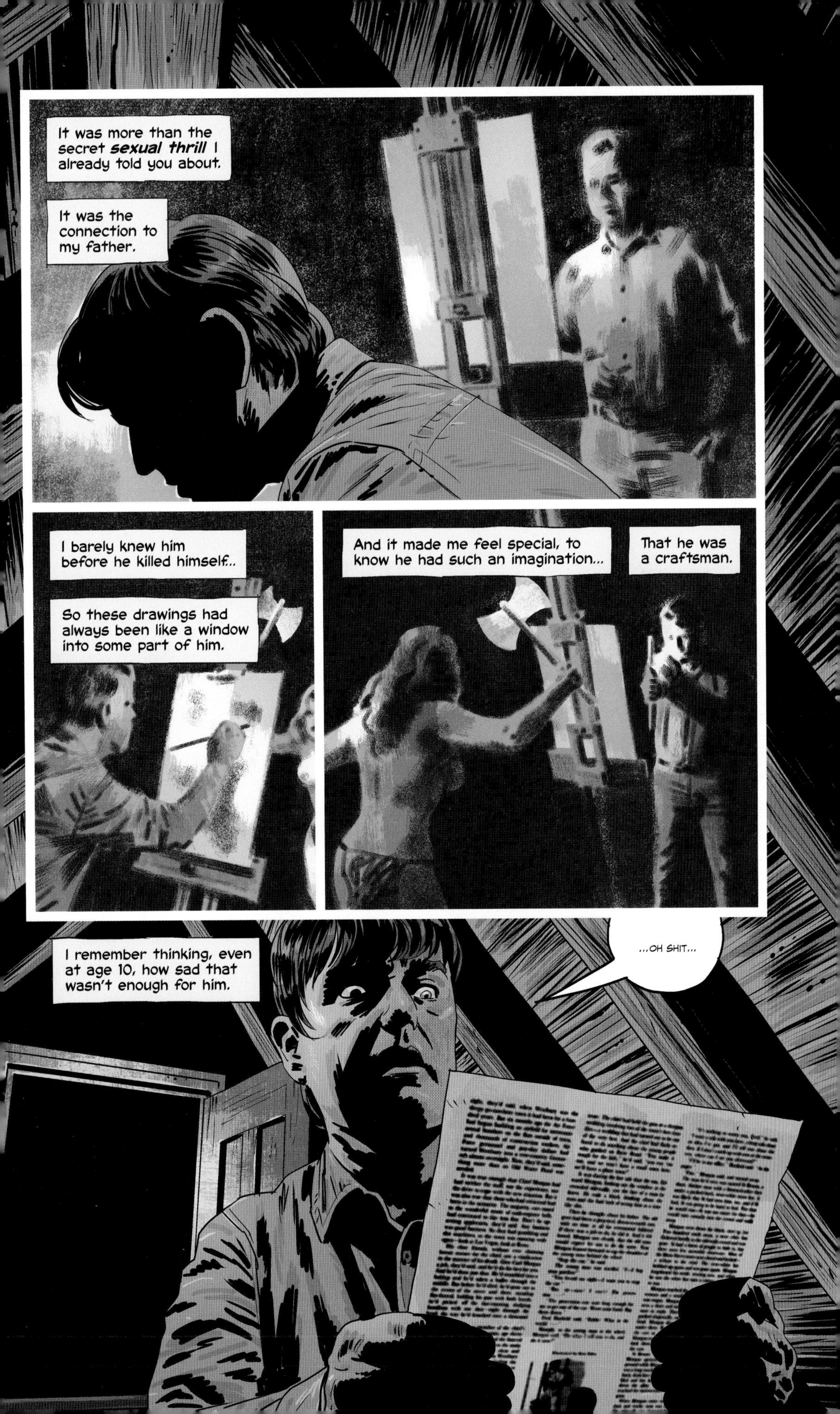

It was more than the secret ***sexual thrill*** I already told you about.
It was the connection to my father.
I barely knew him before he killed himself...
So these drawings had always been like a window into some part of him.
And it made me feel special, to know he had such an imagination...
That he was a craftsman.
I remember thinking, even at age 10, how sad that wasn't enough for him.
...OH SHIT...

Yep, that's right...
I found one more.
I almost flipped right past it, because I was thinking about Dad instead of the demon...
But *there* it was, smiling at me yet again.
HEY, ARE YOU *OKAY*...?

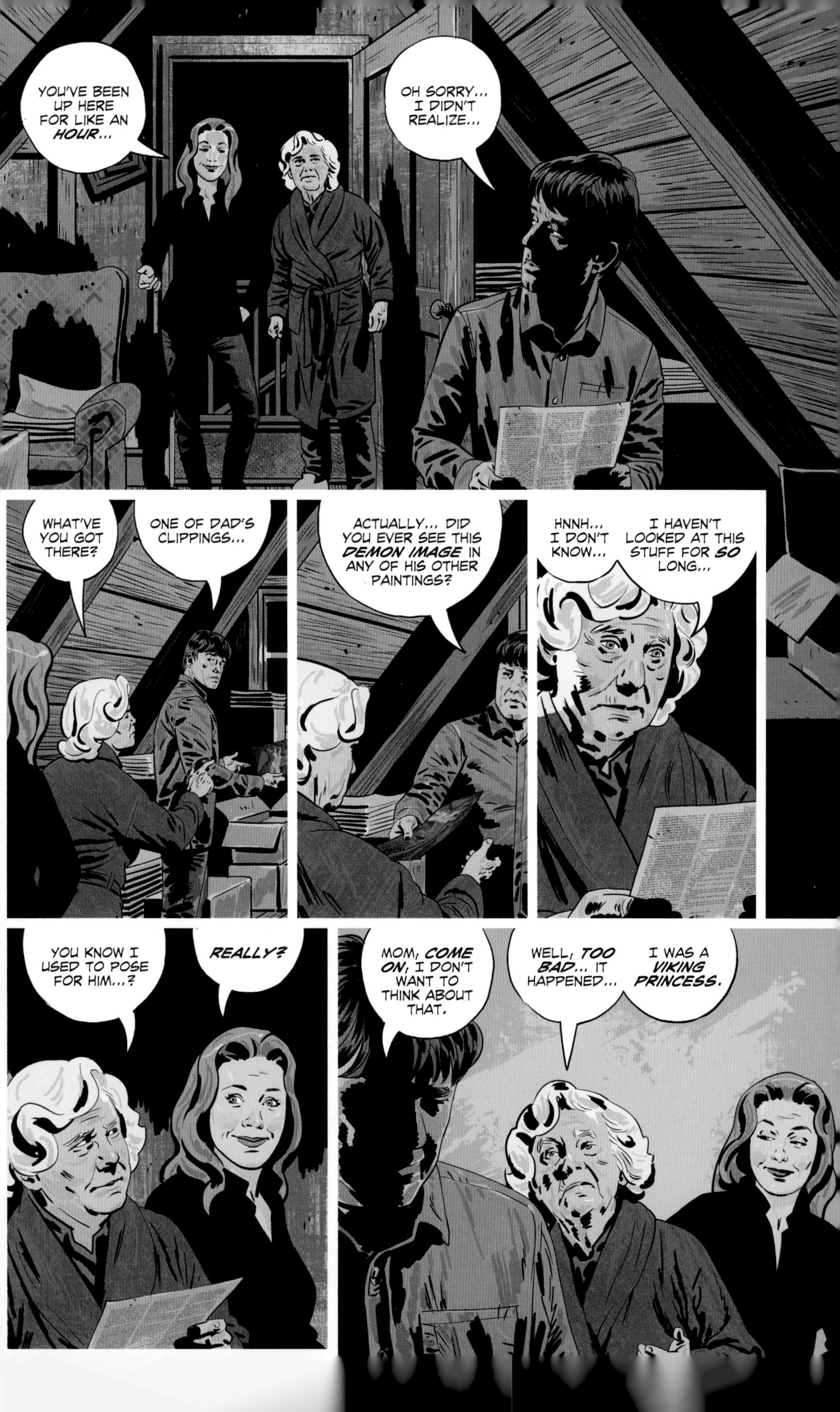

YOU'VE BEEN UP HERE FOR LIKE AN HOUR...
OH SORRY... I DIDN'T REALIZE...
WHAT'VE YOU GOT THERE?
ONE OF DAD'S CLIPPINGS...
ACTUALLY... DID YOU EVER SEE THIS DEMON IMAGE IN ANY OF HIS OTHER PAINTINGS?
HNNH... I DON'T KNOW...
I HAVEN'T LOOKED AT THIS STUFF FOR SO LONG...
YOU KNOW I USED TO POSE FOR HIM...?
REALLY?
MOM, COME ON, I DON'T WANT TO THINK ABOUT THAT.
WELL, TOO BAD... IT HAPPENED...
I WAS A VIKING PRINCESS.

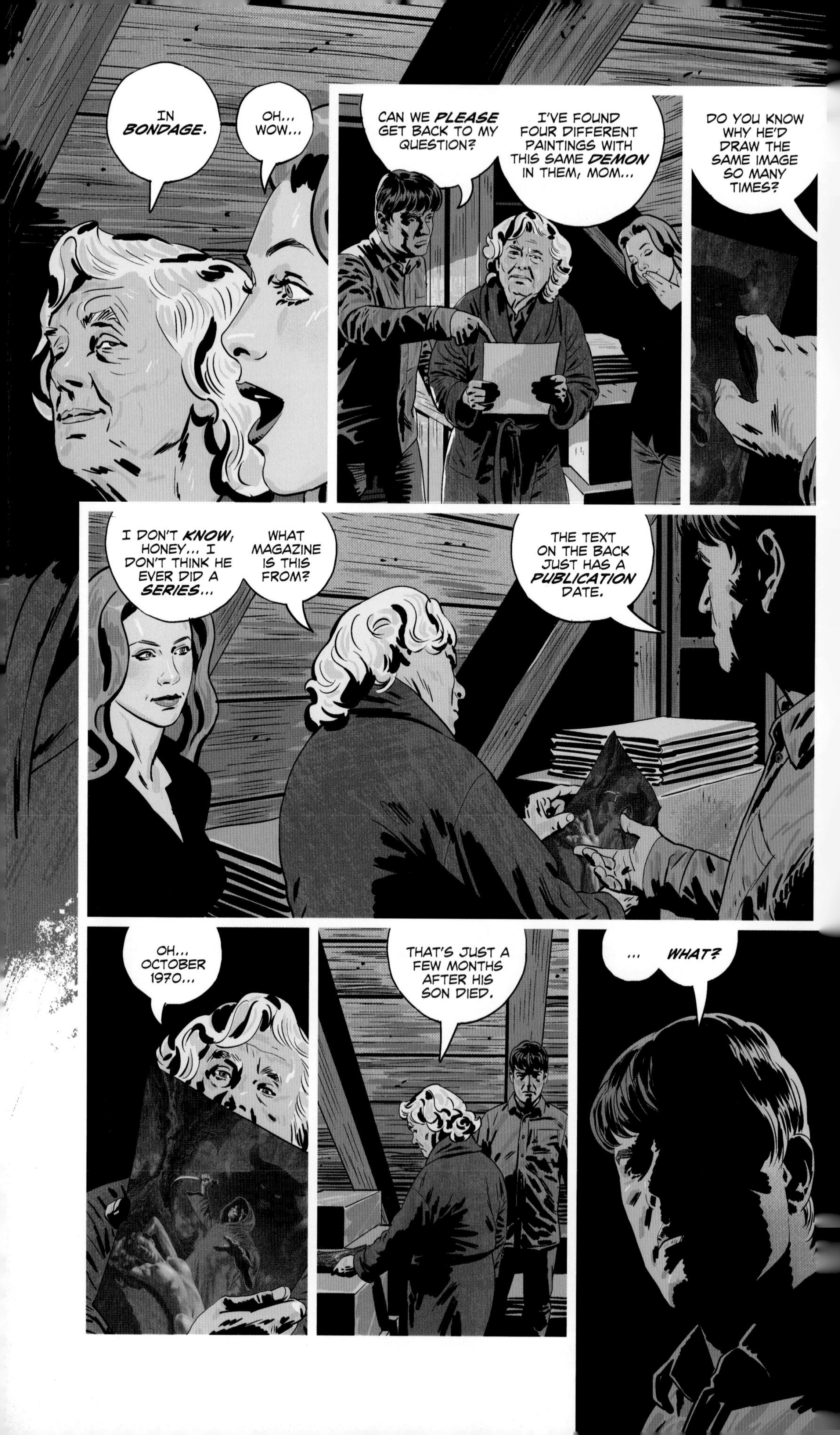
IN *BONDAGE.*
OH... WOW...
CAN WE *PLEASE* GET BACK TO MY QUESTION?
I'VE FOUND FOUR DIFFERENT PAINTINGS WITH THIS SAME *DEMON* IN THEM, MOM...
DO YOU KNOW WHY HE'D DRAW THE SAME IMAGE SO MANY TIMES?
I DON'T *KNOW,* HONEY... I DON'T THINK HE EVER DID A *SERIES...*
WHAT MAGAZINE IS THIS FROM?
THE TEXT ON THE BACK JUST HAS A *PUBLICATION* DATE.
OH... OCTOBER 1970...
THAT'S JUST A FEW MONTHS AFTER HIS SON DIED.
... *WHAT?*

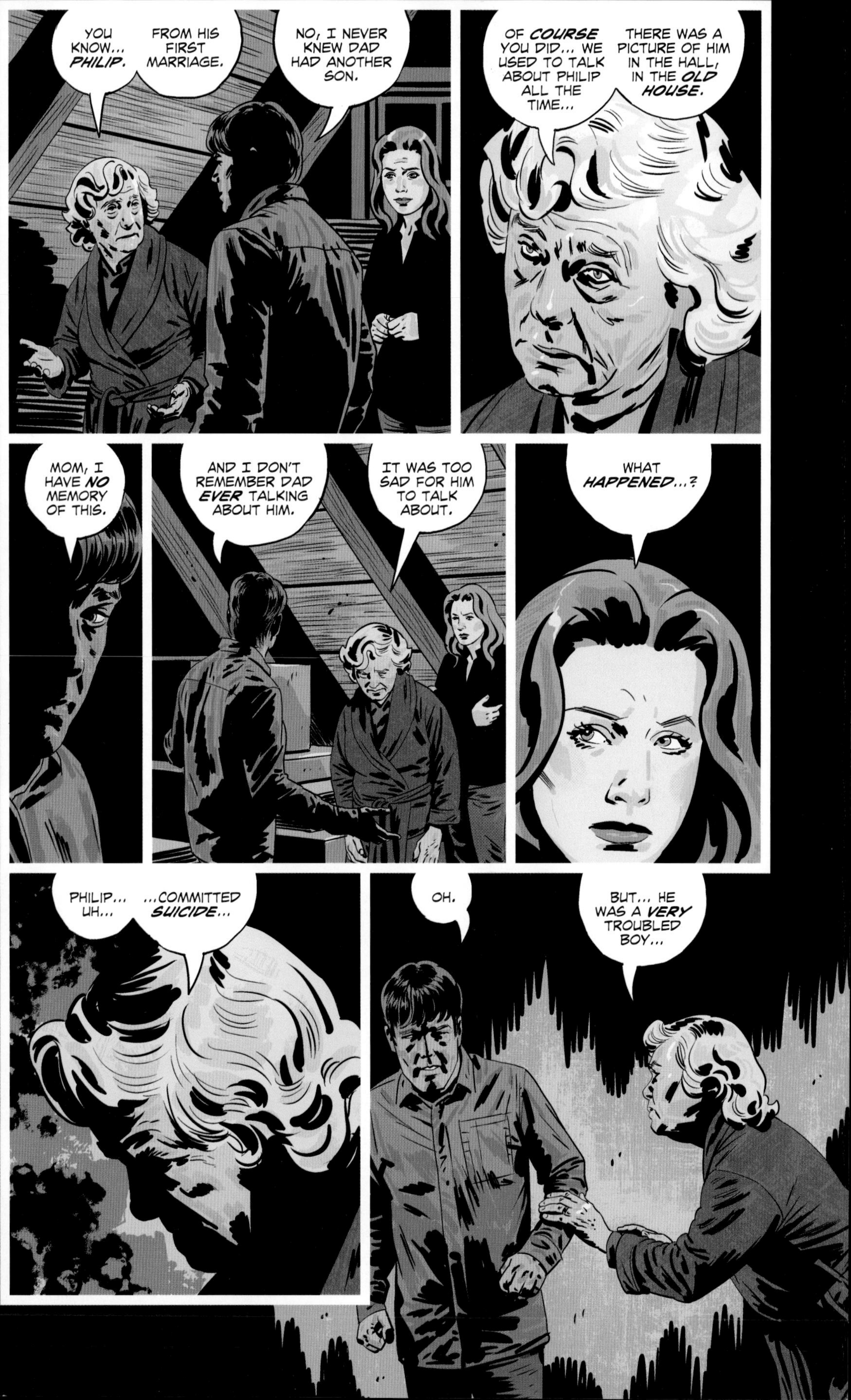

YOU KNOW... PHILIP.
FROM HIS FIRST MARRIAGE.
NO, I NEVER KNEW DAD HAD ANOTHER SON.
OF COURSE YOU DID... WE USED TO TALK ABOUT PHILIP ALL THE TIME...
THERE WAS A PICTURE OF HIM IN THE HALL, IN THE OLD HOUSE.
MOM, I HAVE NO MEMORY OF THIS.
AND I DON'T REMEMBER DAD EVER TALKING ABOUT HIM.
IT WAS TOO SAD FOR HIM TO TALK ABOUT.
WHAT HAPPENED...?
PHILIP... UH...
...COMMITTED SUICIDE...
OH.
BUT... HE WAS A VERY TROUBLED BOY...

And what Mom meant by that, of course, was "he was much more troubled than ***you***, Dylan."

Her voice had that tone, of someone who just brought up something they wish they hadn't...

Like mentioning your cat to someone whose cat just died.

Or bringing up a previously unknown brother who committed suicide... to your son who has tried to ***kill himself*** twice.

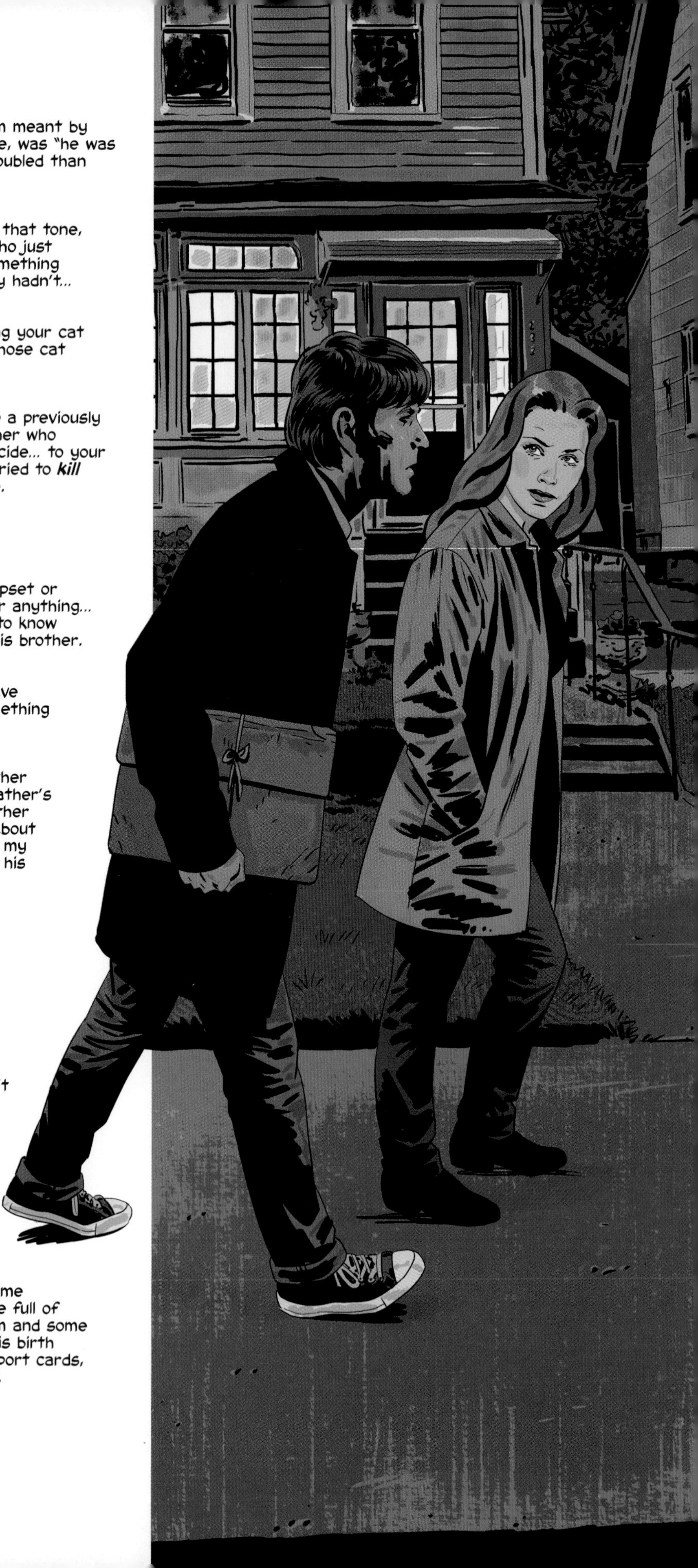

But I wasn't upset or spinning out or anything... I just wanted to know more about this brother.

How could I have forgotten something that big?

Were there other parts of my father's life that I'd either never known about or wiped from my memory after his death?

But Mom didn't ***really*** know anything about ***Philip***, either... Just the few things Dad had told her.

The best she can do is give me an old envelope full of pictures of him and some paperwork... His birth certificate, report cards, stuff like that.

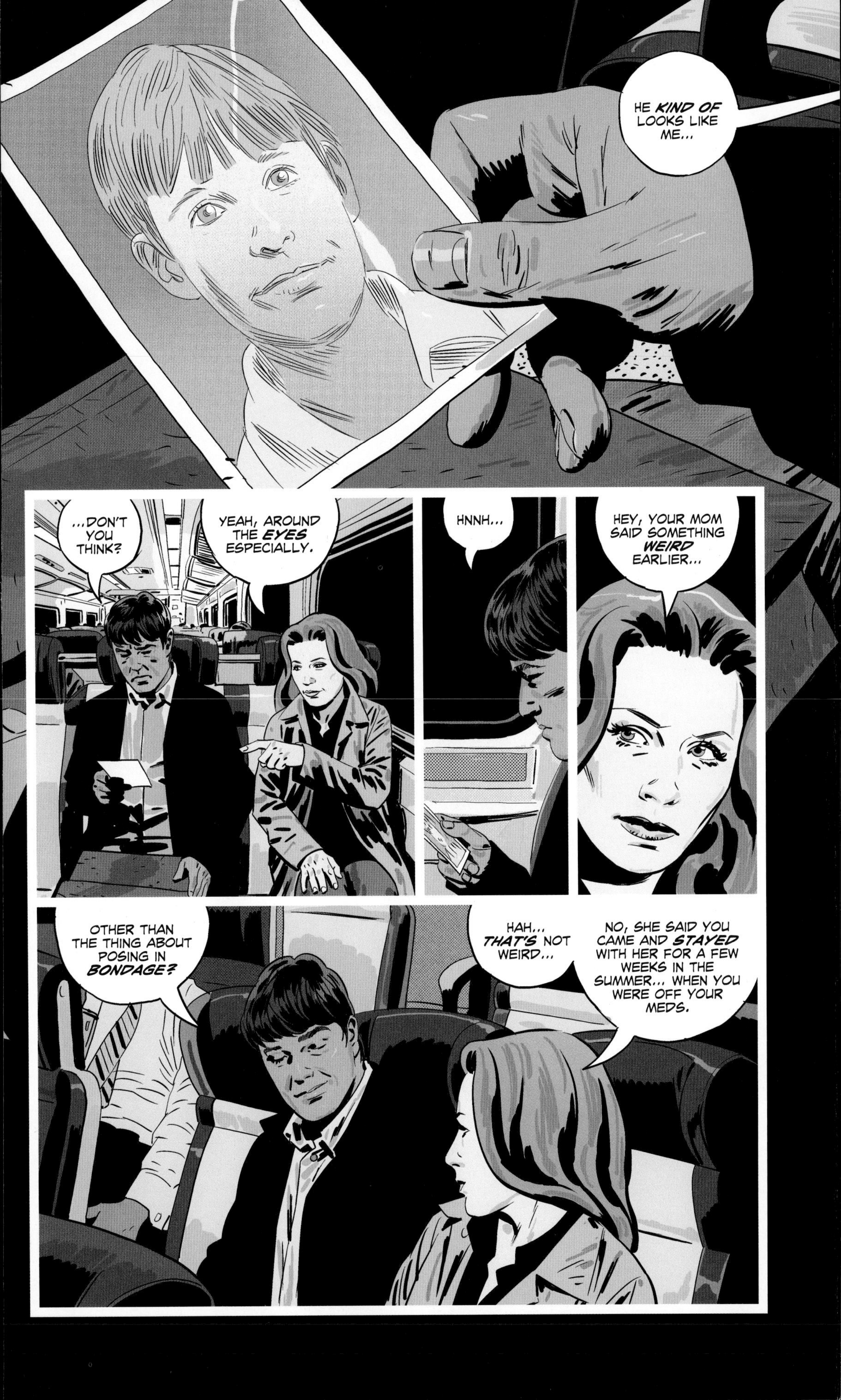
HE KIND OF LOOKS LIKE ME...
...DON'T YOU THINK?
YEAH, AROUND THE EYES ESPECIALLY.
HNNH...
HEY, YOUR MOM SAID SOMETHING WEIRD EARLIER...
OTHER THAN THE THING ABOUT POSING IN BONDAGE?
HAH... THAT'S NOT WEIRD...
NO, SHE SAID YOU CAME AND STAYED WITH HER FOR A FEW WEEKS IN THE SUMMER... WHEN YOU WERE OFF YOUR MEDS.

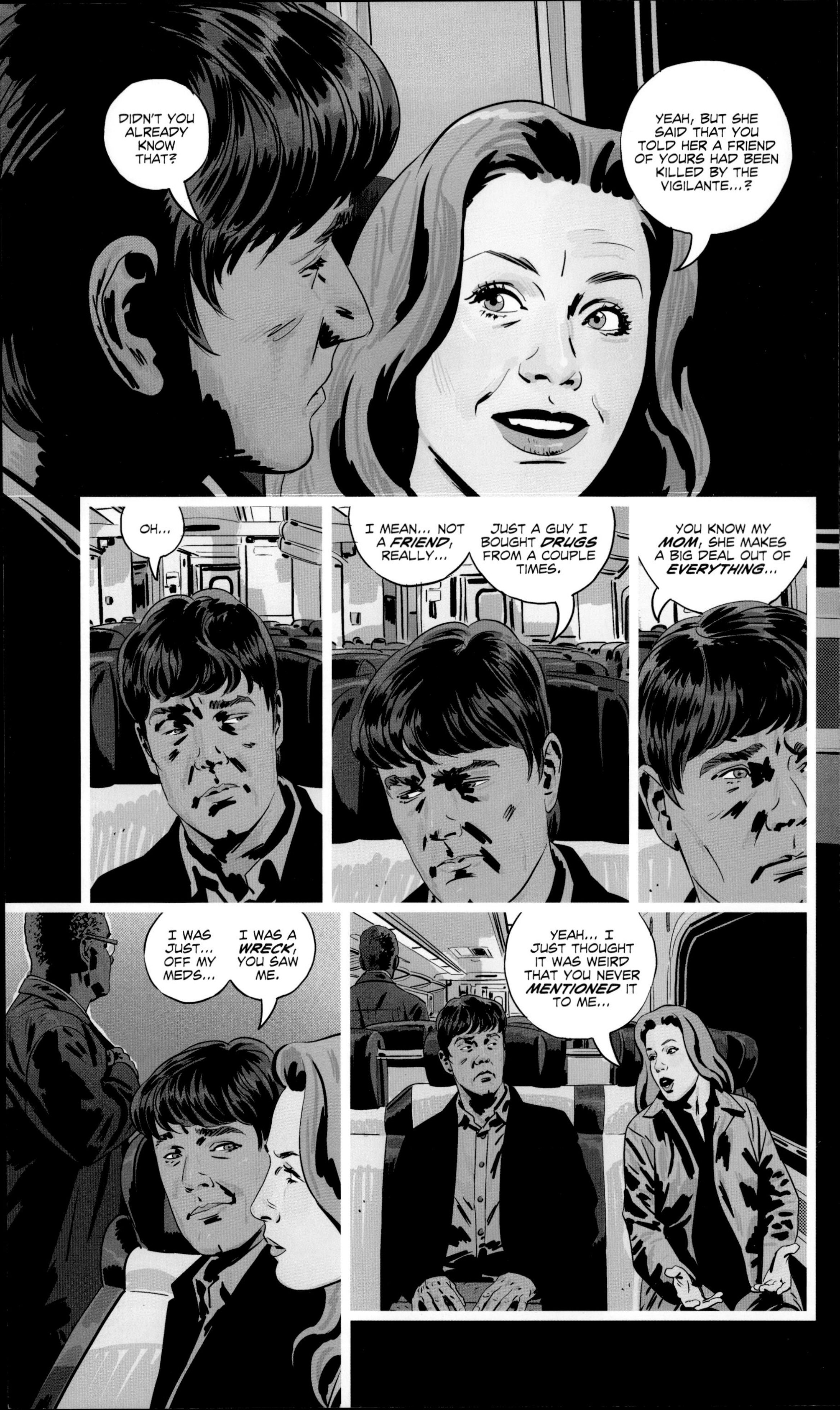
DIDN'T YOU ALREADY KNOW THAT?
YEAH, BUT SHE SAID THAT YOU TOLD HER A FRIEND OF YOURS HAD BEEN KILLED BY THE VIGILANTE...?
OH...
I MEAN... NOT A FRIEND, REALLY...
JUST A GUY I BOUGHT DRUGS FROM A COUPLE TIMES.
YOU KNOW MY MOM, SHE MAKES A BIG DEAL OUT OF EVERYTHING...
I WAS JUST... OFF MY MEDS...
I WAS A WRECK, YOU SAW ME.
YEAH... I JUST THOUGHT IT WAS WEIRD THAT YOU NEVER MENTIONED IT TO ME...

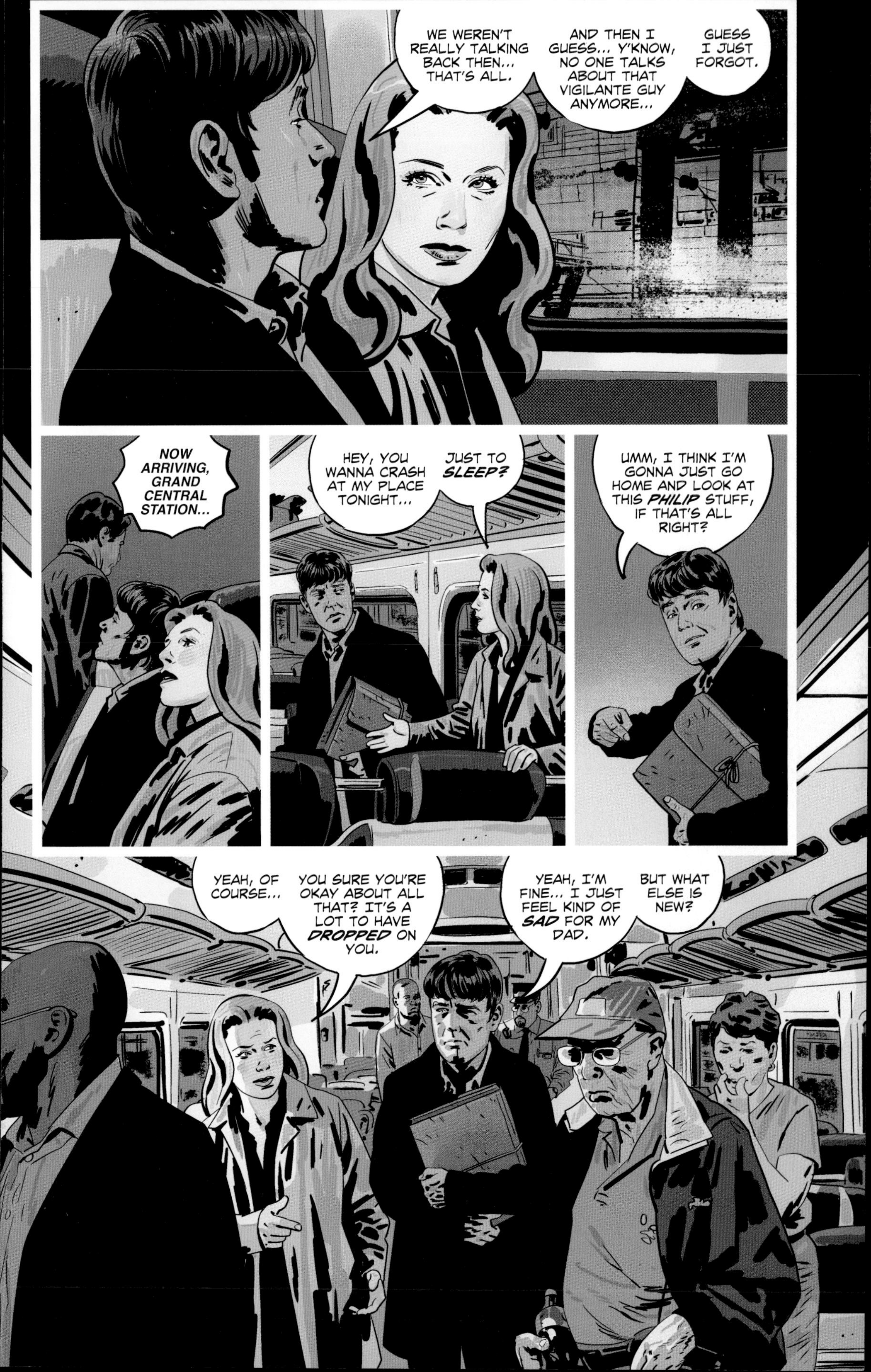
WE WEREN'T REALLY TALKING BACK THEN... THAT'S ALL.
AND THEN I GUESS... Y'KNOW, NO ONE TALKS ABOUT THAT VIGILANTE GUY ANYMORE...
GUESS I JUST FORGOT.
NOW ARRIVING, GRAND CENTRAL STATION...
HEY, YOU WANNA CRASH AT MY PLACE TONIGHT...
JUST TO *SLEEP?*
UMM, I THINK I'M GONNA JUST GO HOME AND LOOK AT THIS *PHILIP* STUFF, IF THAT'S ALL RIGHT?
YEAH, OF COURSE...
YOU SURE YOU'RE OKAY ABOUT ALL THAT? IT'S A LOT TO HAVE *DROPPED* ON YOU.
YEAH, I'M FINE... I JUST FEEL KIND OF *SAD* FOR MY DAD.
BUT WHAT ELSE IS NEW?

So, you might be wondering right now, why did you need to hear about all this stuff before I got to the action again?

And I mean, I guess there are a few reasons...

One, because it's just ***what happened***... I started obsessing about the demon and then I found out I had a half-brother who killed himself.

But mainly I wanted you to know, because I wanted you to understand how it affected me.

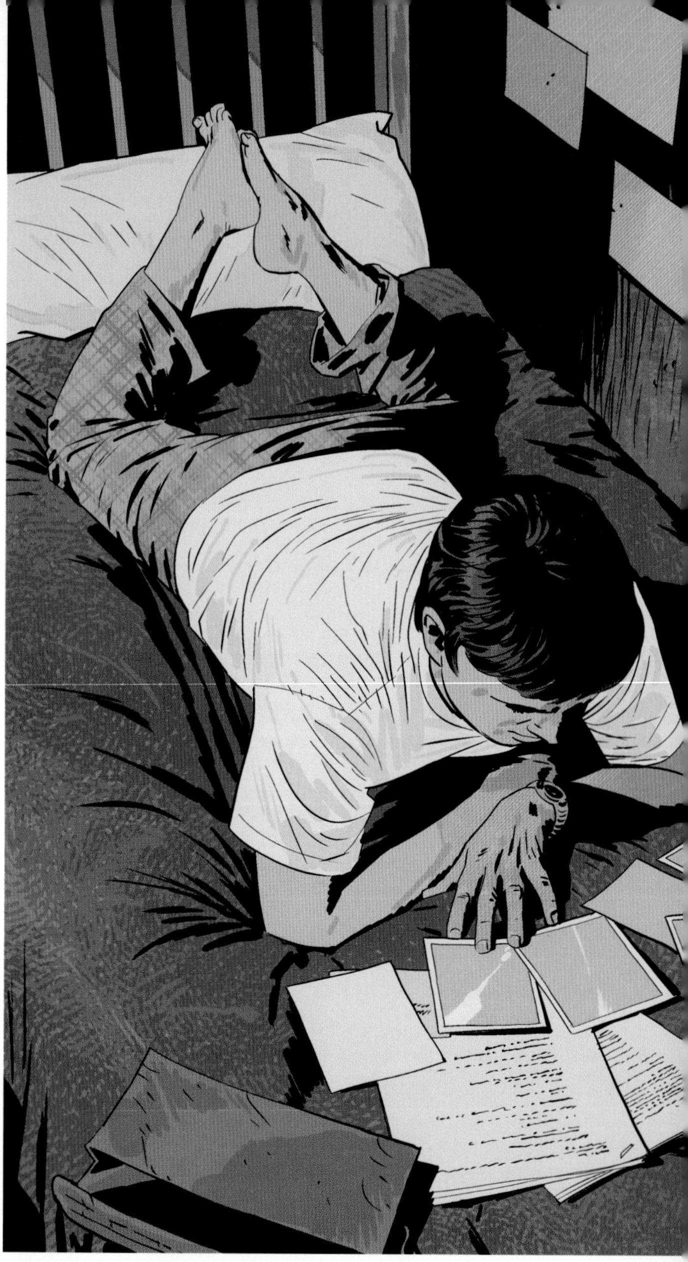

See, there were only a half a dozen photos of Philip in that envelope, along with some other odds and ends...

And honestly, it's just pathetic these few things are all that Dad held onto.

Not the kind of pathetic that makes you angry, but the kind that breaks your heart... that small, fragile kind.

I thought of my father as a young man, full of hope... and then I thought of him in his later years...

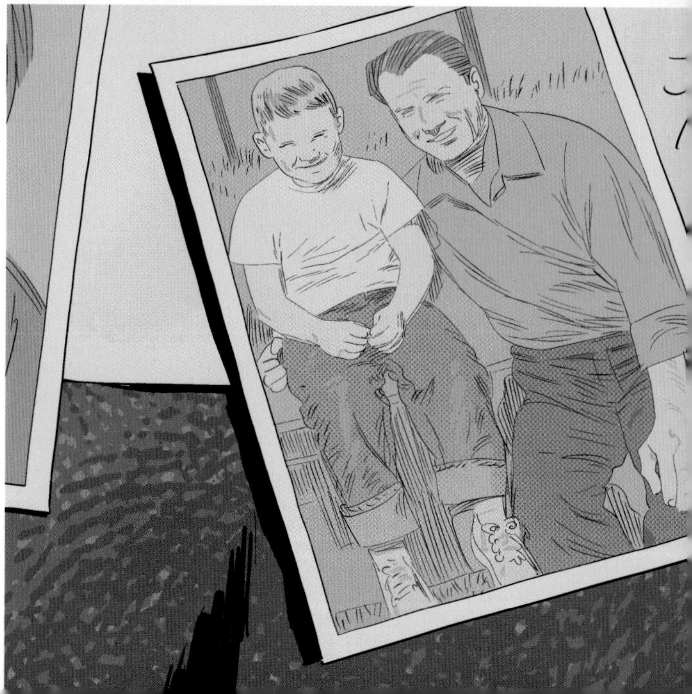

I pictured him sitting alone in his studio, regretting that he didn't have more pictures of his son...

Probably regretting so many things, really.

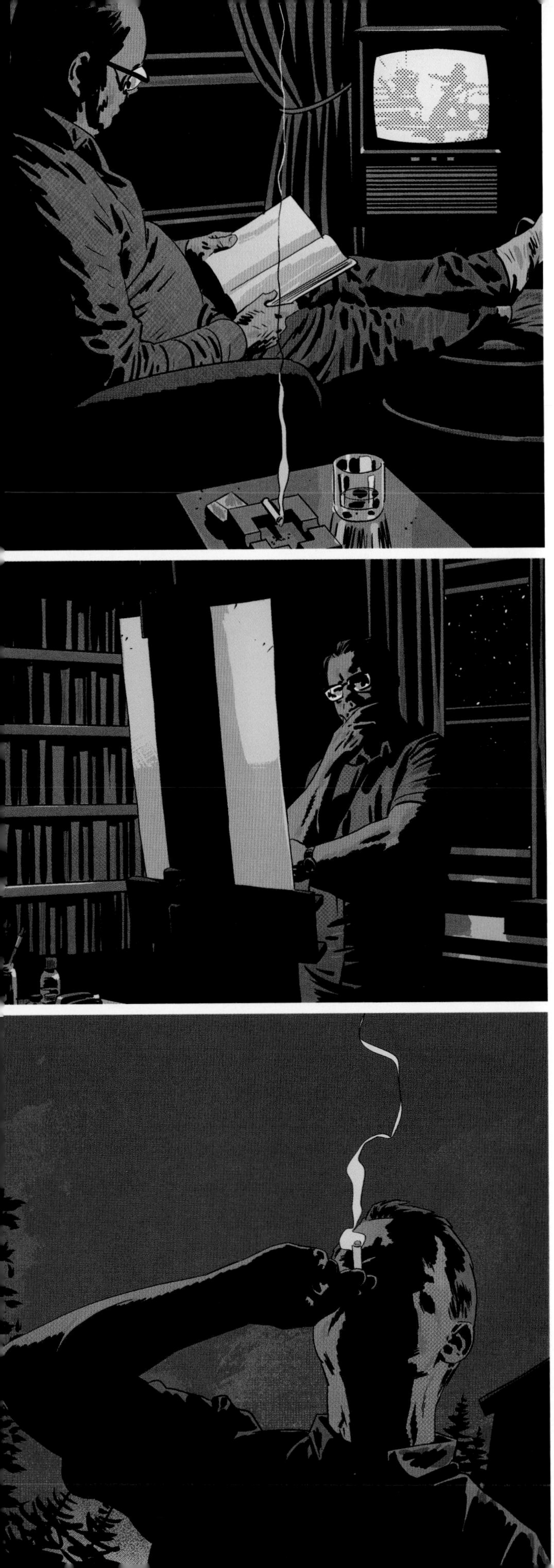

I guess it's different for people whose fathers ***didn't*** commit suicide, but if yours did, then he's probably a fairly tragic figure in your memory...

That familial memory that shapes who you are.

That's how it always was for me. My father was legendary and tragic and sad... all at one time.

And if I had to pick one word that described him best, it would've been a tie between "lonely" and "isolated."

Anyway, as I was looking at the pictures of his dead son that night, I remembered a story Mom told me, about when Dad tried to start a commercial art studio.

One of the freelancers they used was terrible, but he was connected to the mafia somehow...

So when they stopped giving him work, two big guys came by and roughed up Dad's partner and told them to keep hiring the guy... Which, of course, they did.

No one wants to get their teeth broken over a few drawings.

But the studio shut down not long after that...

And Dad gave up on his dream and did whatever he had to to support his family...

Which fell apart anyway.

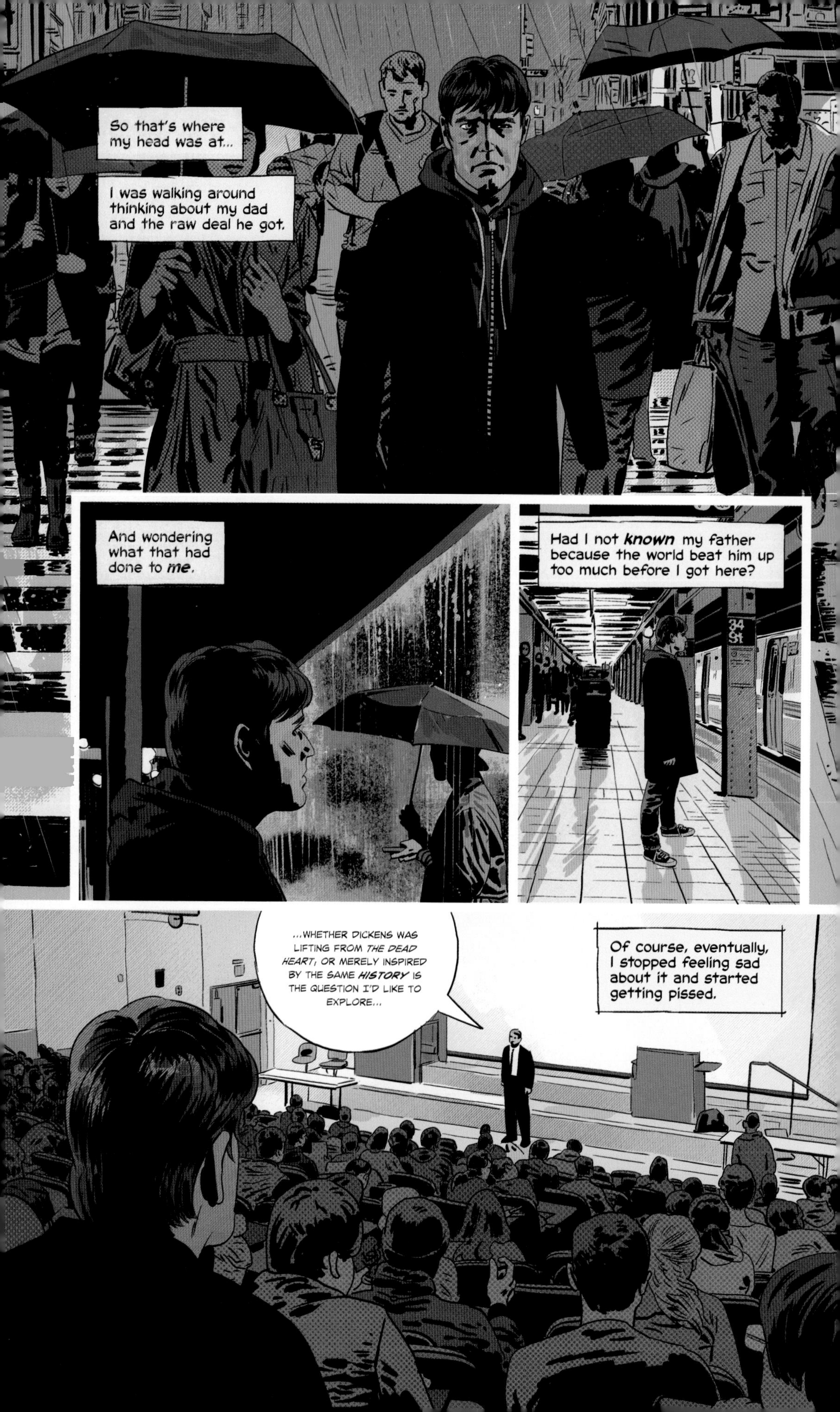
So that's where my head was at...
I was walking around thinking about my dad and the raw deal he got.
And wondering what that had done to *me*.
Had I not ***known*** my father because the world beat him up too much before I got here?
...WHETHER DICKENS WAS LIFTING FROM *THE DEAD HEART*, OR MERELY INSPIRED BY THE SAME ***HISTORY*** IS THE QUESTION I'D LIKE TO EXPLORE...
Of course, eventually, I stopped feeling sad about it and started getting pissed.

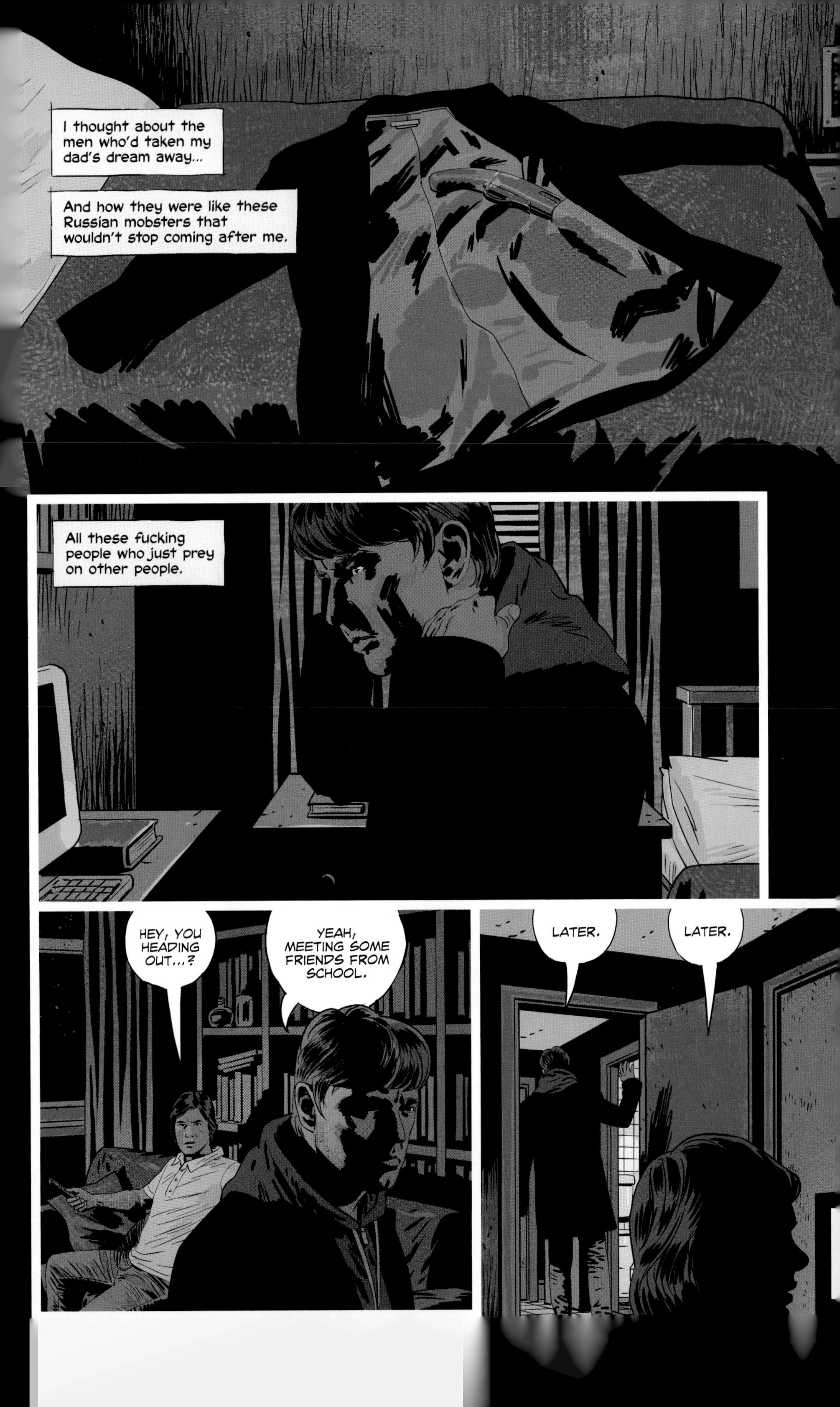

I thought about the men who'd taken my dad's dream away...
And how they were like these Russian mobsters that wouldn't stop coming after me.
All these fucking people who just prey on other people.
HEY, YOU HEADING OUT...?
YEAH, MEETING SOME FRIENDS FROM SCHOOL.
LATER.
LATER.

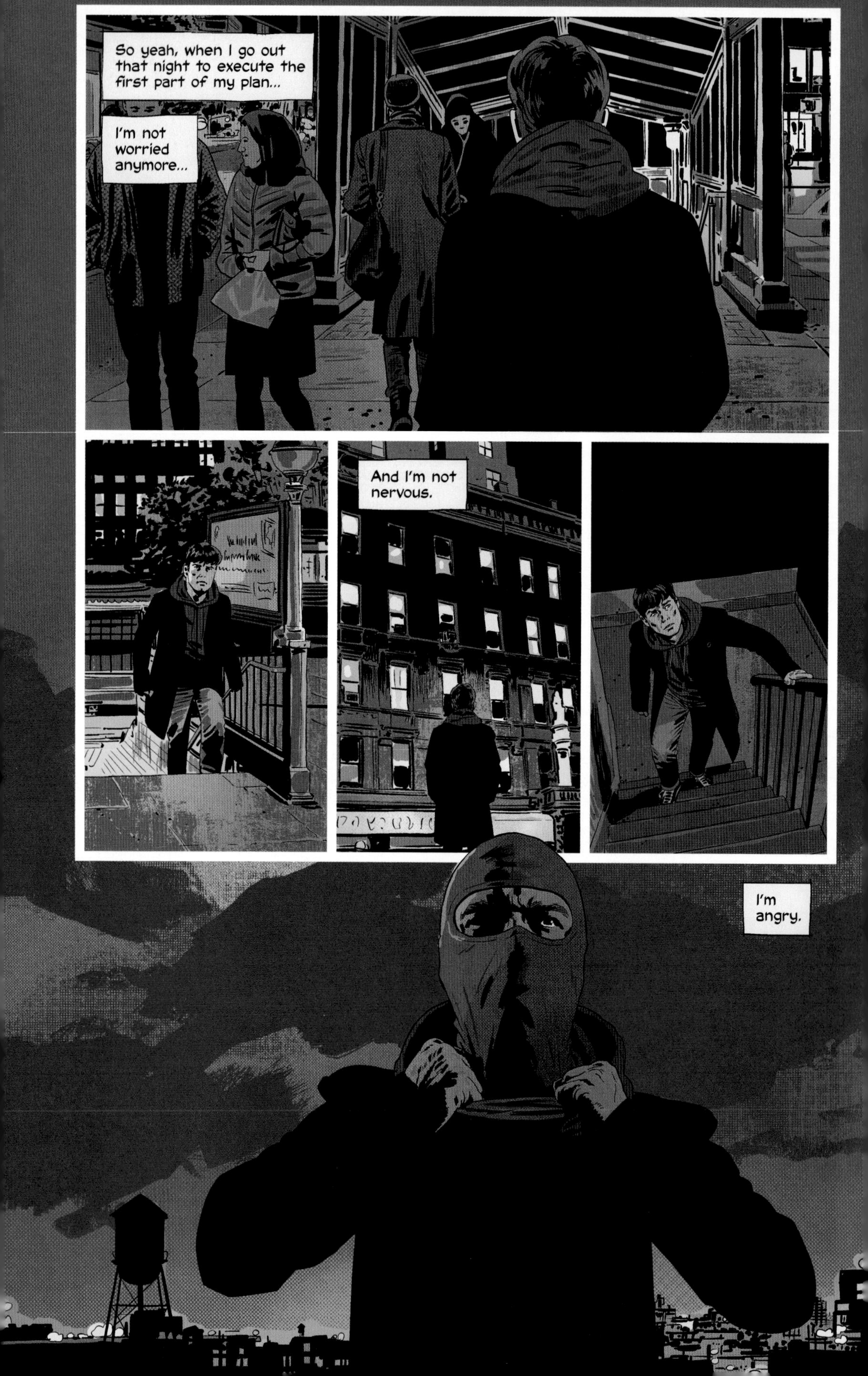
So yeah, when I go out that night to execute the first part of my plan...
I'm not worried anymore...
And I'm not nervous.
I'm angry.

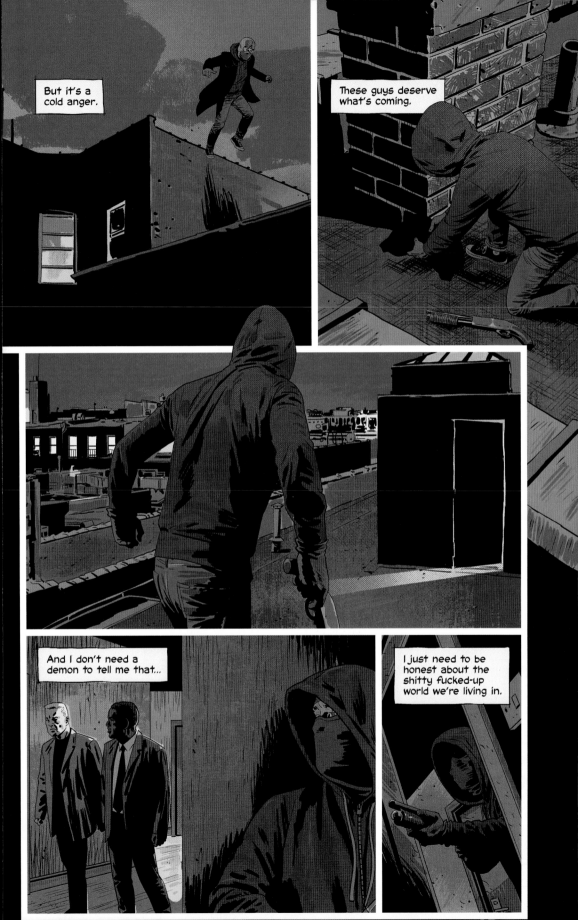

But it's a cold anger.

These guys deserve what's coming.

And I don't need a demon to tell me that...

I just need to be honest about the shitty fucked-up world we're living in.

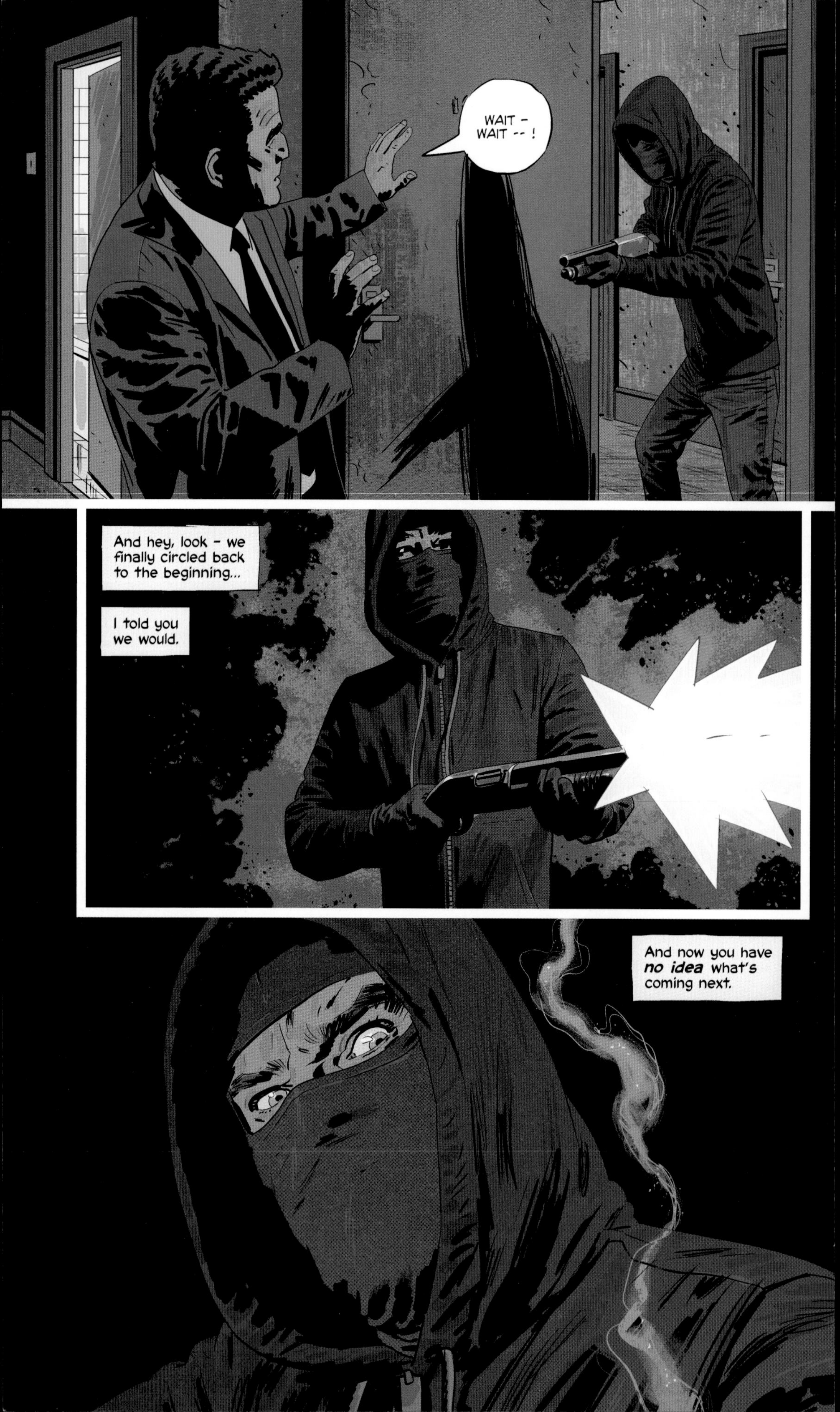
WAIT -
WAIT -- !
And hey, look - we finally circled back to the beginning...
I told you we would.
And now you have *no idea* what's coming next.

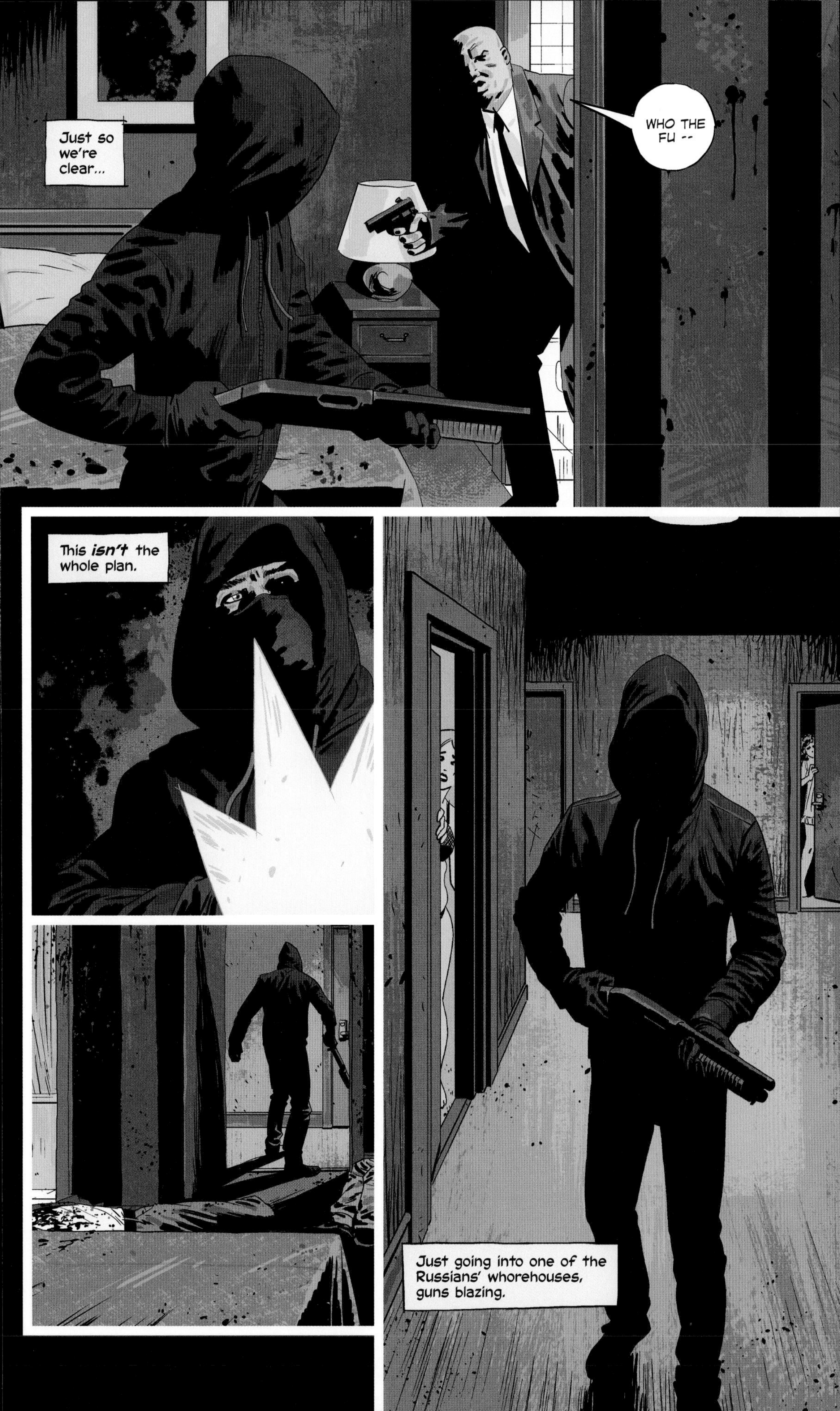
Just so we're clear...
WHO THE FU --
This *isn't* the whole plan.
Just going into one of the Russians' whorehouses, guns blazing.

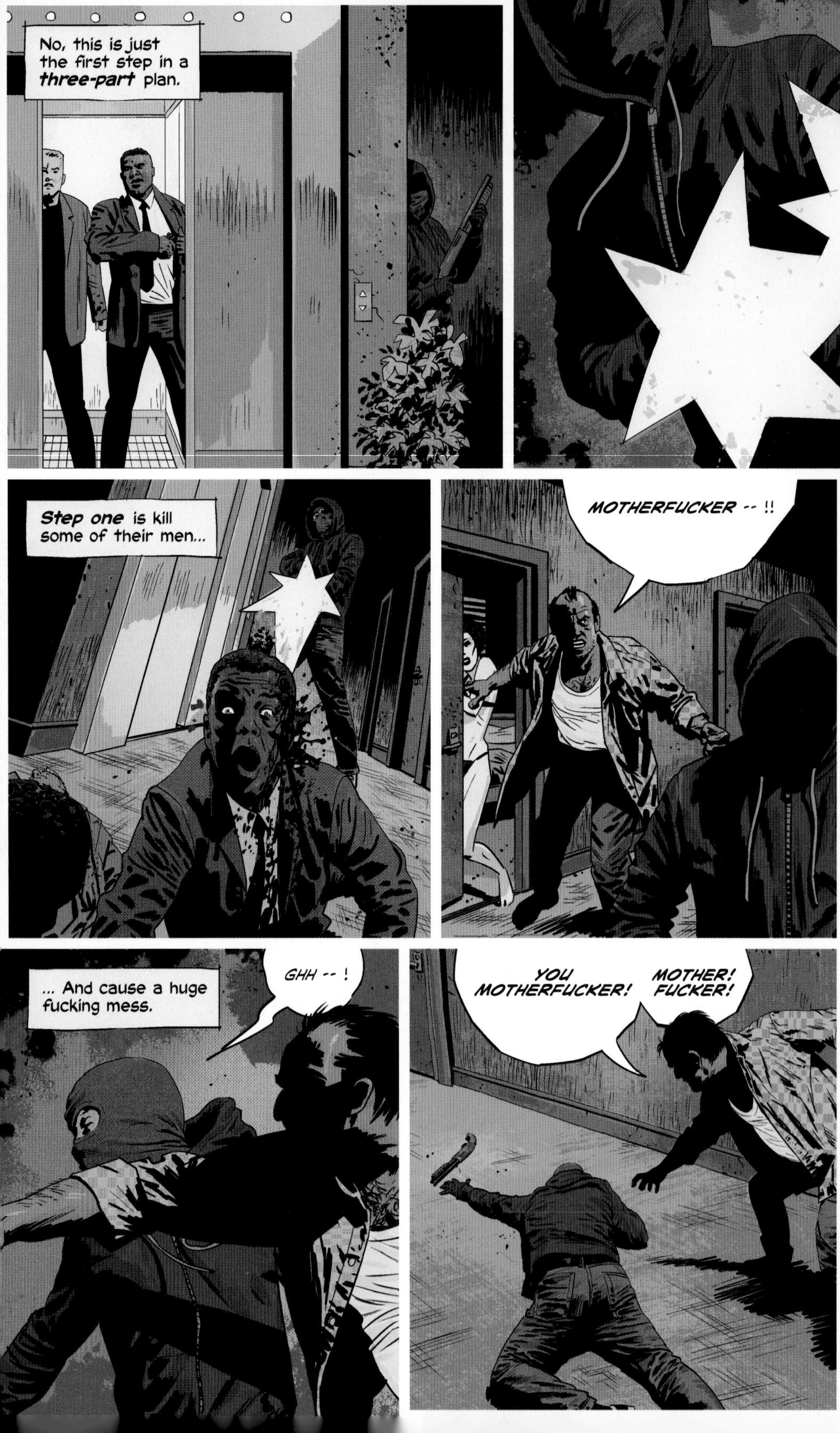

No, this is just the first step in a ***three-part*** plan.
Step one is kill some of their men...
MOTHERFUCKER -- !!
... And cause a huge fucking mess.
GHH -- !
YOU MOTHERFUCKER!
MOTHER! FUCKER!

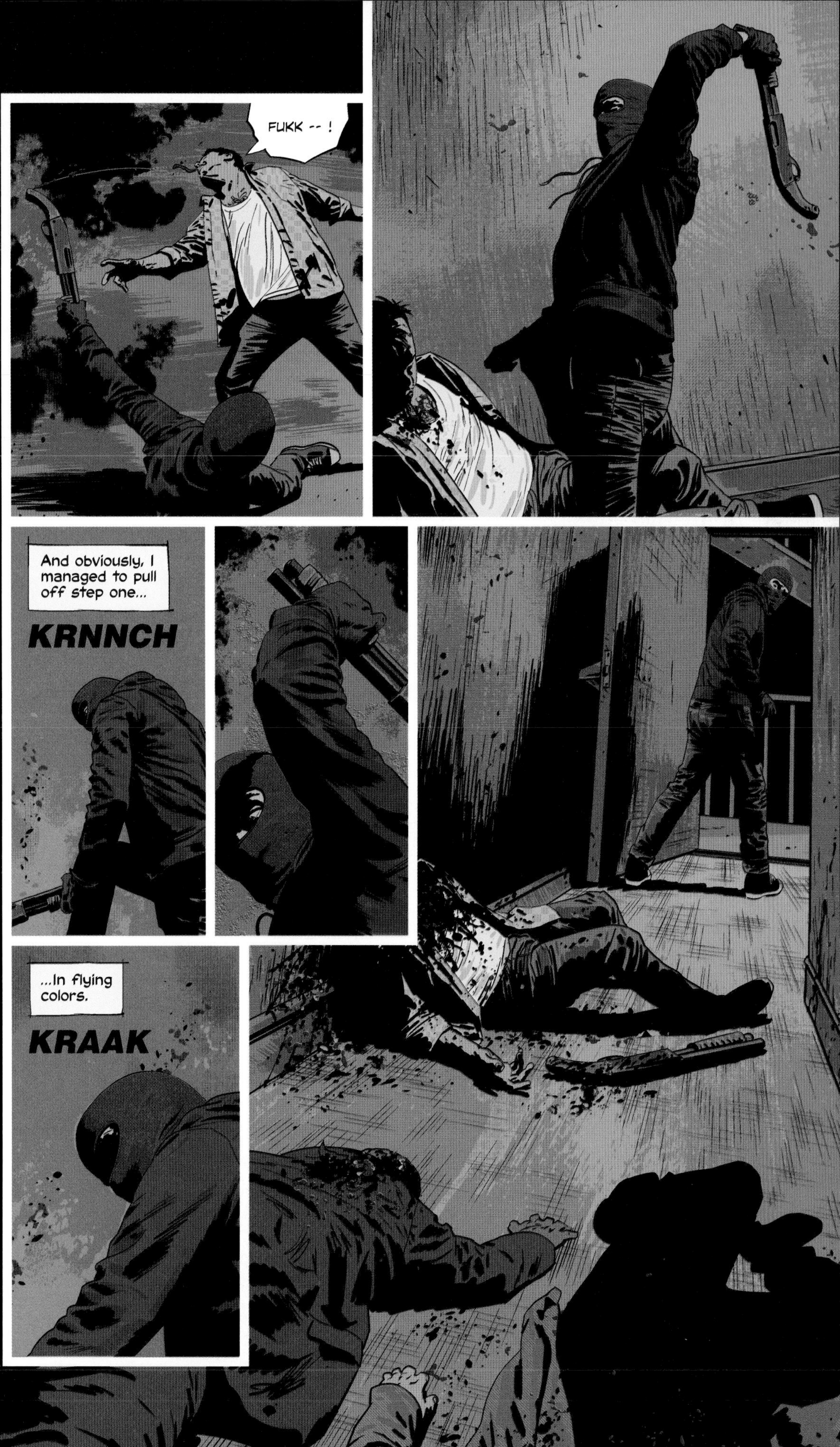

FUKK -- !
And obviously, I managed to pull off step one...
KRNNCH
...In flying colors.
KRAAK

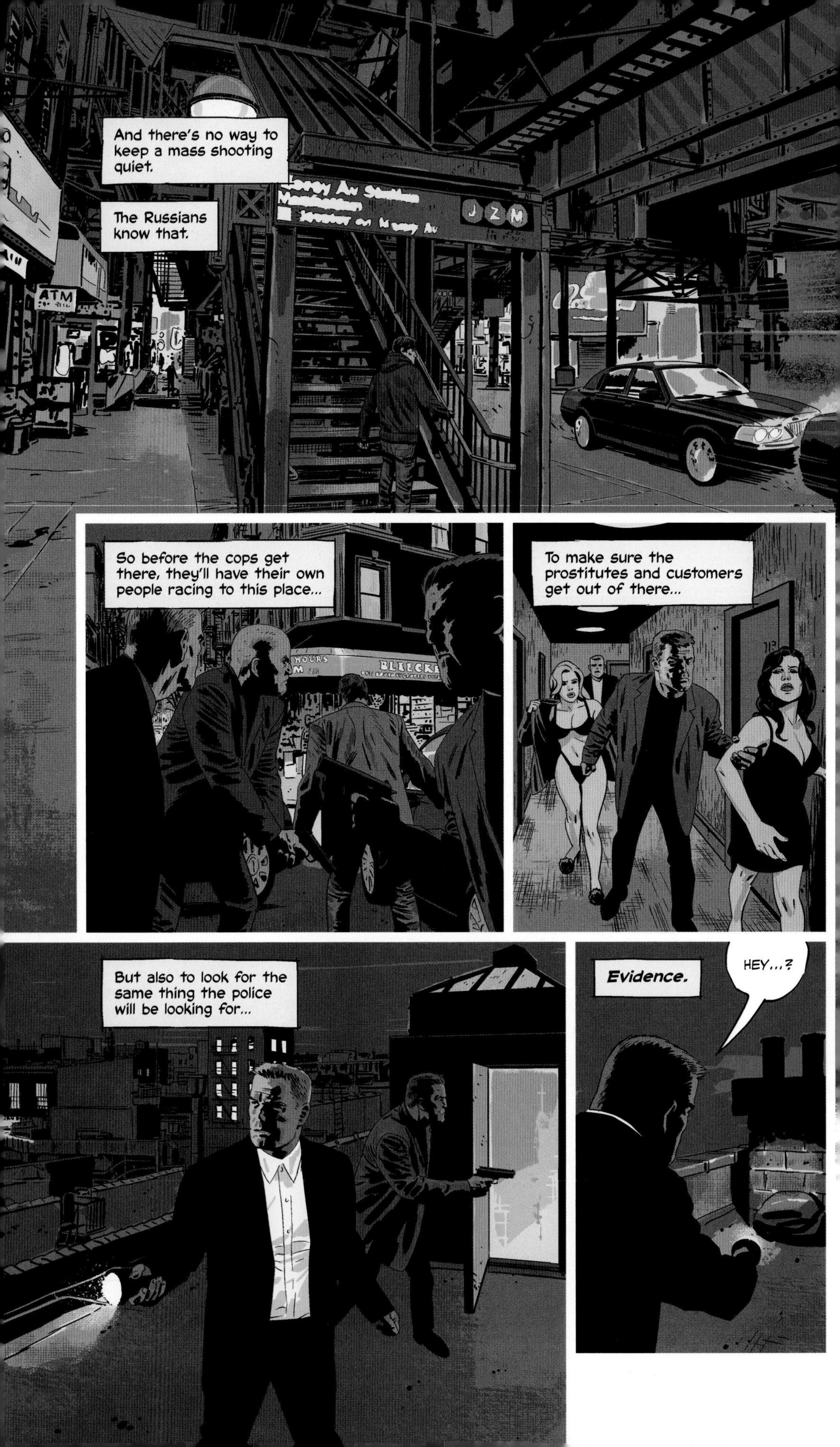

And there's no way to keep a mass shooting quiet.
The Russians know that.
J Z M
ATM
So before the cops get there, they'll have their own people racing to this place...
To make sure the prostitutes and customers get out of there...
But also to look for the same thing the police will be looking for...
Evidence.
HEY...?

And that's where **step two** of my plan comes into play.

HEY -- I FIND SOMETHING OVER HERE.

WHAT IS IT?

OVERCOAT. SOMEONE PUT HERE, LIKE TO HIDE.

Step two is to make them think I fucked up.

LET ME SEE.

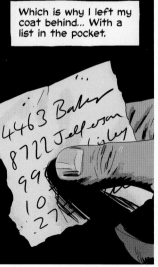

Which is why I left my coat behind... With a list in the pocket.

The **locations** of their other five brothels.

OH... SHIT.

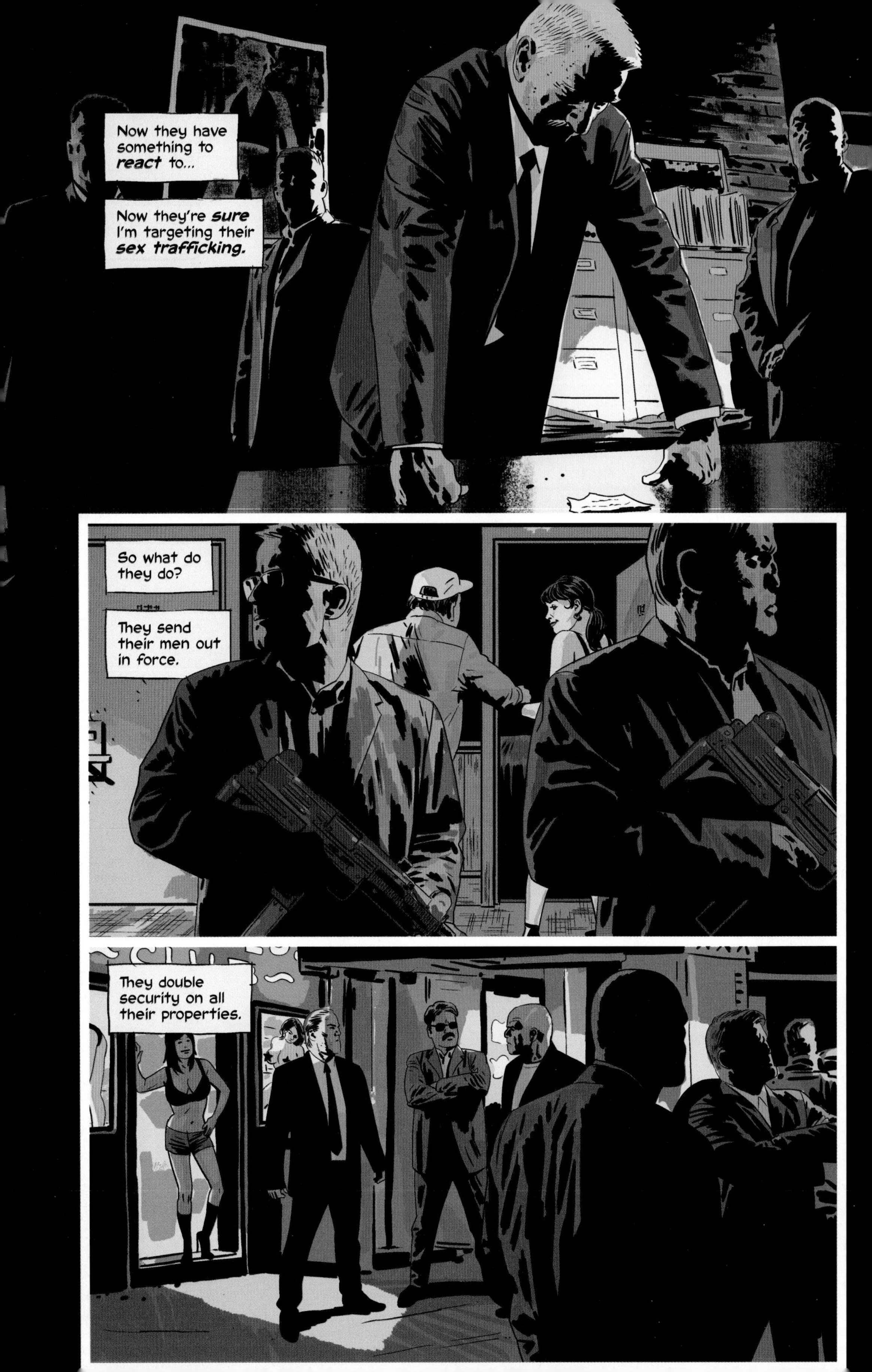
Now they have something to ***react*** to...
Now they're ***sure*** I'm targeting their ***sex trafficking.***
So what do they do?
They send their men out in force.
They double security on all their properties.

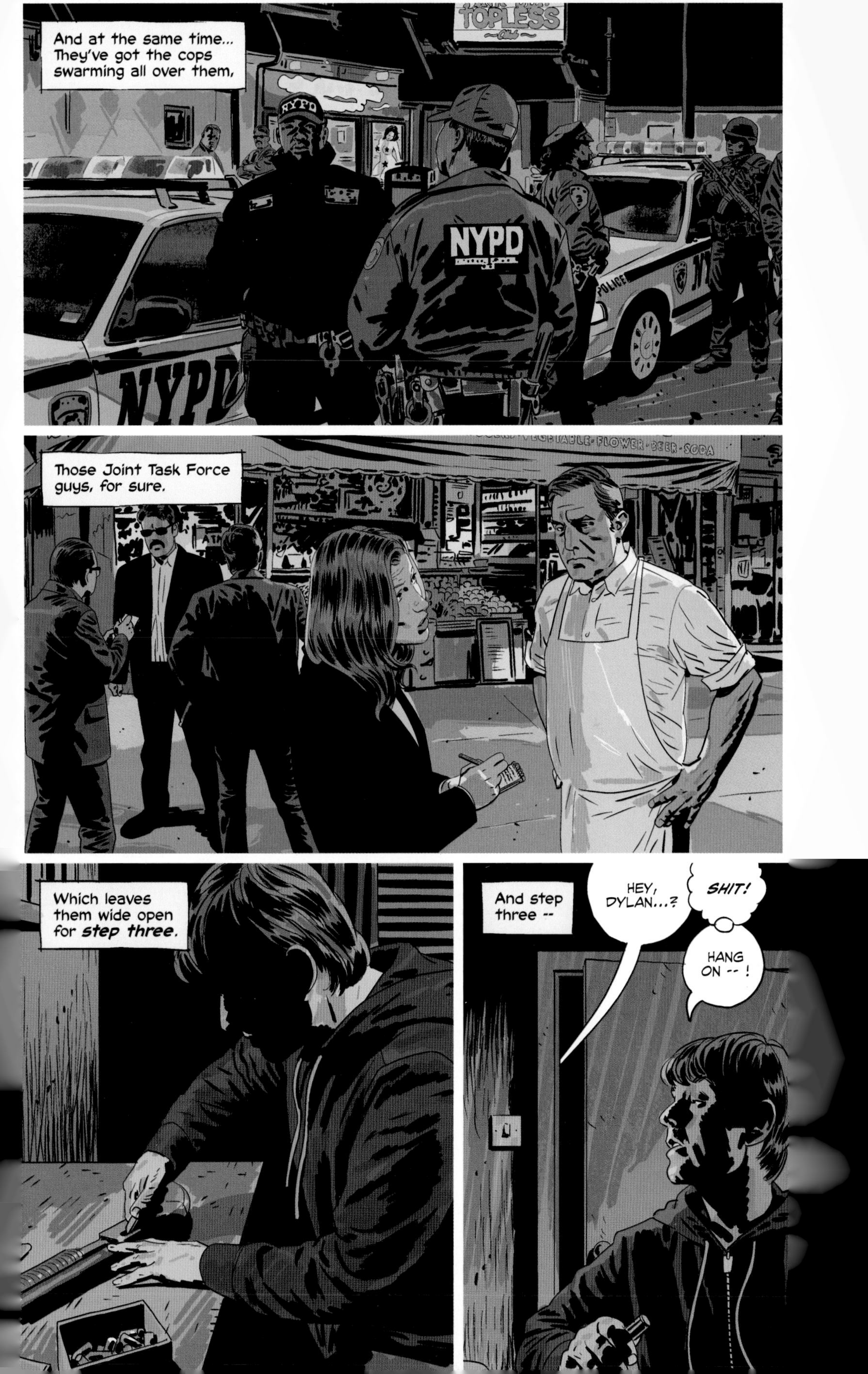
TOPLESS
And at the same time... They've got the cops swarming all over them,
NYPD
NYPD
NYPD
POLICE
VEGETABLE·FLOWER·BEER·SODA
Those Joint Task Force guys, for sure.
Which leaves them wide open for ***step three***.
And step three --
HEY, DYLAN...?
SHIT!
HANG ON -- !

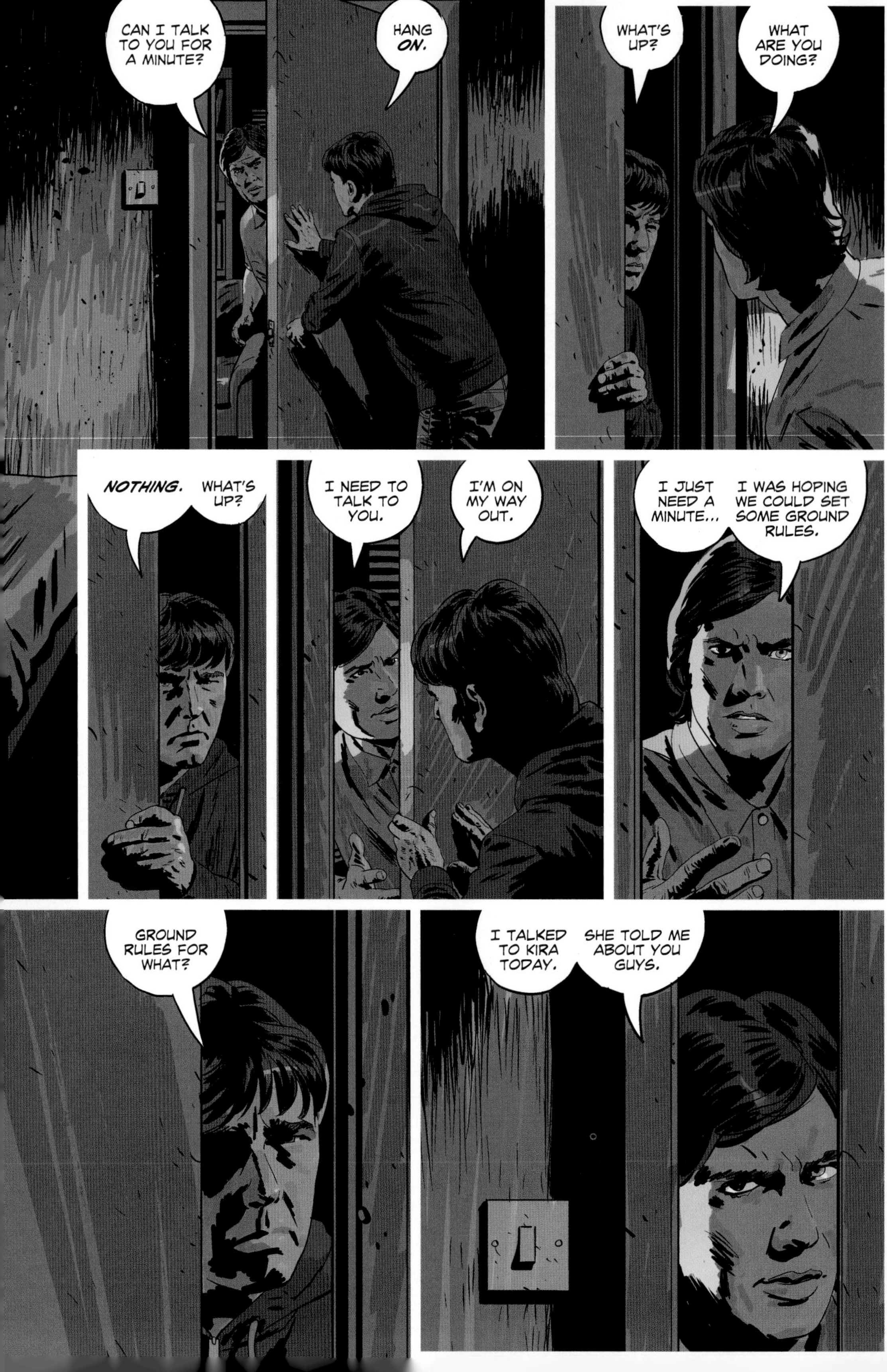
CAN I TALK TO YOU FOR A MINUTE?
HANG *ON.*
WHAT'S UP?
WHAT ARE YOU DOING?
NOTHING.
WHAT'S UP?
I NEED TO TALK TO YOU.
I'M ON MY WAY OUT.
I JUST NEED A MINUTE...
I WAS HOPING WE COULD SET SOME GROUND RULES.
GROUND RULES FOR WHAT?
I TALKED TO KIRA TODAY.
SHE TOLD ME ABOUT YOU GUYS.

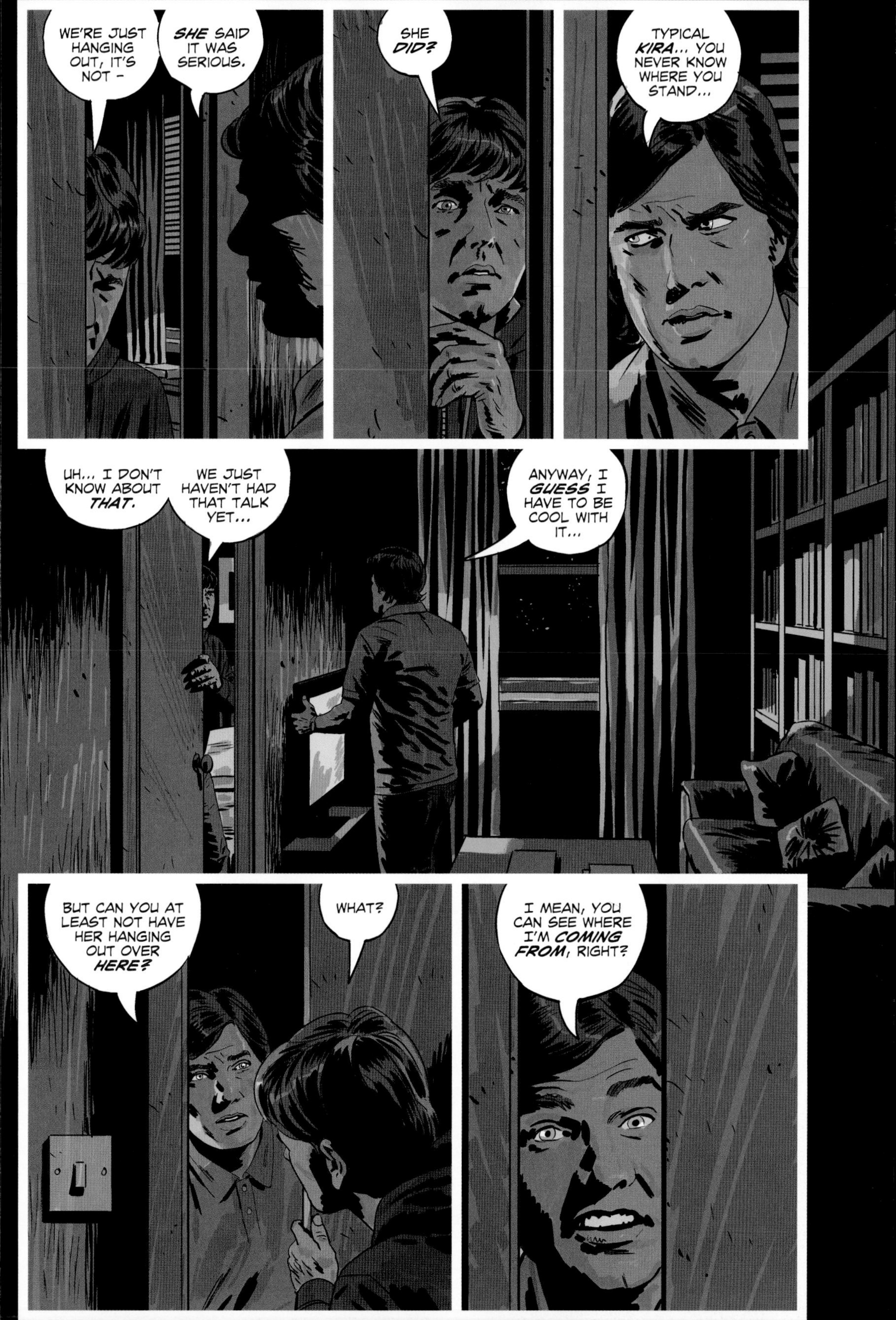
WE'RE JUST HANGING OUT, IT'S NOT -
SHE SAID IT WAS SERIOUS.
SHE DID?
TYPICAL KIRA... YOU NEVER KNOW WHERE YOU STAND...
UH... I DON'T KNOW ABOUT THAT.
WE JUST HAVEN'T HAD THAT TALK YET...
ANYWAY, I GUESS I HAVE TO BE COOL WITH IT...
BUT CAN YOU AT LEAST NOT HAVE HER HANGING OUT OVER HERE?
WHAT?
I MEAN, YOU CAN SEE WHERE I'M COMING FROM, RIGHT?

So, ***here's*** a thing...

Normally -
Historically, I mean -
I'm the kind of guy
who avoids conflict.

And yeah, I know
that's "ironic" since
I'm a vigilante killer...

But I'm talking about
in my ***normal*** life.

Put me in a dark alley
with a child molester
or a mobster and I'm
fine.

But make me talk to
my roommate about
anything even slightly
unpleasant and I'll
avoid it...

Or just agree to
whatever, just
to get along.

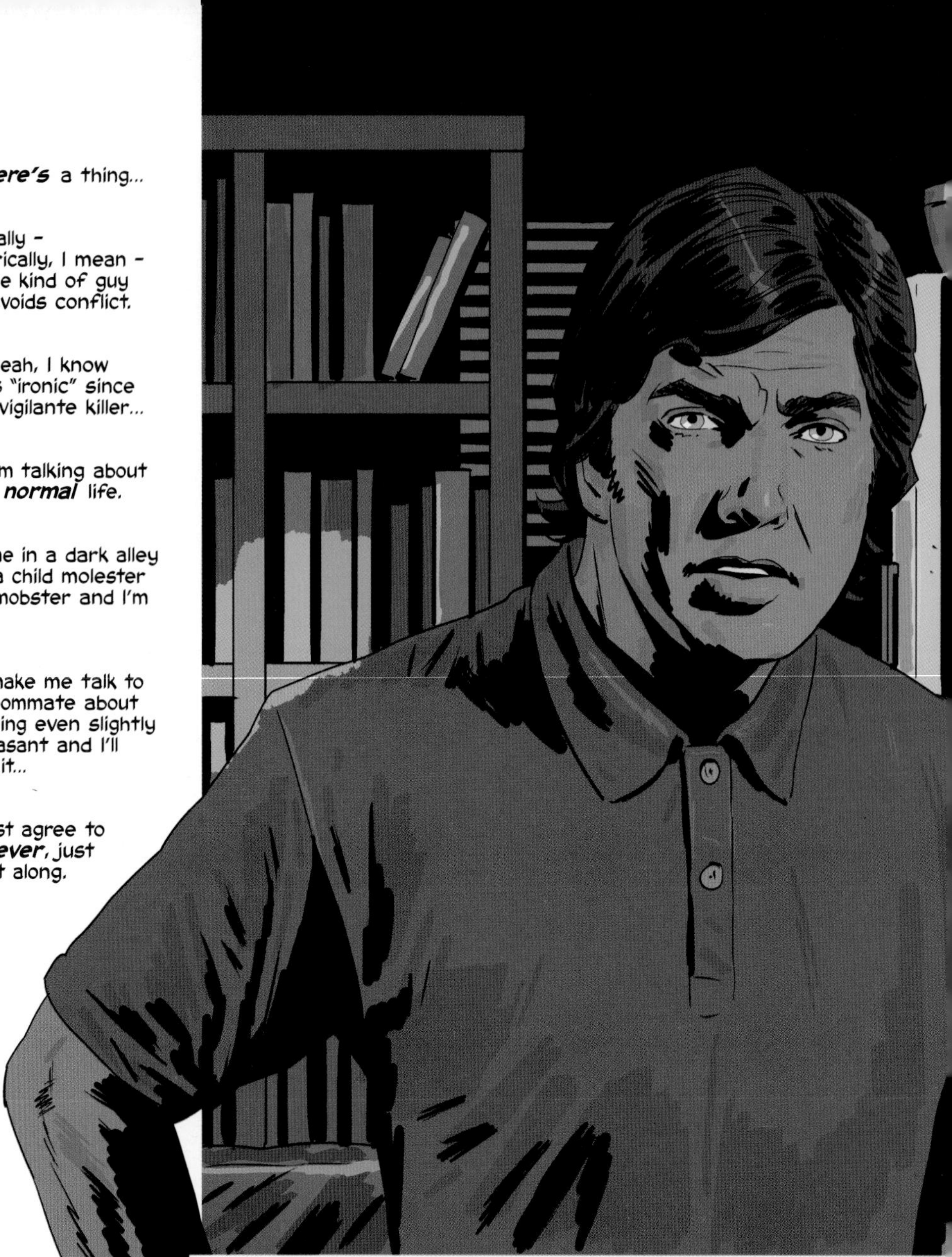

But as
I was
standing
there looking
at Mason
that night,
I heard myself
thinking...

Who the fuck does
this guy think he is...?

And why do I put up
with this bullshit?

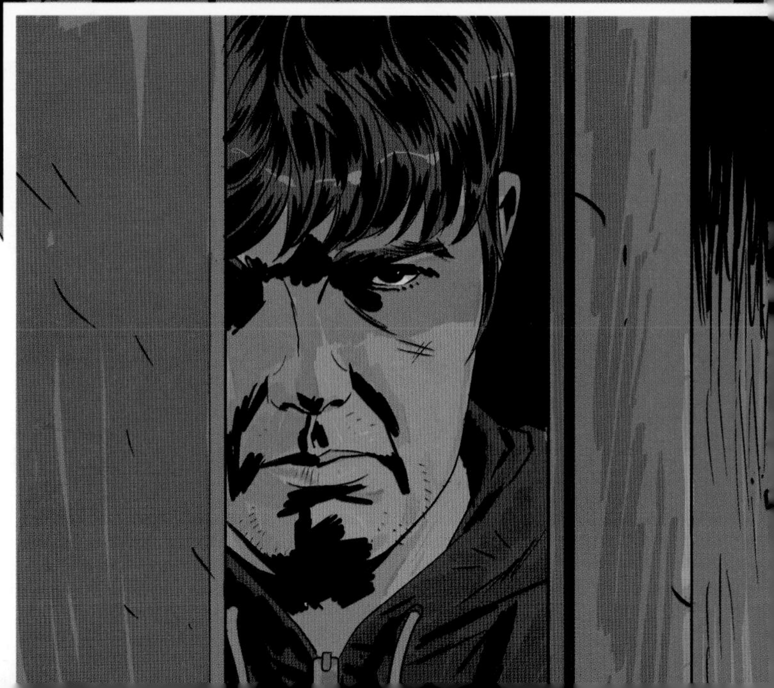

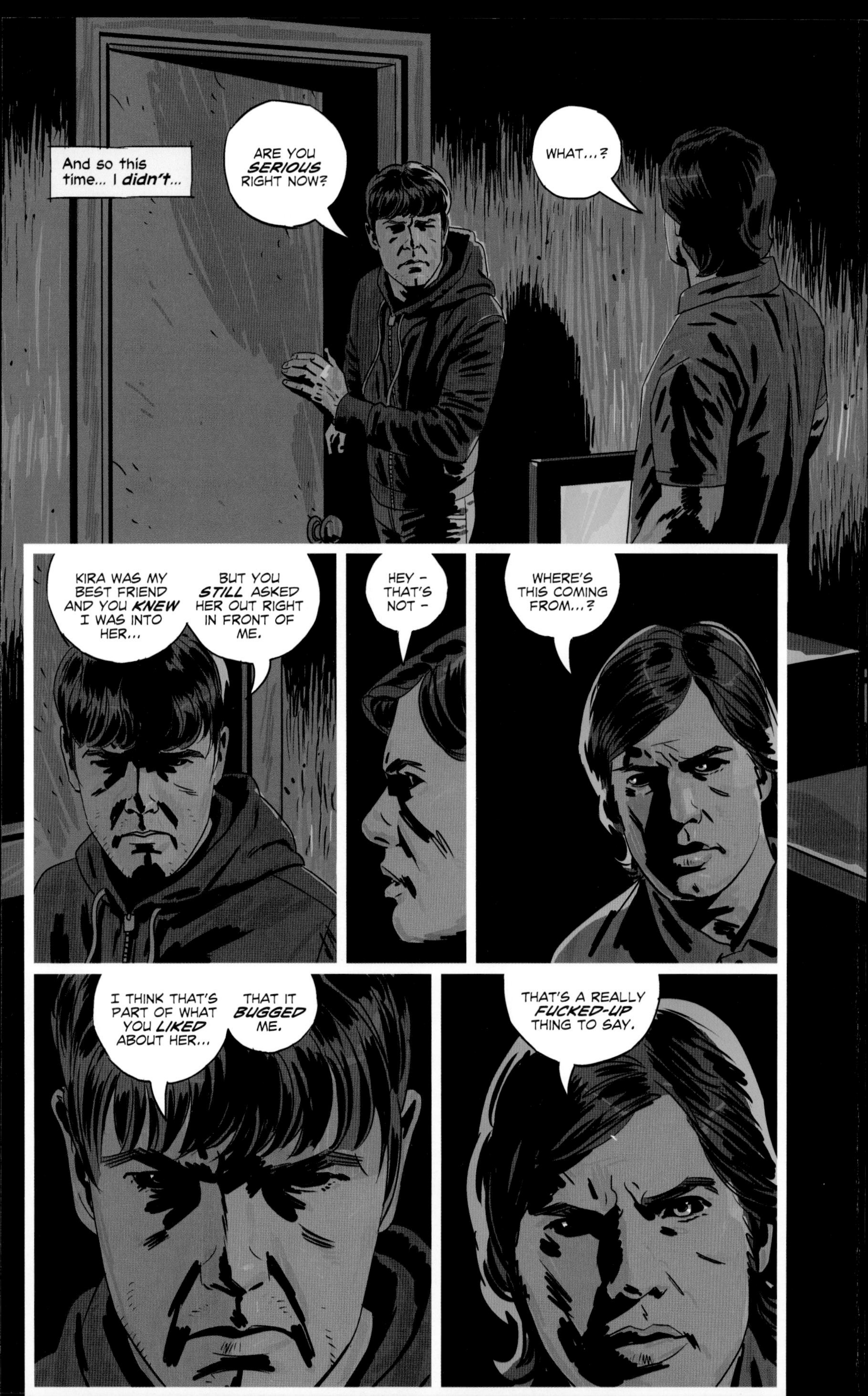
And so this time... I *didn't*...
ARE YOU *SERIOUS* RIGHT NOW?
WHAT...?
KIRA WAS MY BEST FRIEND AND YOU *KNEW* I WAS INTO HER...
BUT YOU *STILL* ASKED HER OUT RIGHT IN FRONT OF ME.
HEY – THAT'S NOT –
WHERE'S THIS COMING FROM...?
I THINK THAT'S PART OF WHAT YOU *LIKED* ABOUT HER...
THAT IT *BUGGED* ME.
THAT'S A REALLY *FUCKED-UP* THING TO SAY.

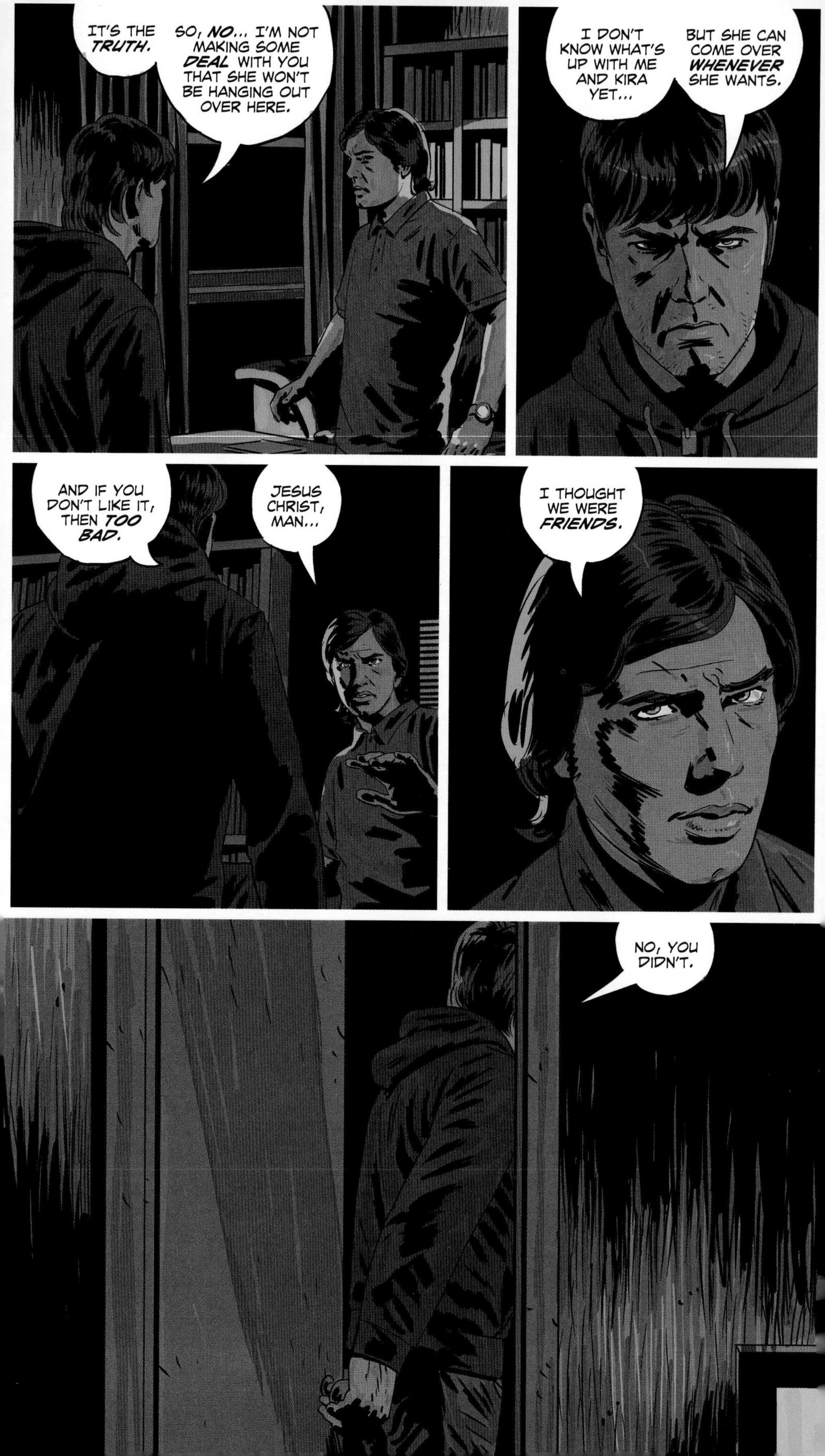
IT'S THE TRUTH.
SO, NO... I'M NOT MAKING SOME DEAL WITH YOU THAT SHE WON'T BE HANGING OUT OVER HERE.
I DON'T KNOW WHAT'S UP WITH ME AND KIRA YET...
BUT SHE CAN COME OVER WHENEVER SHE WANTS.
AND IF YOU DON'T LIKE IT, THEN TOO BAD.
JESUS CHRIST, MAN...
I THOUGHT WE WERE FRIENDS.
NO, YOU DIDN'T.

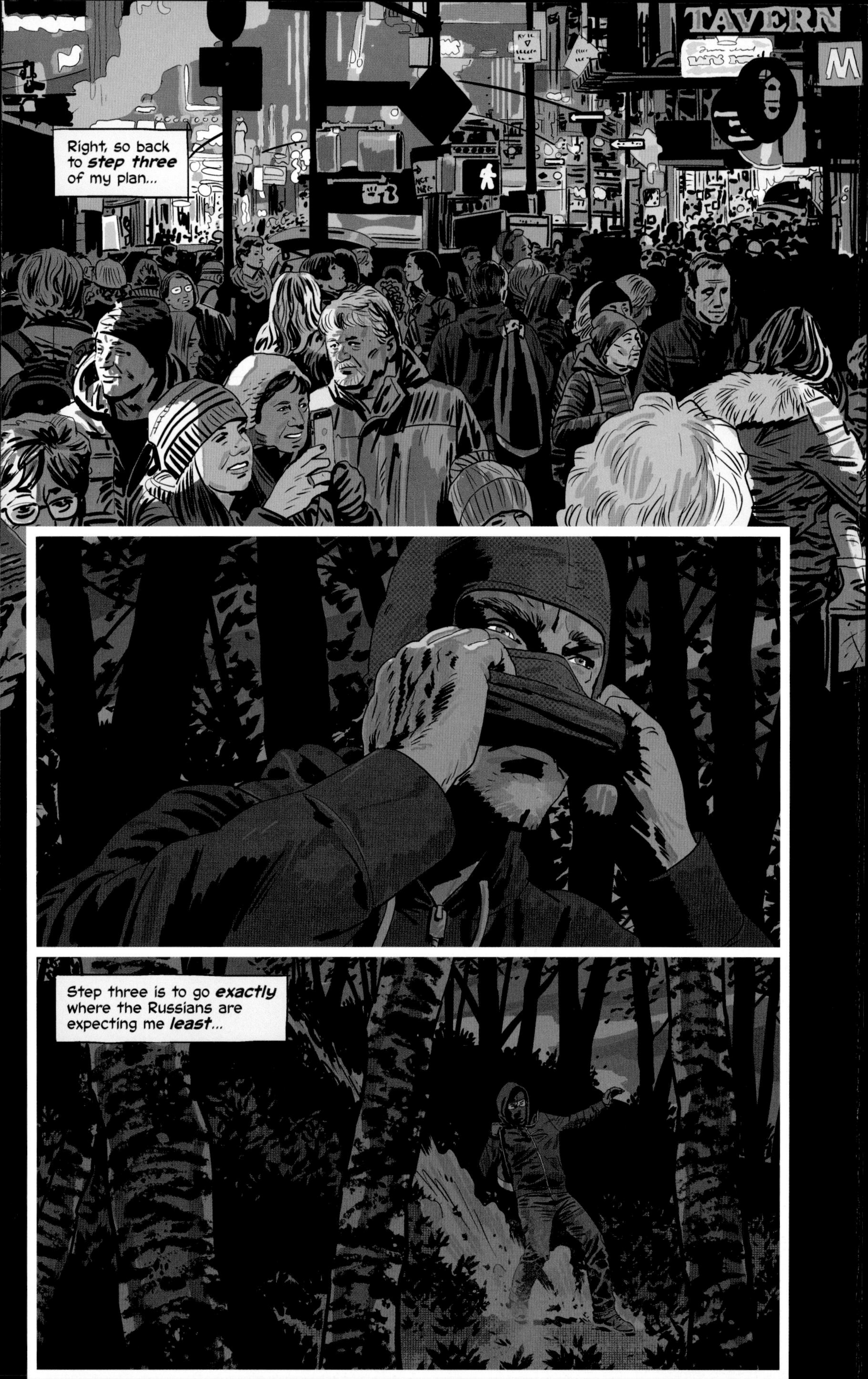
TAVERN
M
Right, so back to step three of my plan...
Step three is to go exactly where the Russians are expecting me least...

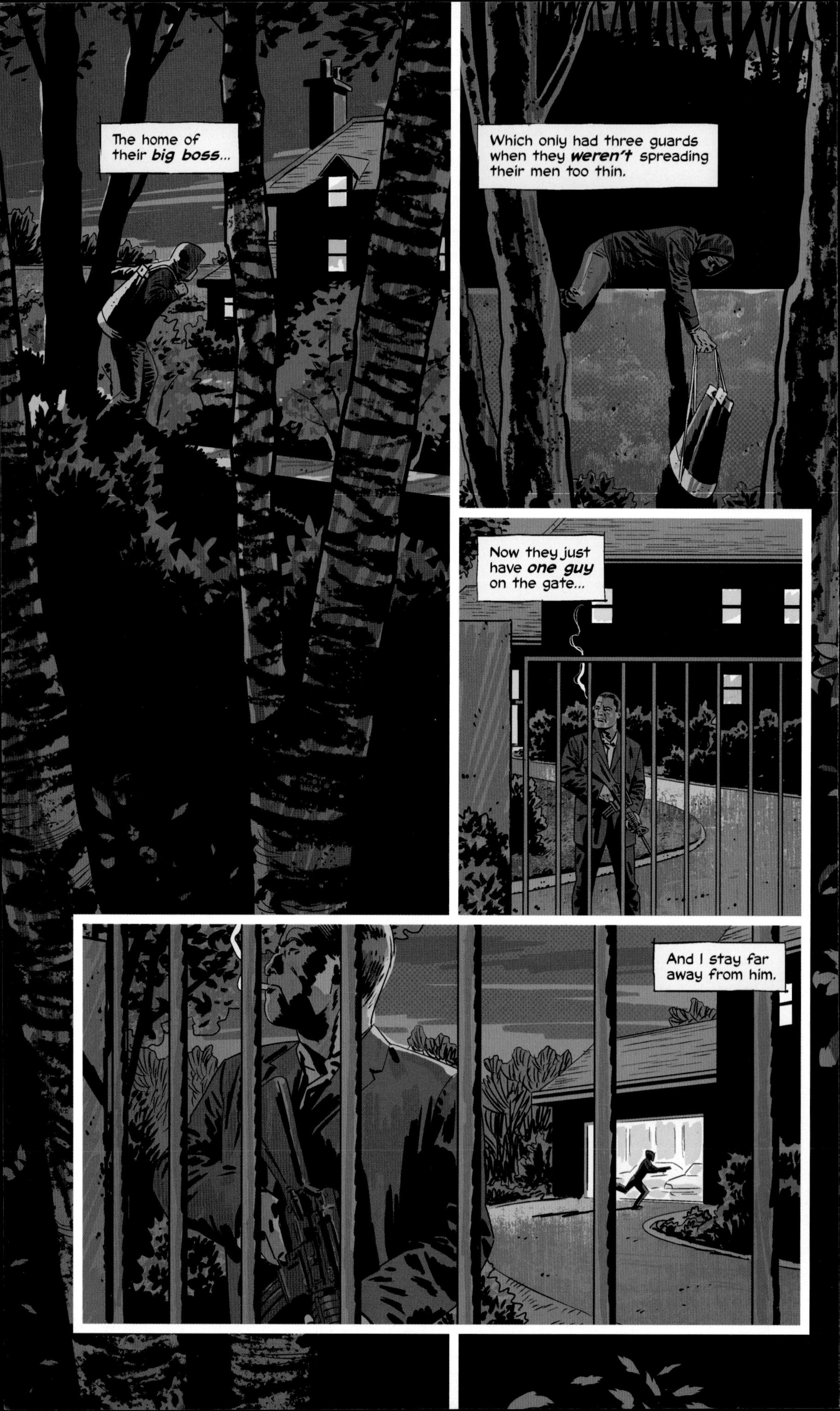

The home of their *big boss*...
Which only had three guards when they ***weren't*** spreading their men too thin.
Now they just have ***one guy*** on the gate...
And I stay far away from him.

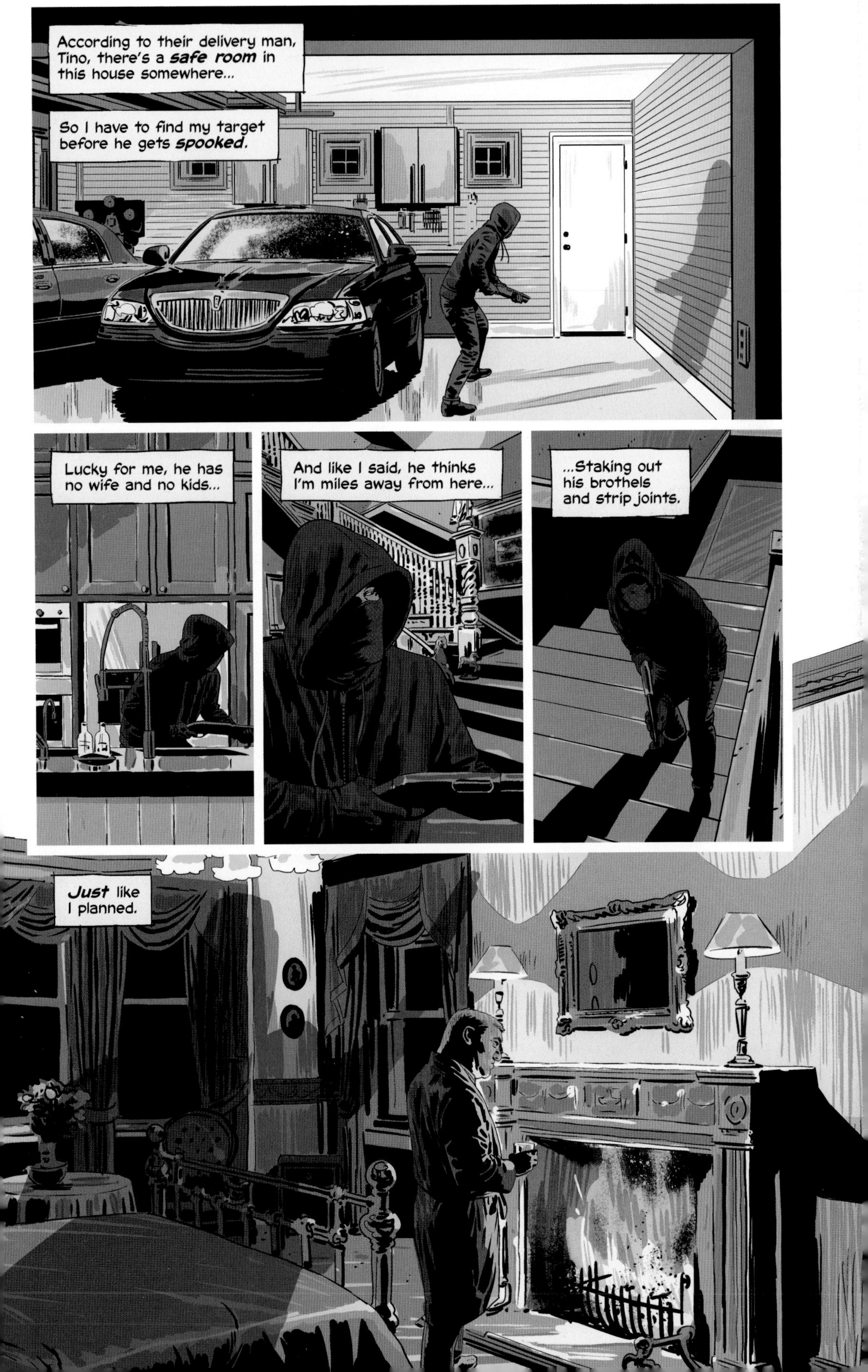
According to their delivery man, Tino, there's a *safe room* in this house somewhere...
So I have to find my target before he gets *spooked.*
Lucky for me, he has no wife and no kids...
And like I said, he thinks I'm miles away from here...
...Staking out his brothels and strip joints.
Just like I planned.

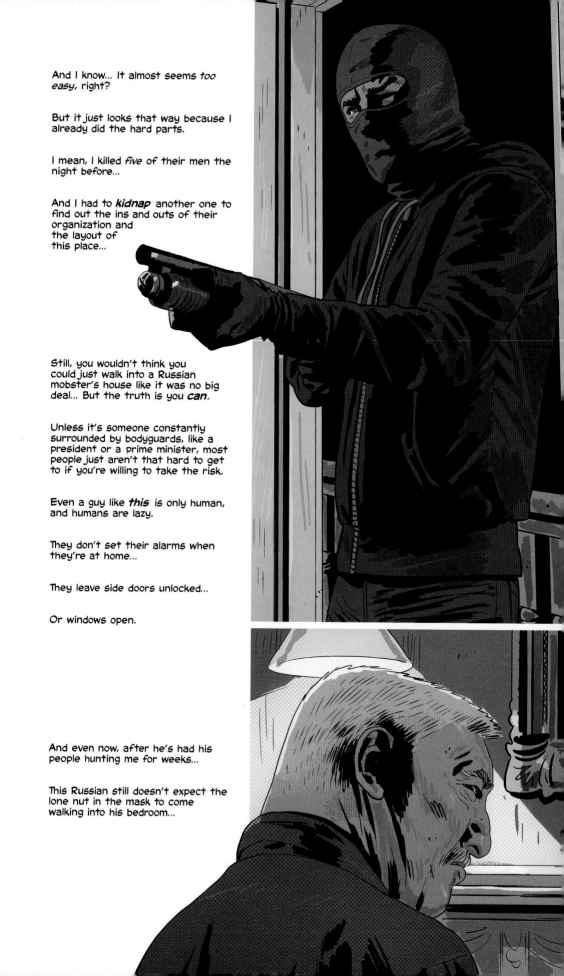

And I know... It almost seems *too easy*, right?

But it just looks that way because I already did the hard parts.

I mean, I killed *five* of their men the night before...

And I had to ***kidnap*** another one to find out the ins and outs of their organization and the layout of this place...

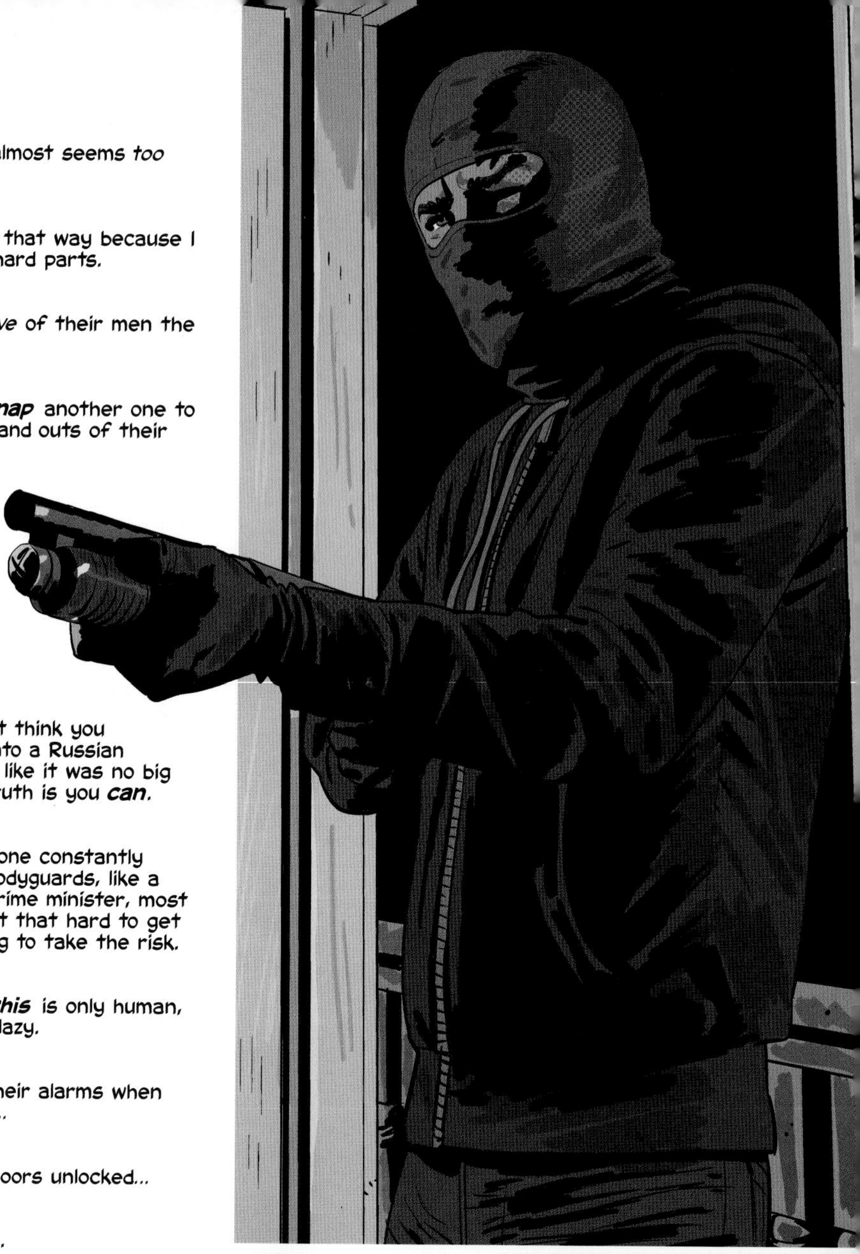

Still, you wouldn't think you could just walk into a Russian mobster's house like it was no big deal... But the truth is you ***can***.

Unless it's someone constantly surrounded by bodyguards, like a president or a prime minister, most people just aren't that hard to get to if you're willing to take the risk.

Even a guy like ***this*** is only human, and humans are lazy.

They don't set their alarms when they're at home...

They leave side doors unlocked...

Or windows open.

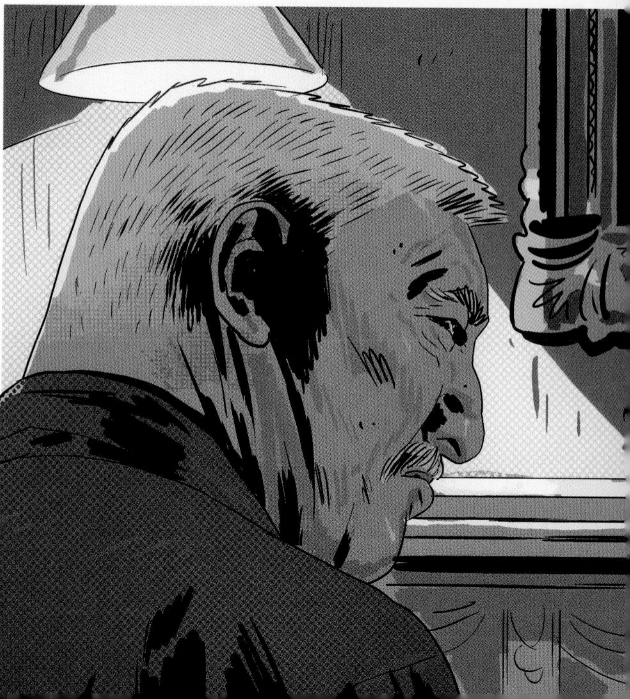

And even now, after he's had his people hunting me for weeks...

This Russian still doesn't expect the lone nut in the mask to come walking into his bedroom...

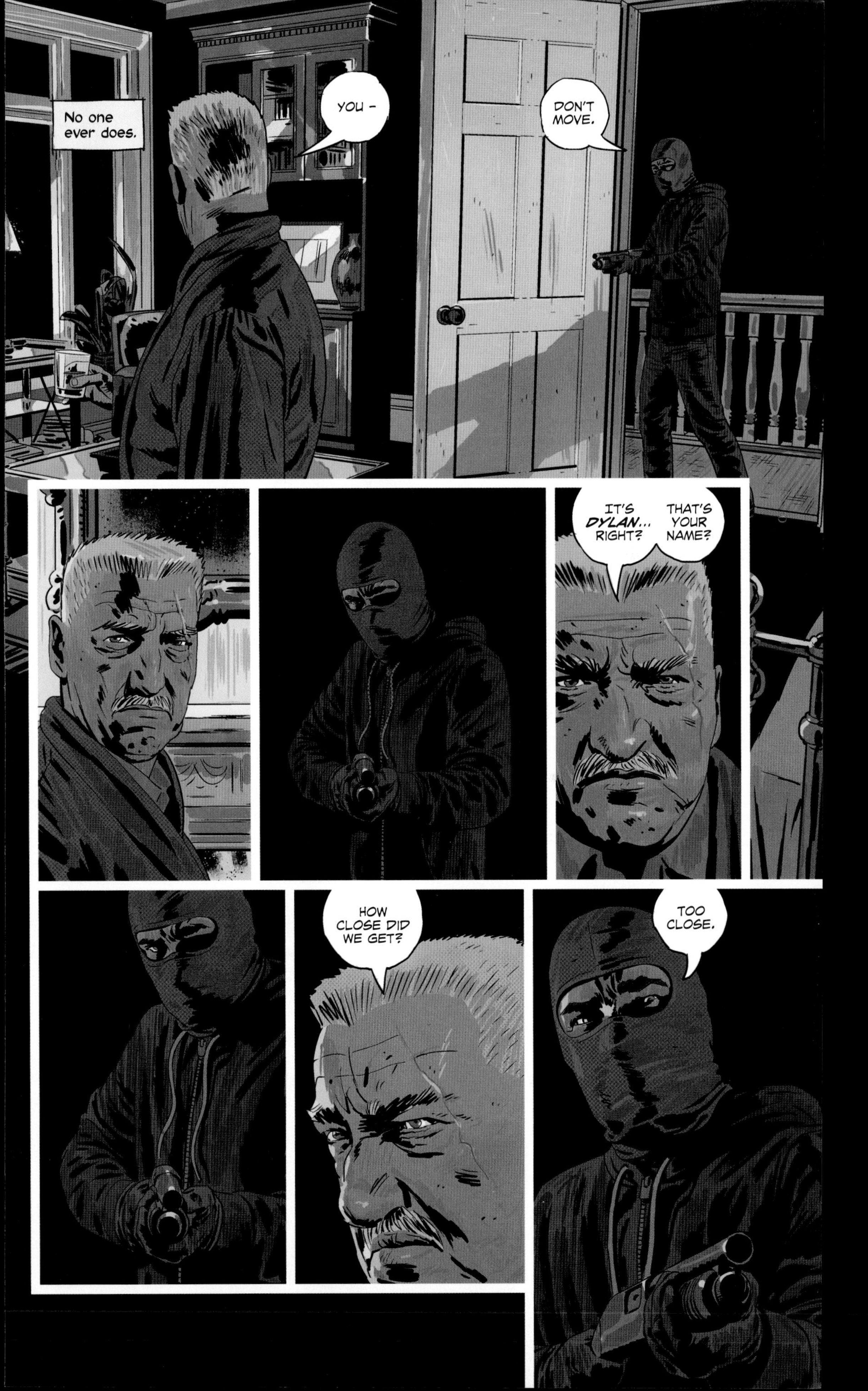
No one ever does.
YOU -
DON'T MOVE.
IT'S *DYLAN*... RIGHT?
THAT'S YOUR NAME?
HOW CLOSE DID WE GET?
TOO CLOSE.

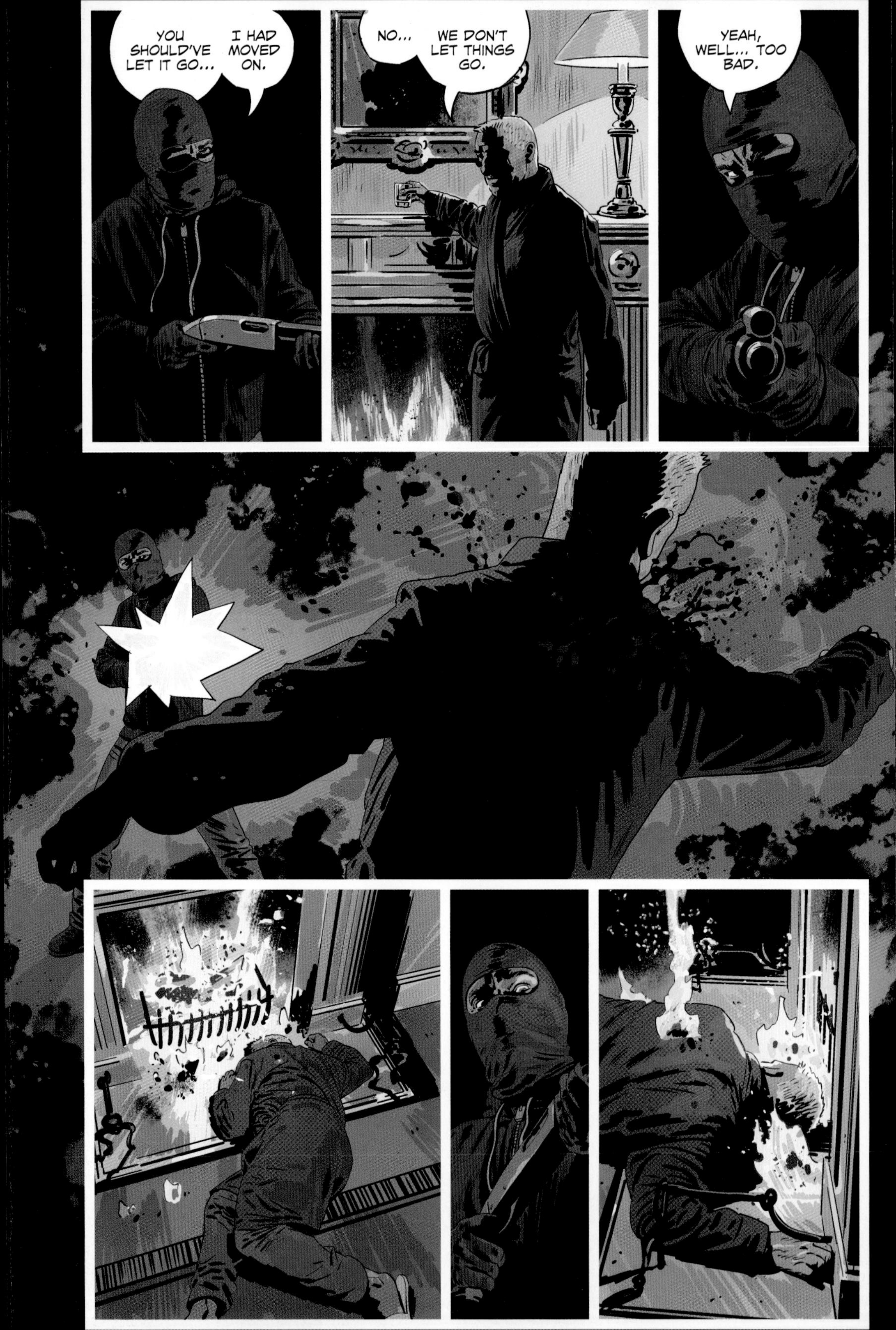
YOU SHOULD'VE LET IT GO...
I HAD MOVED ON.
NO...
WE DON'T LET THINGS GO.
YEAH, WELL... TOO BAD.

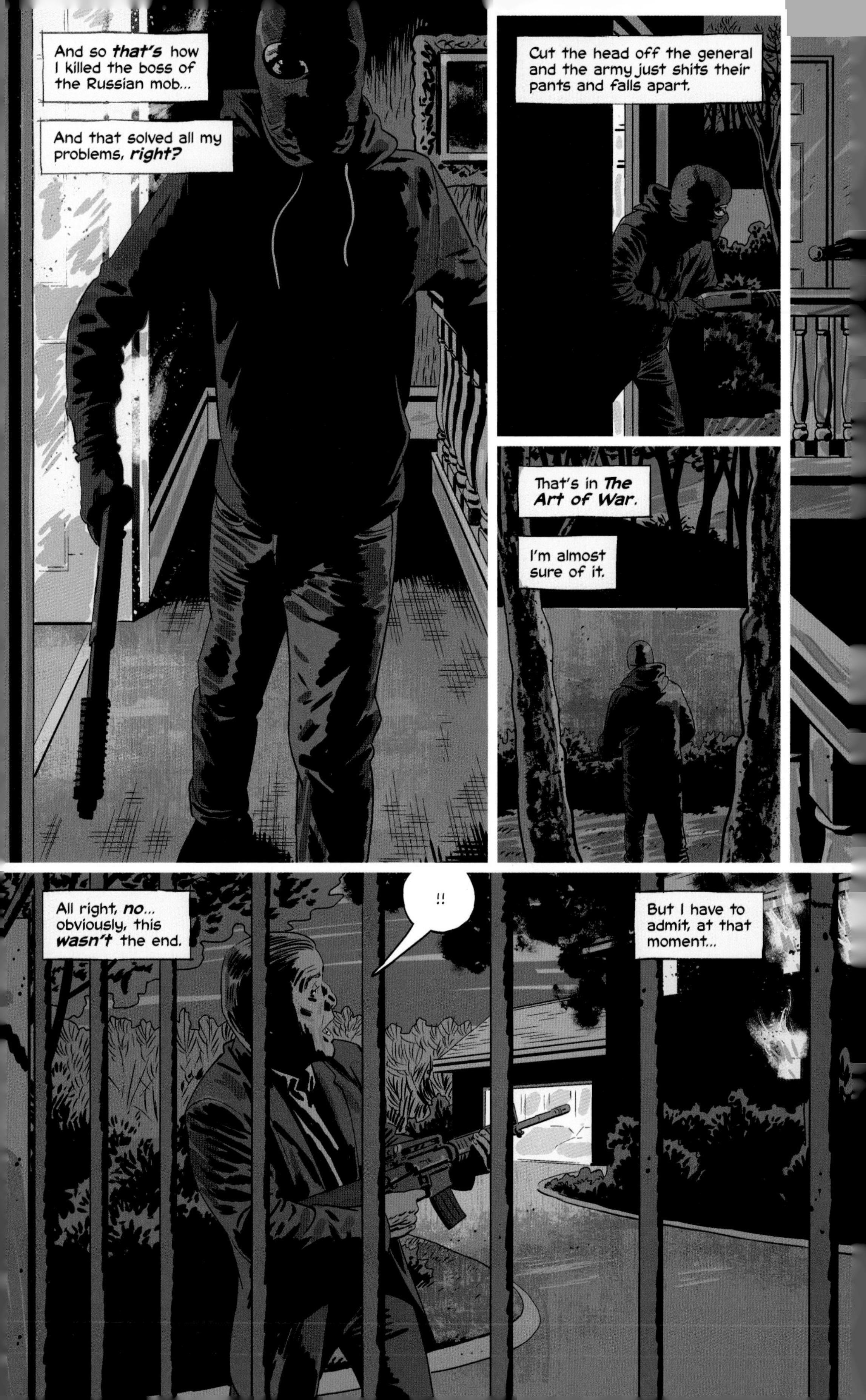
And so *that's* how I killed the boss of the Russian mob...
And that solved all my problems, *right?*
Cut the head off the general and the army just shits their pants and falls apart.
That's in *The Art of War*.
I'm almost sure of it.
All right, *no*... obviously, this *wasn't* the end.
!!
But I have to admit, at that moment...

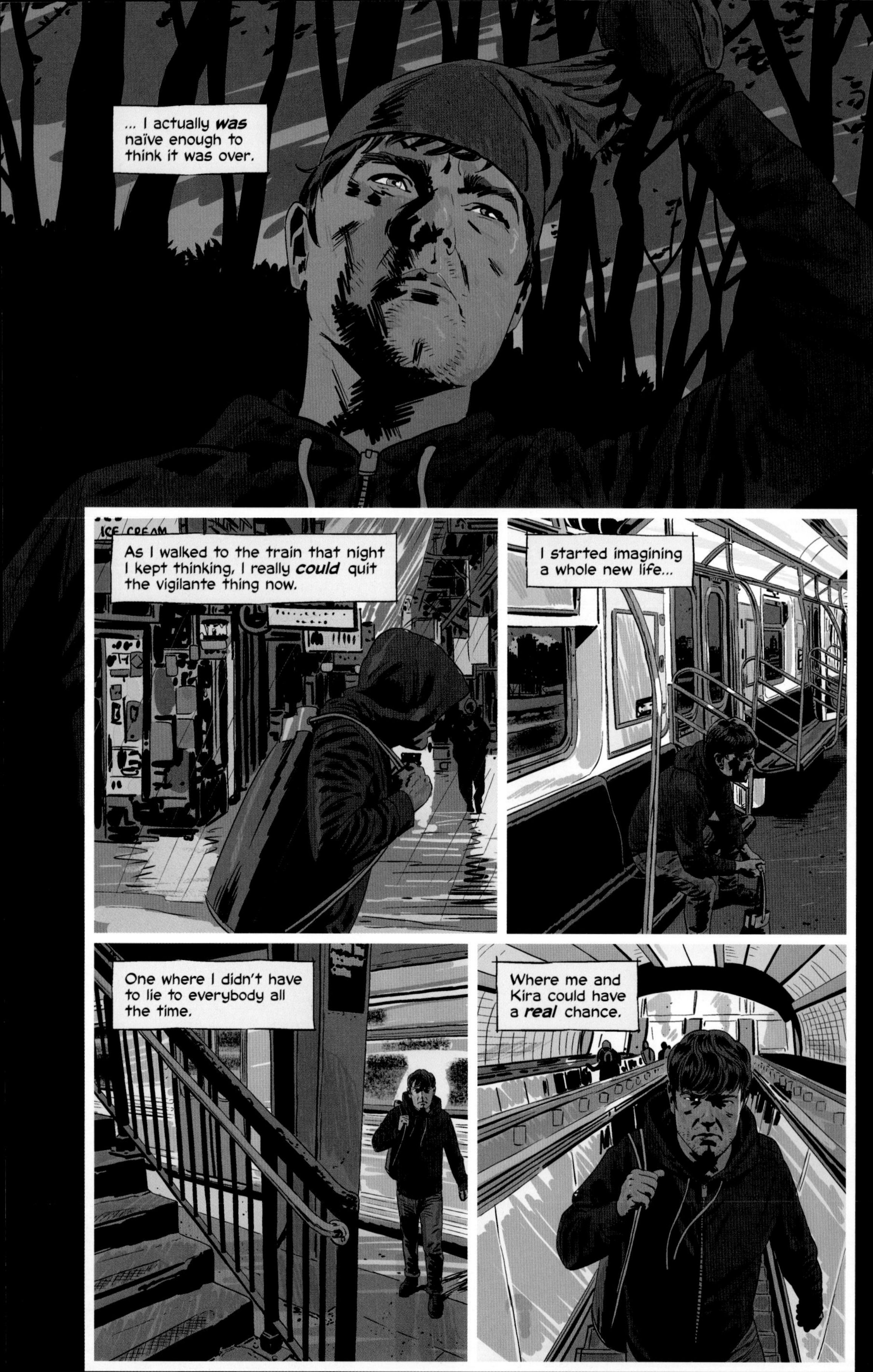
... I actually *was* naïve enough to think it was over.
As I walked to the train that night I kept thinking, I really *could* quit the vigilante thing now.
ICE CREAM
I started imagining a whole new life...
One where I didn't have to lie to everybody all the time.
Where me and Kira could have a *real* chance.

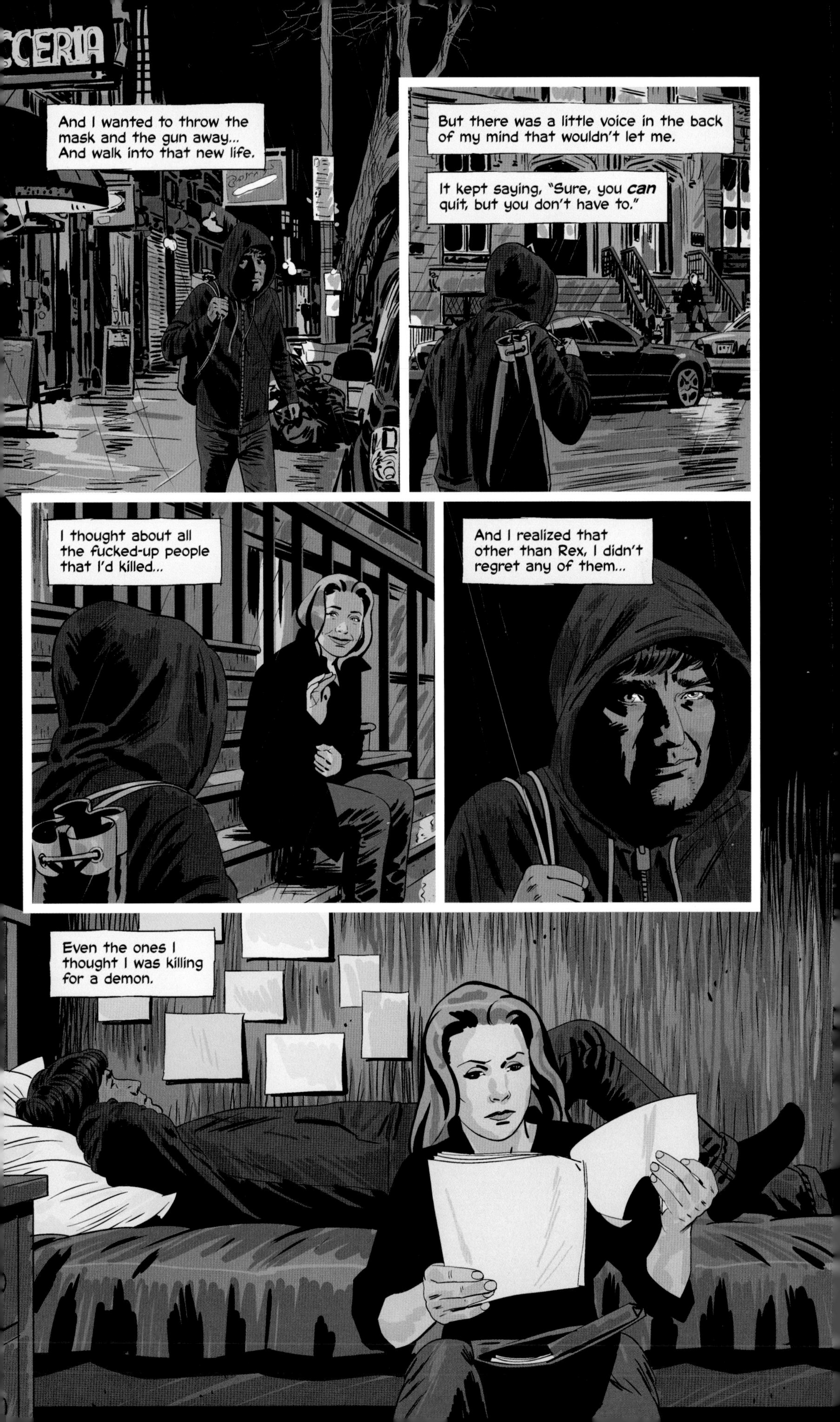

CCERIA
And I wanted to throw the mask and the gun away... And walk into that new life.
But there was a little voice in the back of my mind that wouldn't let me.
It kept saying, "Sure, you *can* quit, but you don't have to."
I thought about all the fucked-up people that I'd killed...
And I realized that other than Rex, I didn't regret any of them...
Even the ones I thought I was killing for a demon.

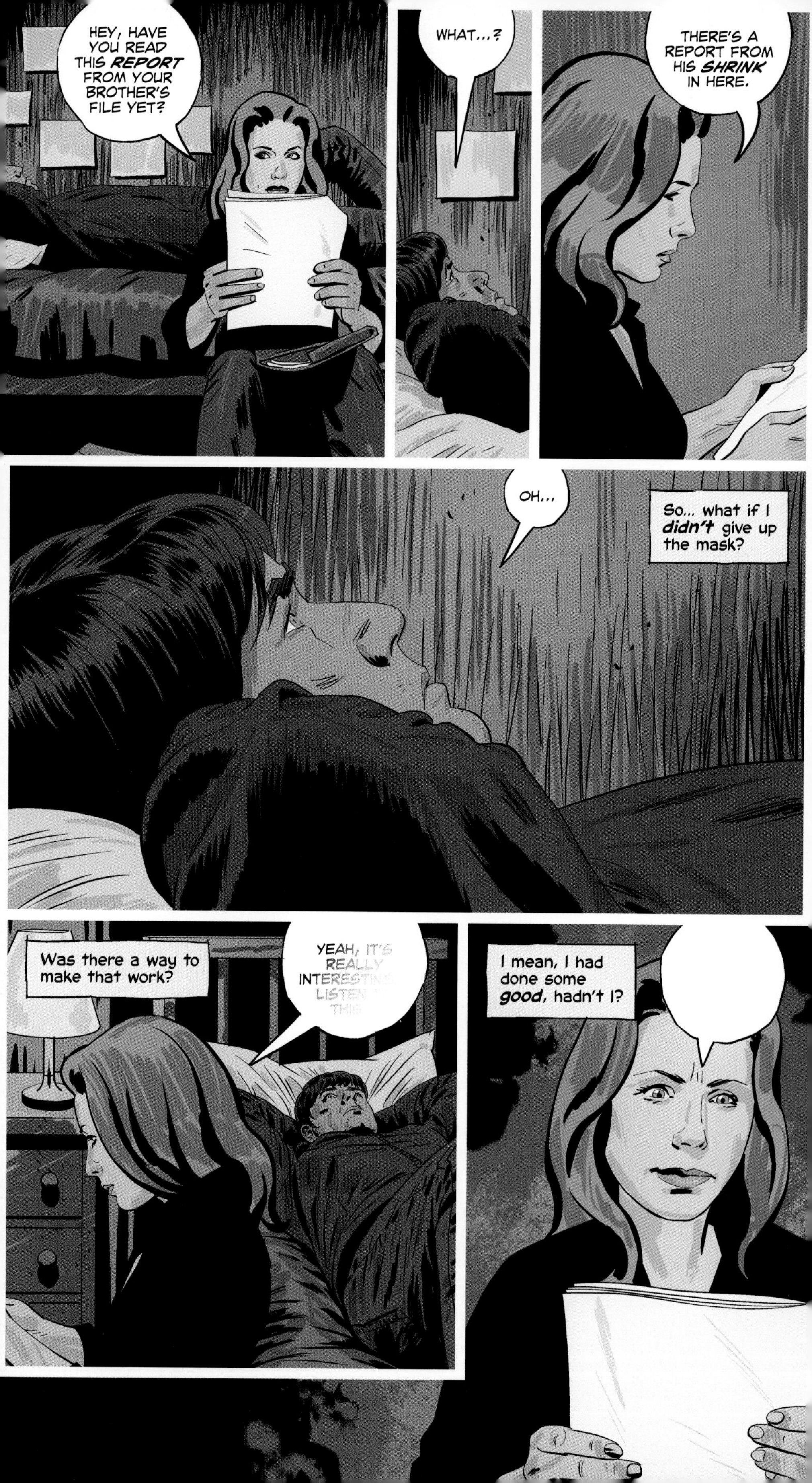
HEY, HAVE YOU READ THIS *REPORT* FROM YOUR BROTHER'S FILE YET?
WHAT...?
THERE'S A REPORT FROM HIS *SHRINK* IN HERE.
OH...
So... what if I ***didn't*** give up the mask?
Was there a way to make that work?
YEAH, IT'S REALLY INTERESTIN LISTEN
I mean, I had done some ***good***, hadn't I?

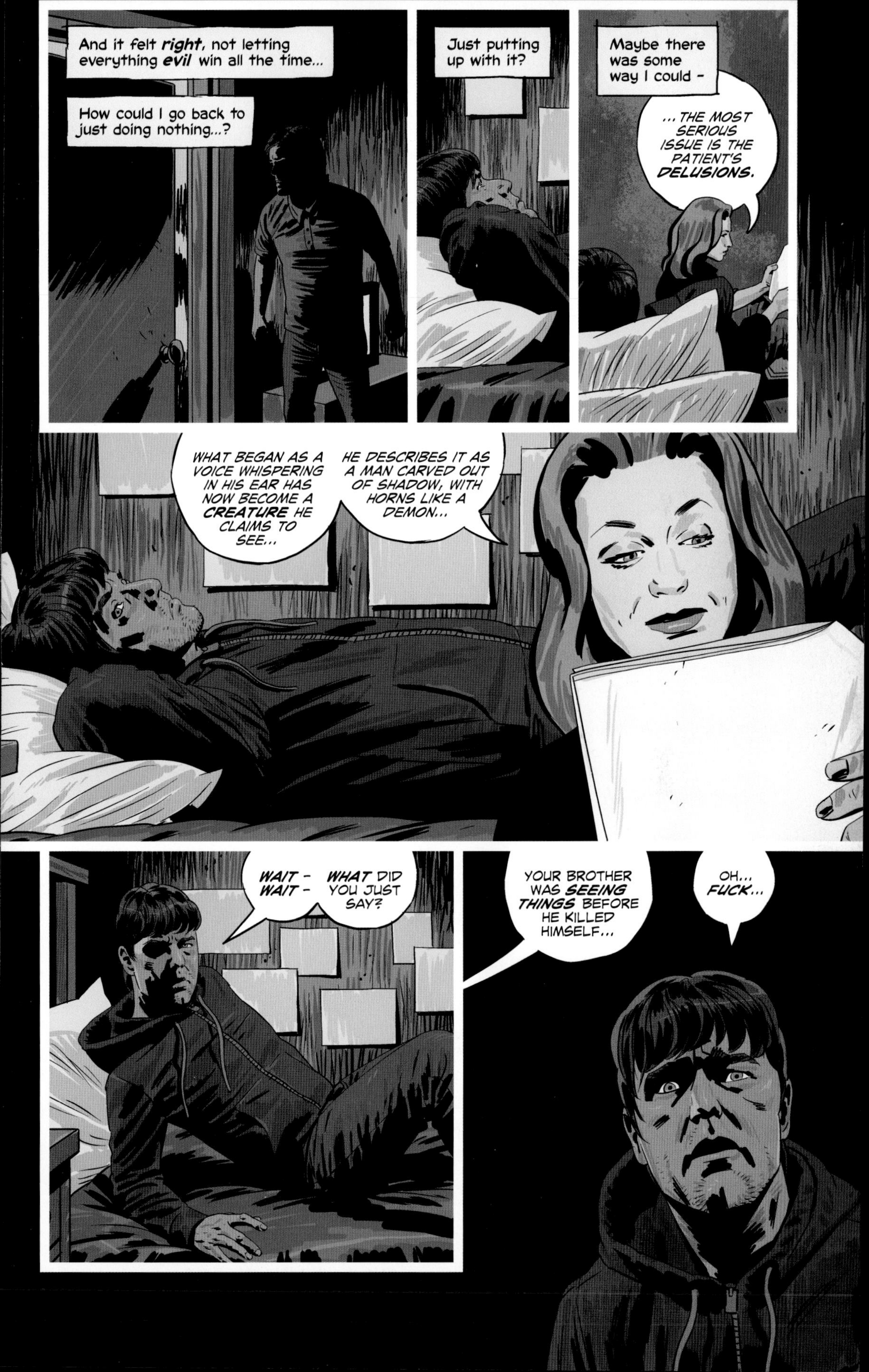

And it felt **right**, not letting everything **evil** win all the time...
How could I go back to just doing nothing...?
Just putting up with it?
Maybe there was some way I could -
...THE MOST SERIOUS ISSUE IS THE PATIENT'S **DELUSIONS**.
WHAT BEGAN AS A VOICE WHISPERING IN HIS EAR HAS NOW BECOME A **CREATURE** HE CLAIMS TO SEE...
HE DESCRIBES IT AS A MAN CARVED OUT OF SHADOW, WITH HORNS LIKE A DEMON...
WAIT - **WAIT** -
WHAT DID YOU JUST SAY?
YOUR BROTHER WAS **SEEING THINGS** BEFORE HE KILLED HIMSELF...
OH... **FUCK**...

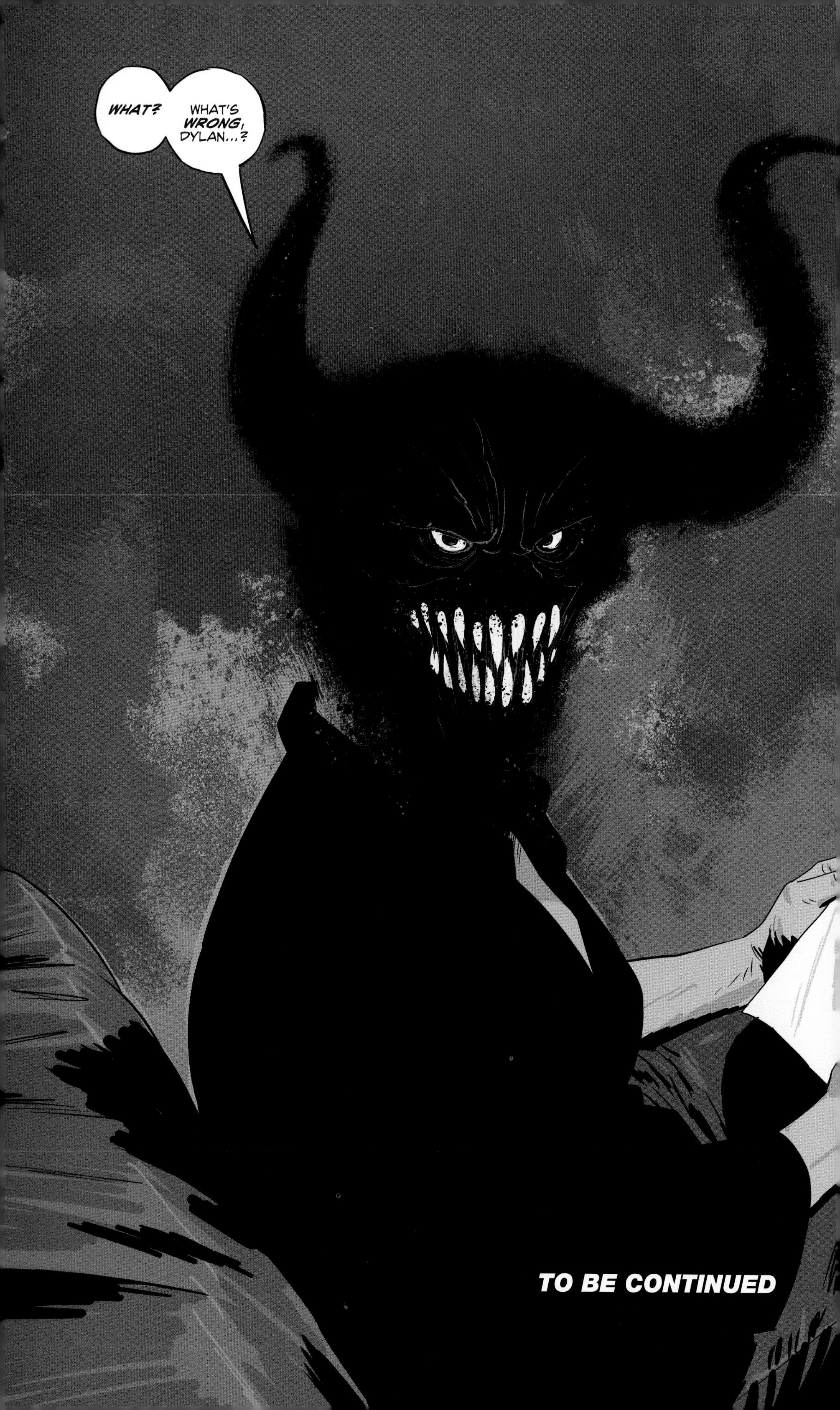

WHAT?
WHAT'S WRONG, DYLAN...?
TO BE CONTINUED

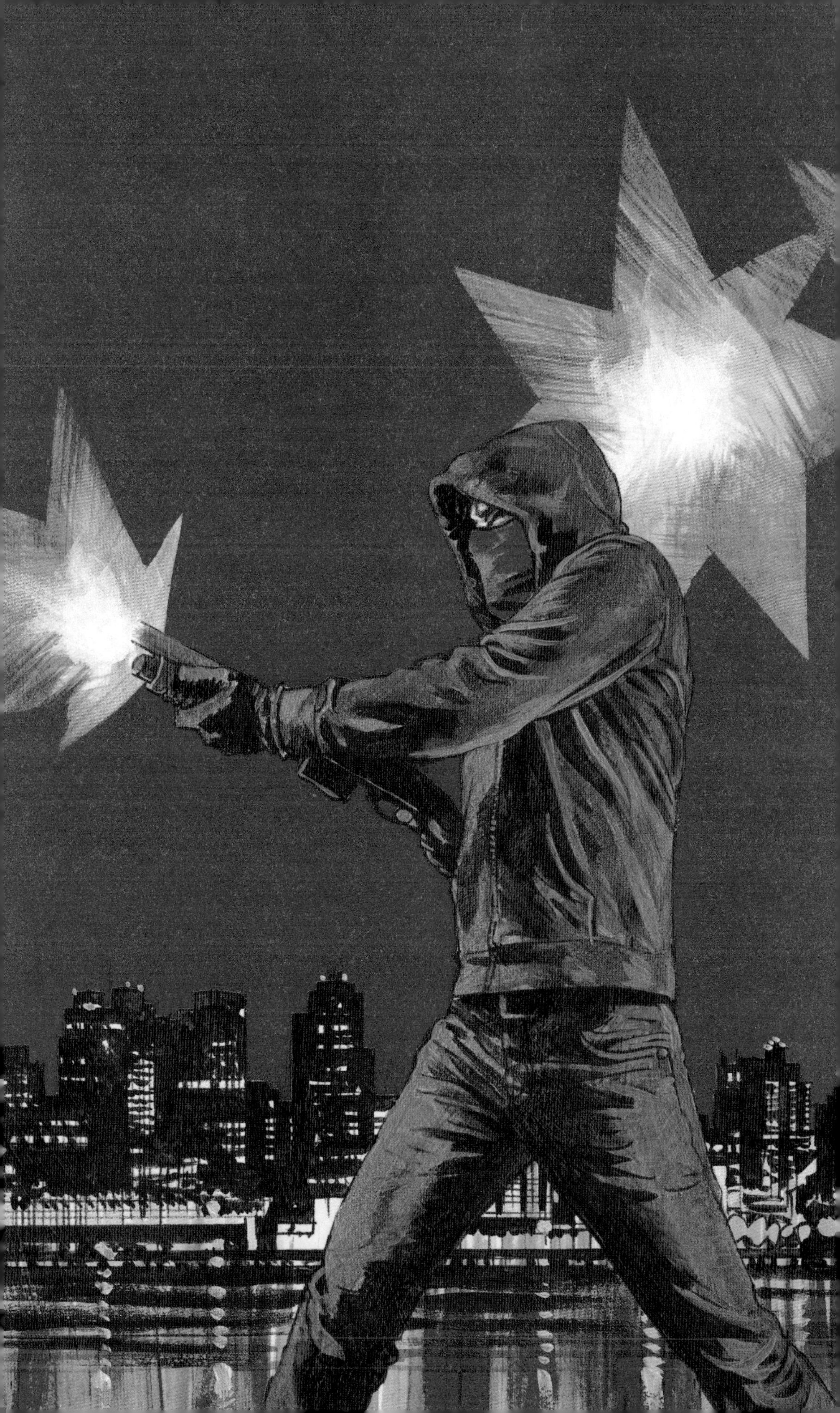

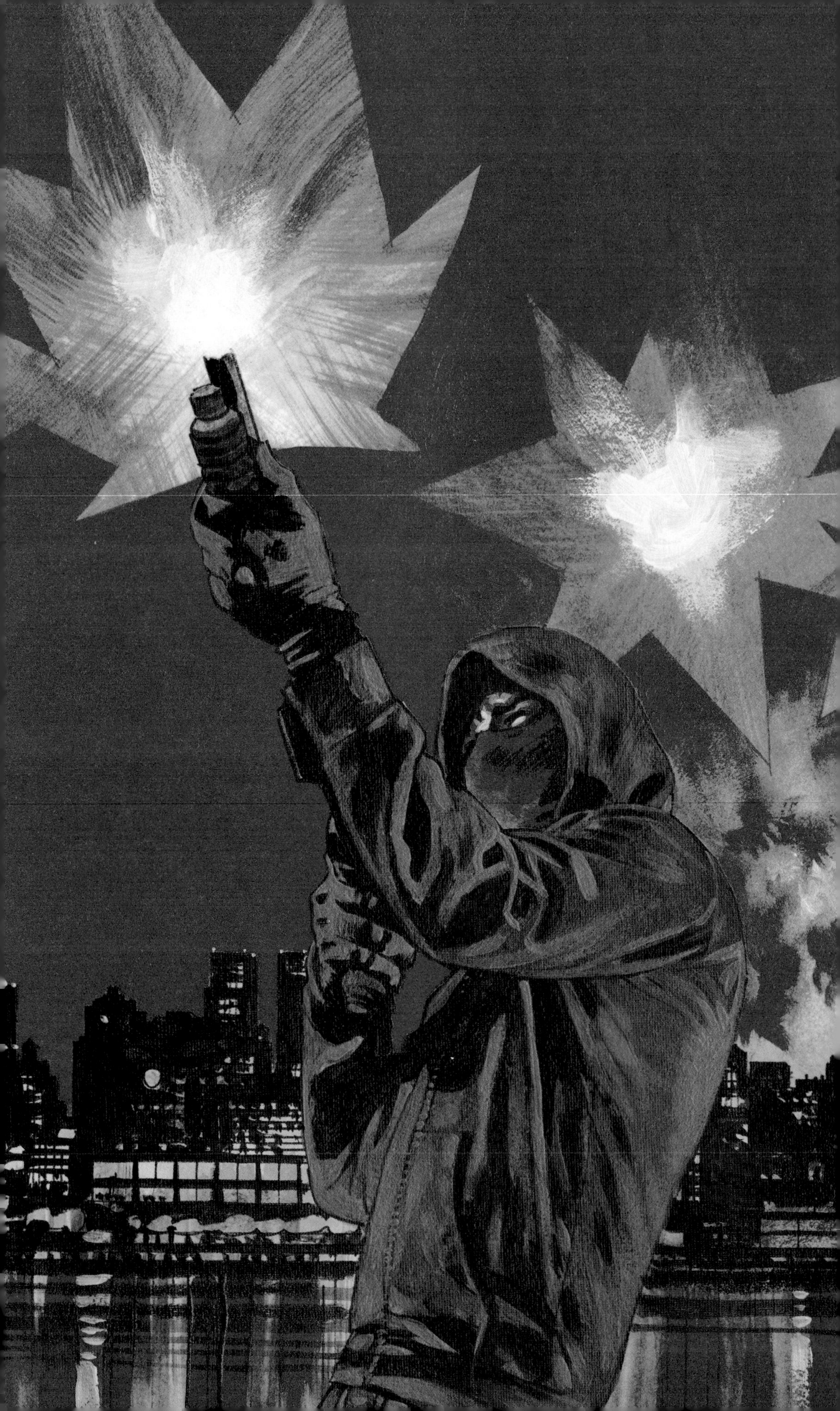

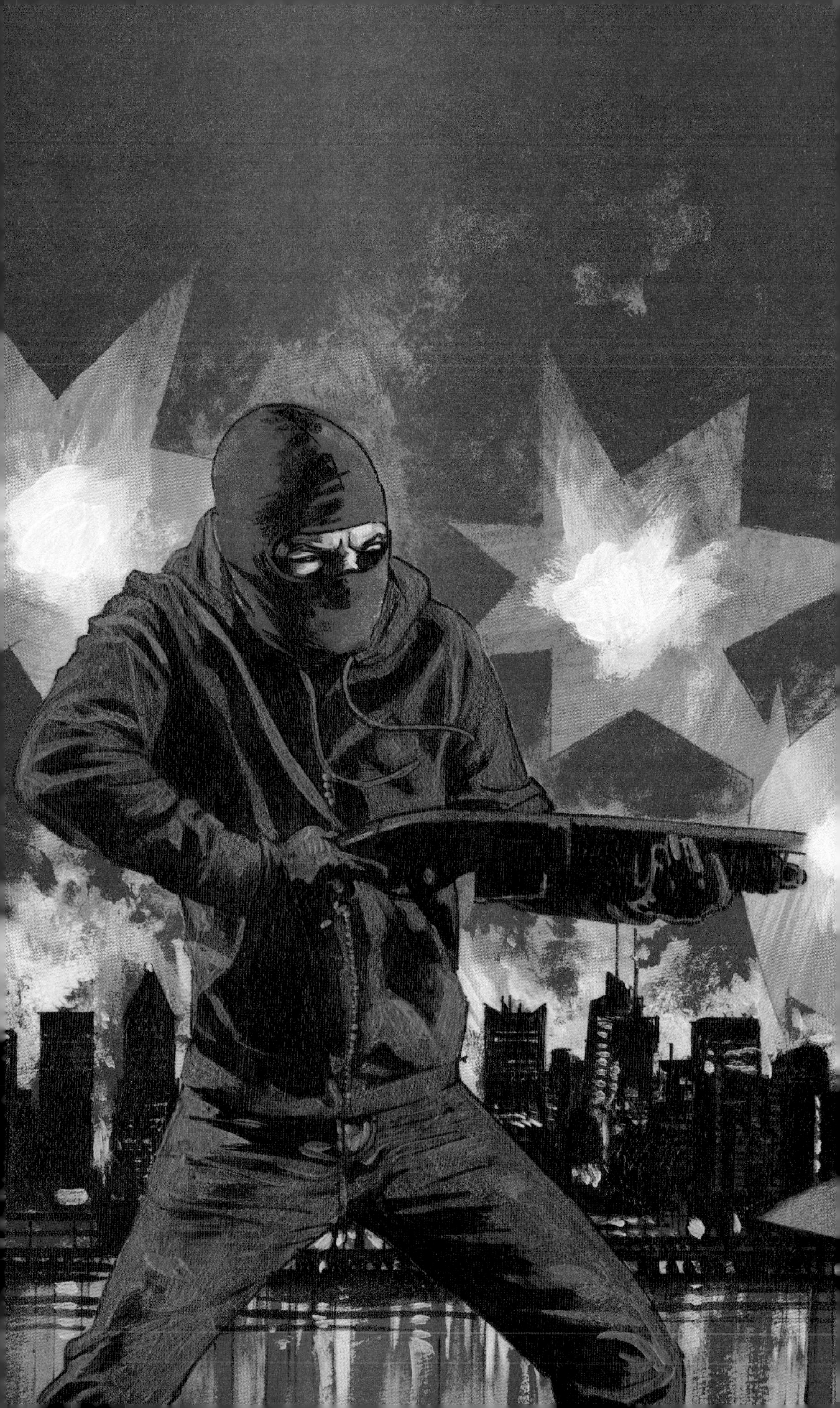

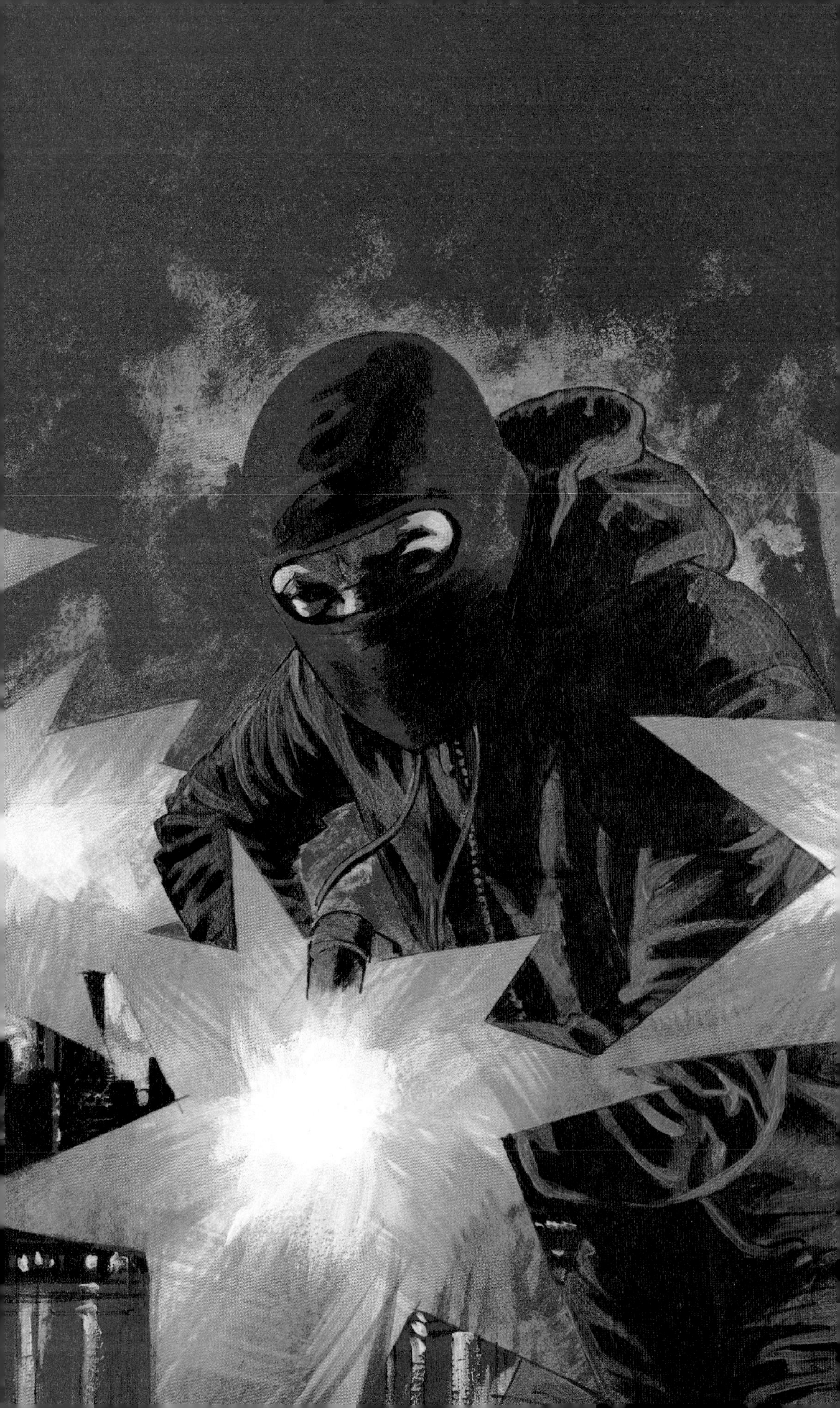

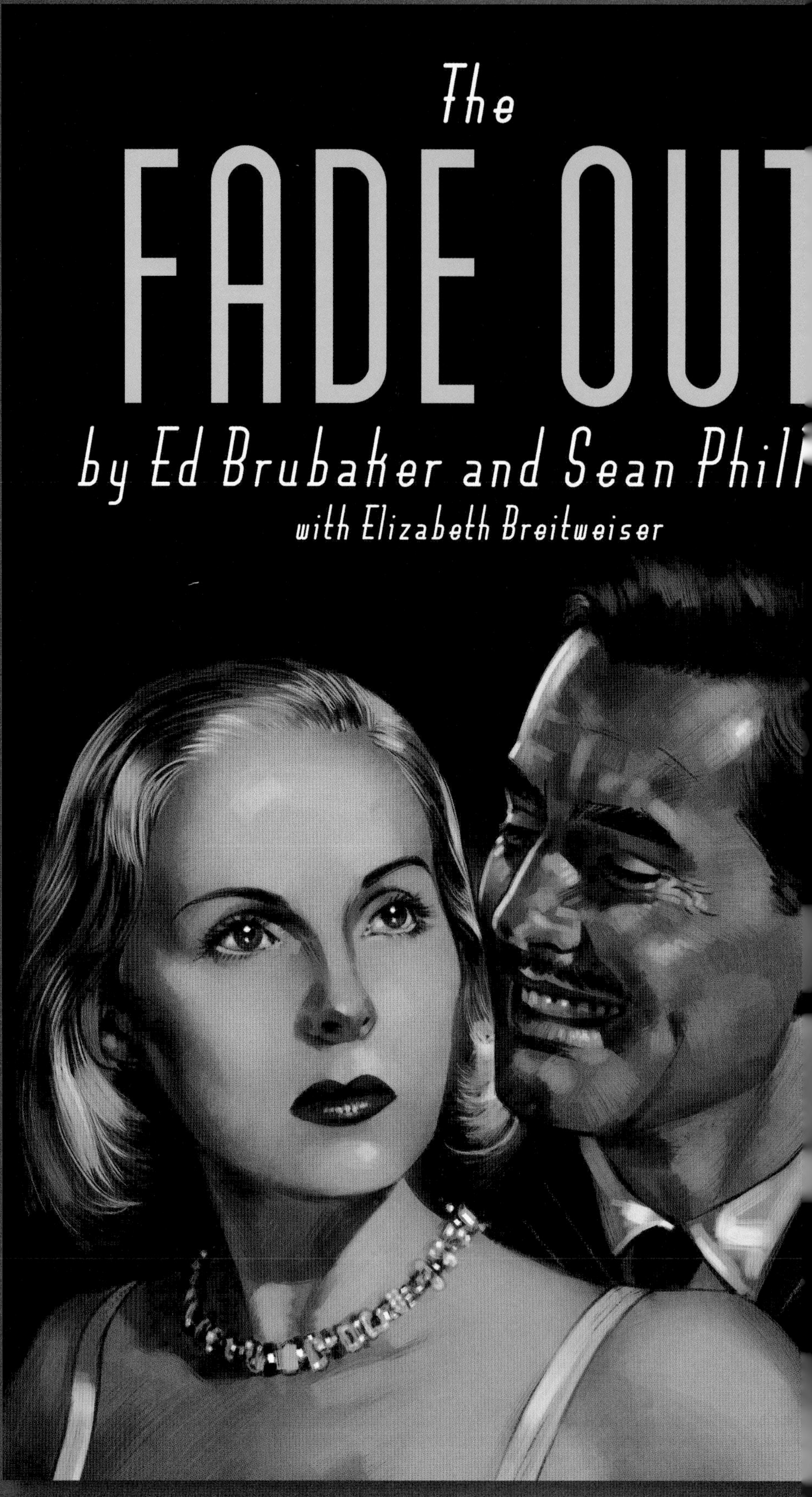
The
FADE OUT
by Ed Brubaker and Sean Phill
with Elizabeth Breitweiser

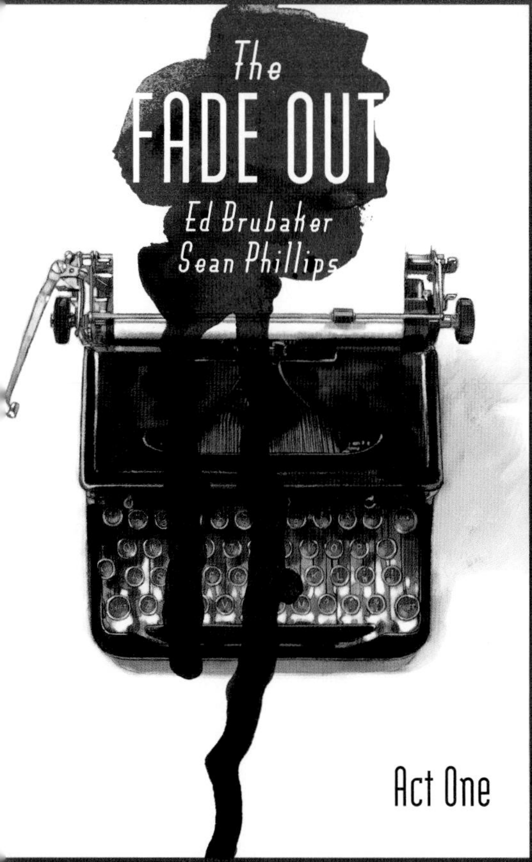
The
FADE OUT
Ed Brubaker
Sean Phillips
Act One

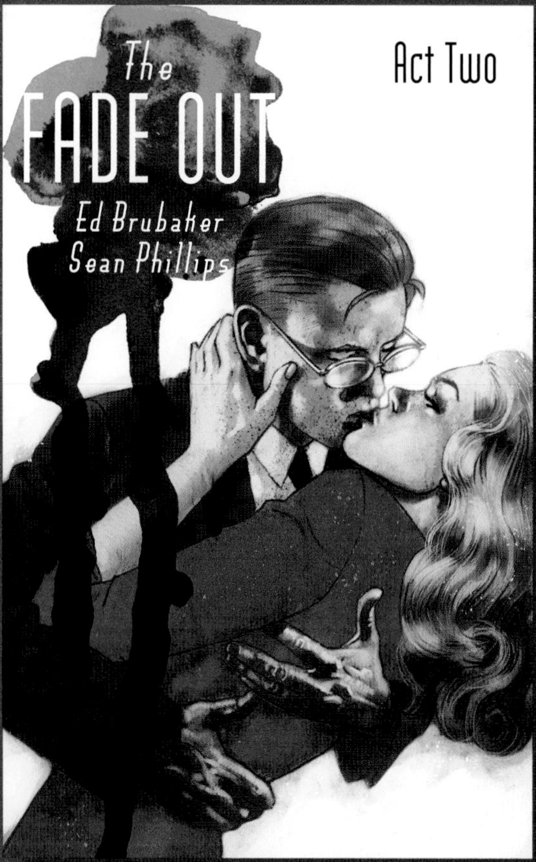
The
FADE OUT
Act Two
Ed Brubaker
Sean Phillips

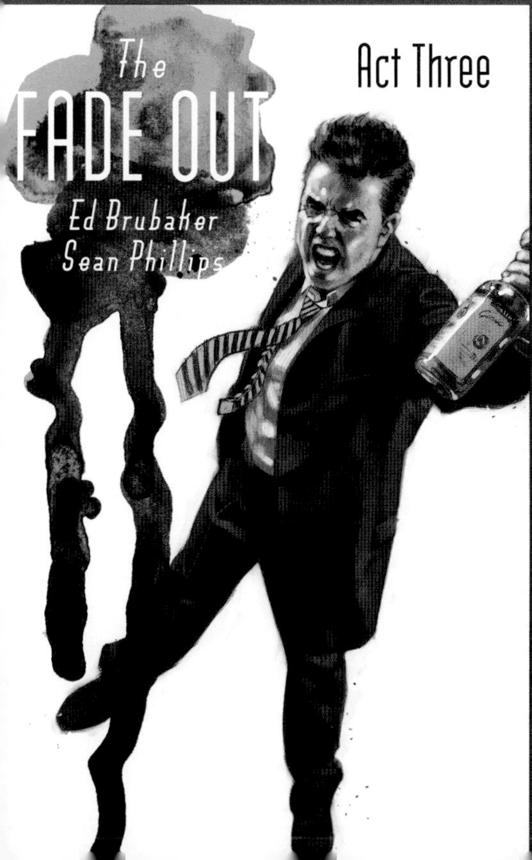
The
FADE OUT
Act Three
Ed Brubaker
Sean Phillips

"One of comics dream teams delivers their best story yet in ***THE FADE OUT****, an old Hollywood murder mystery draped against HUAC and the Red Scare."*

- ***New York Magazine***

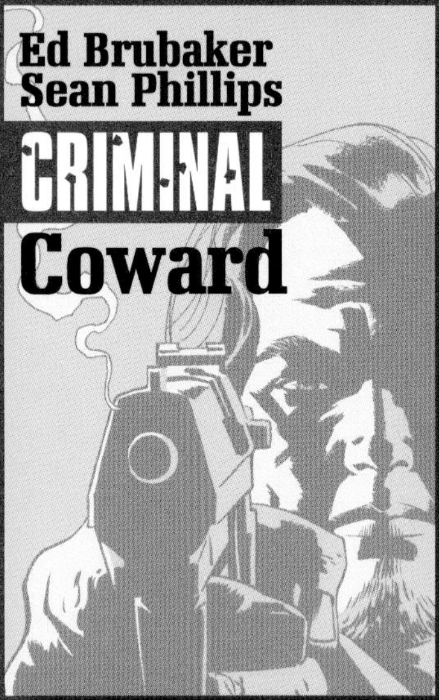
Ed Brubaker
Sean Phillips
CRIMINAL
Coward

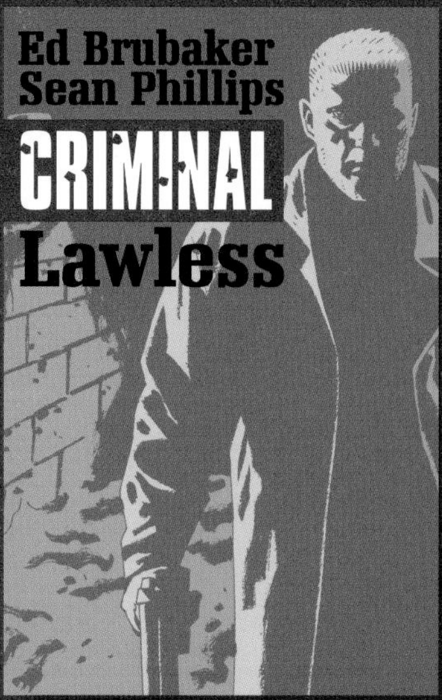
Ed Brubaker
Sean Phillips
CRIMINAL
Lawless

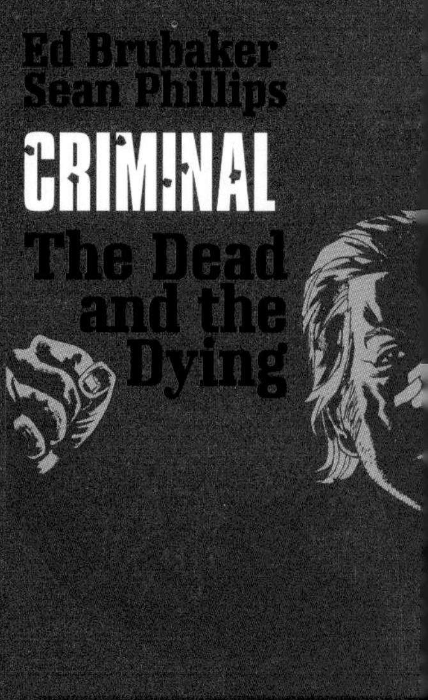
Ed Brubaker
Sean Phillips
CRIMINAL
The Dead and the Dying

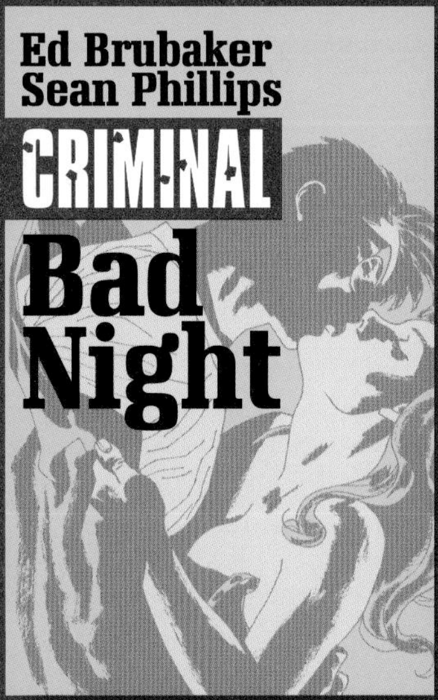
Ed Brubaker
Sean Phillips
CRIMINAL
Bad Night

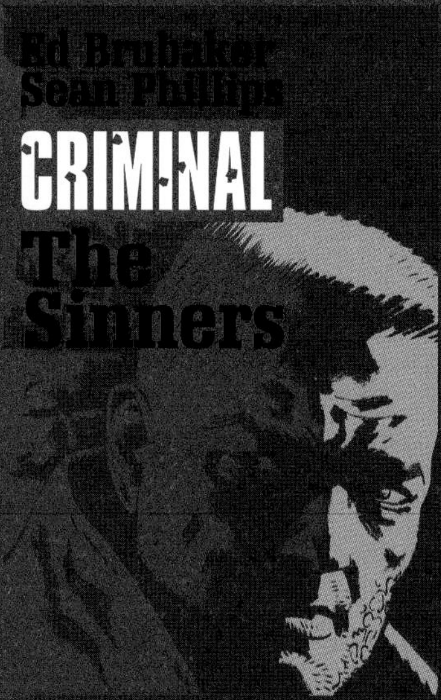
Ed Brubaker
Sean Phillips
CRIMINAL
The Sinners

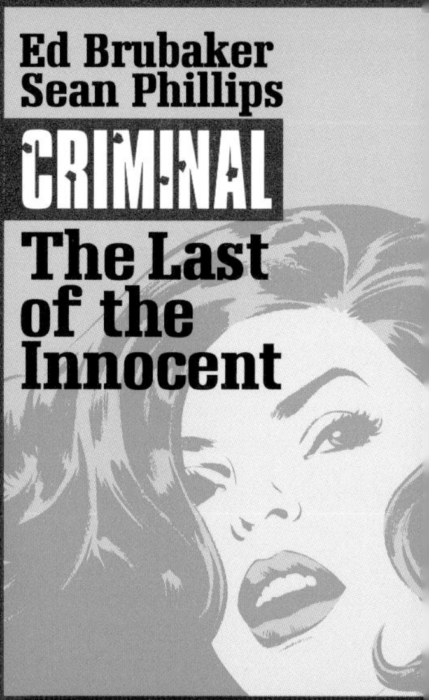
Ed Brubaker
Sean Phillips
CRIMINAL
The Last of the Innocent

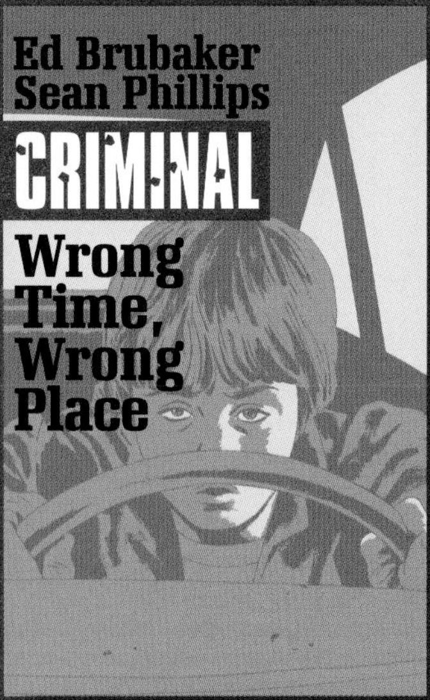
Ed Brubaker
Sean Phillips
CRIMINAL
Wrong Time, Wrong Place

"***CRIMINAL*** *is equal parts John Woo's* ***THE KILLER***, *Stanley Kubrick's* ***THE KILLING***, *and Francis Ford Coppola's* ***THE GODFATHER.***"

- ***Playboy Magazine***

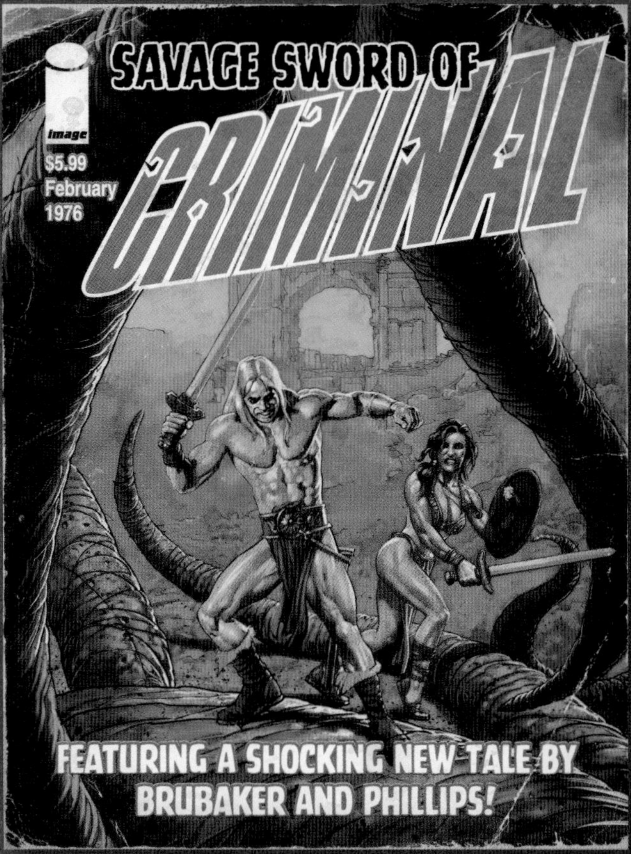
SAVAGE SWORD OF
CRIMINAL
image
$5.99
February
1976
FEATURING A SHOCKING NEW TALE BY
BRUBAKER AND PHILLIPS!

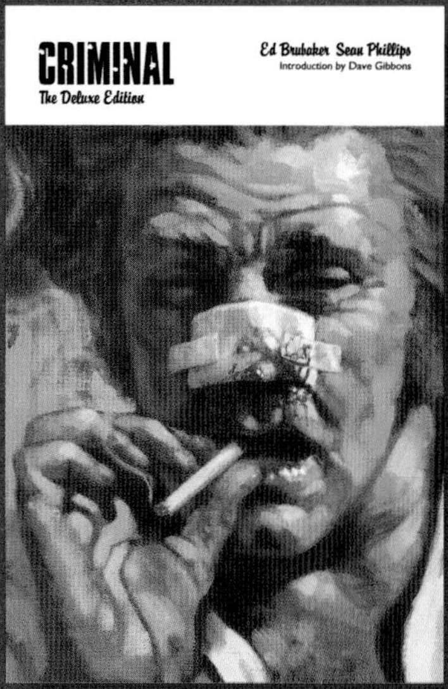
CRIMINAL
The Deluxe Edition
Ed Brubaker Sean Phillips
Introduction by Dave Gibbons

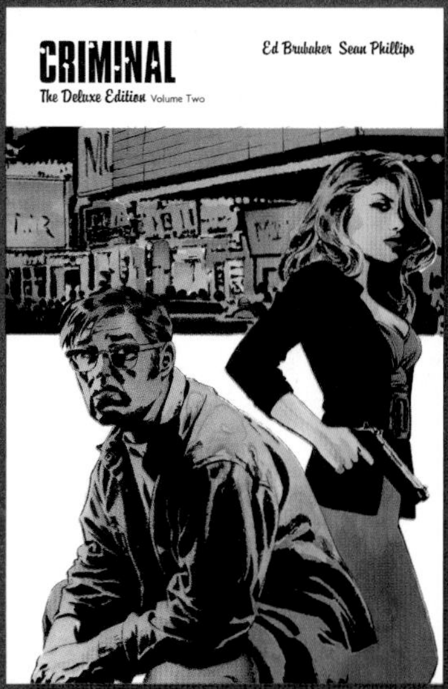
CRIMINAL
The Deluxe Edition Volume Two
Ed Brubaker Sean Phillips

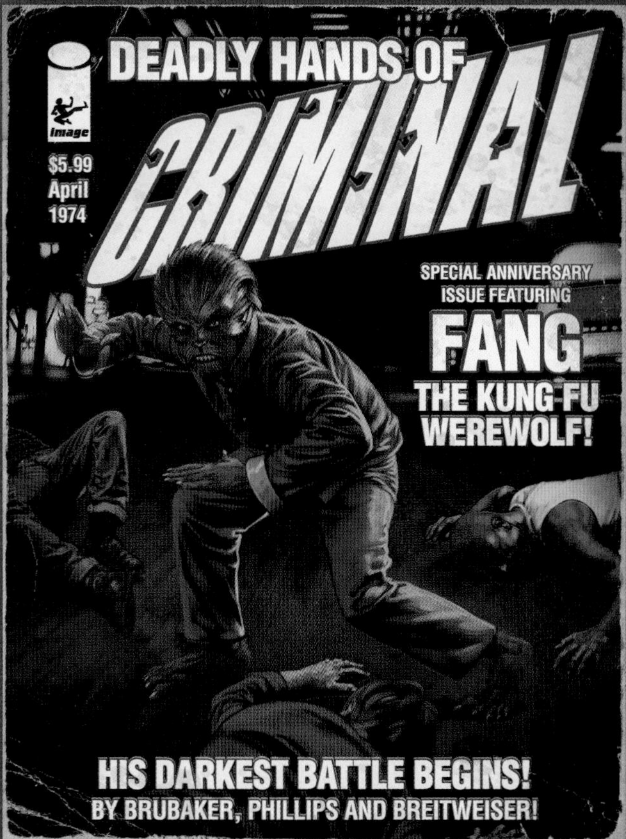
DEADLY HANDS OF
CRIMINAL
image
$5.99
April
1974
SPECIAL ANNIVERSARY
ISSUE FEATURING
FANG
THE KUNG FU
WEREWOLF!
HIS DARKEST BATTLE BEGINS!
BY BRUBAKER, PHILLIPS AND BREITWEISER!

Multiple Eisner Award-Winning Series

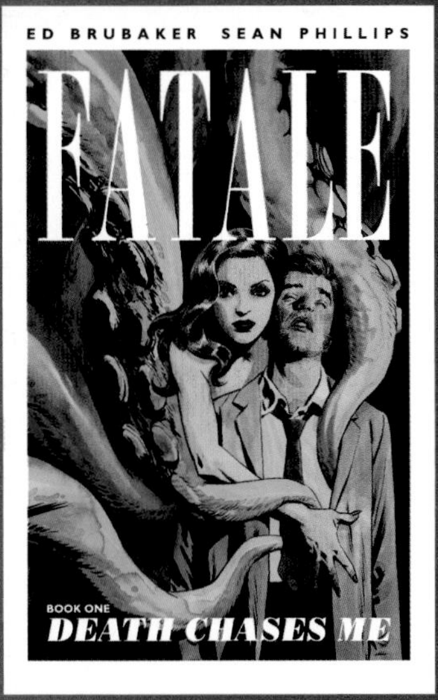
ED BRUBAKER SEAN PHILLIPS
FATALE
BOOK ONE
DEATH CHASES ME

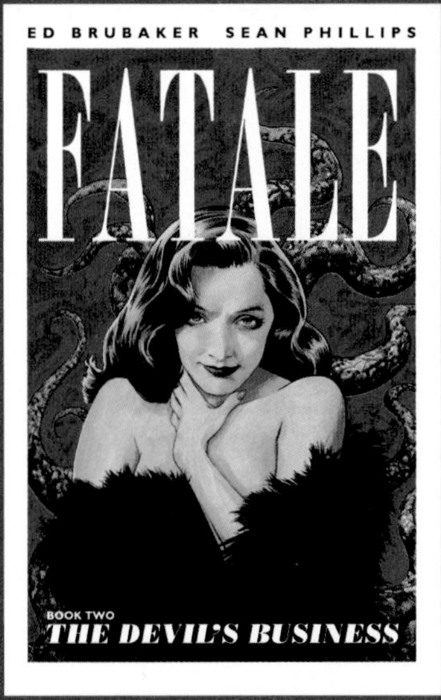
ED BRUBAKER SEAN PHILLIPS
FATALE
BOOK TWO
THE DEVIL'S BUSINESS

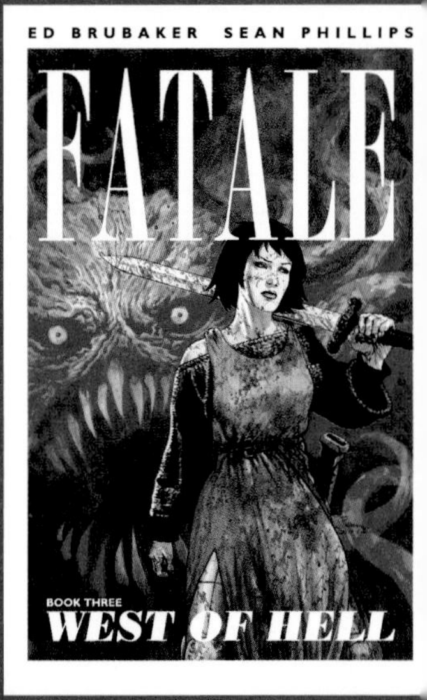
ED BRUBAKER SEAN PHILLIPS
FATALE
BOOK THREE
WEST OF HELL

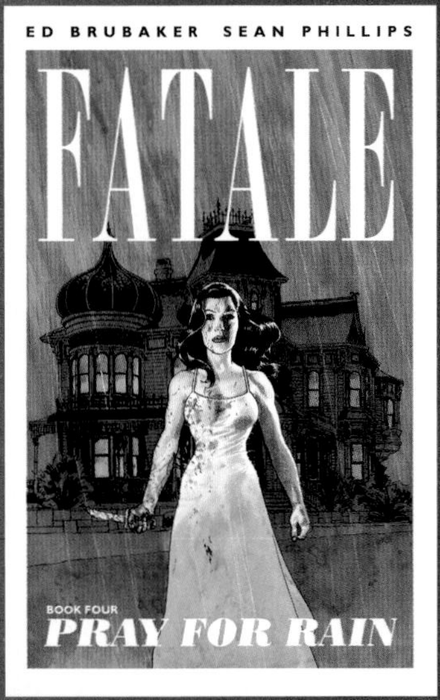
ED BRUBAKER SEAN PHILLIPS
FATALE
BOOK FOUR
PRAY FOR RAIN

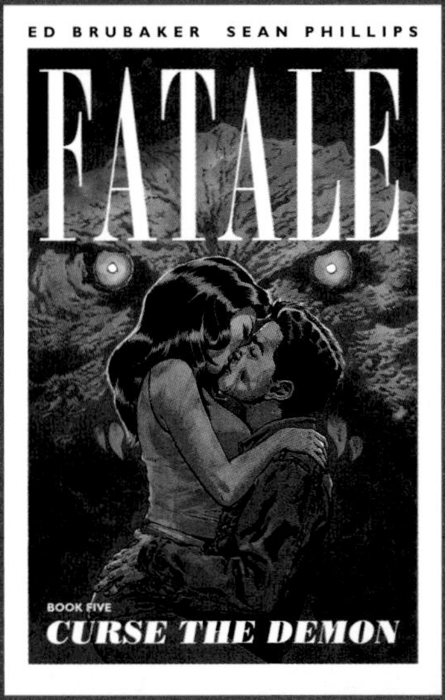
ED BRUBAKER SEAN PHILLIPS
FATALE
BOOK FIVE
CURSE THE DEMON

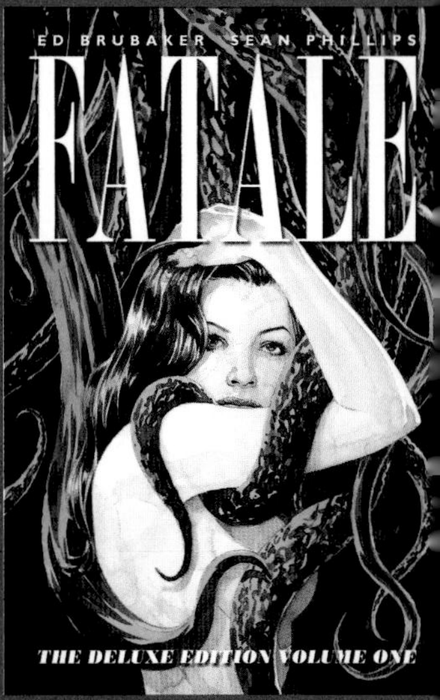
ED BRUBAKER SEAN PHILLIPS
FATALE
THE DELUXE EDITION VOLUME ONE

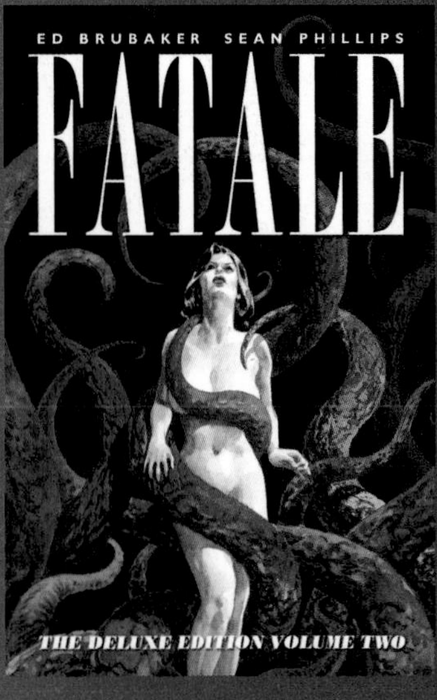
ED BRUBAKER SEAN PHILLIPS
FATALE
THE DELUXE EDITION VOLUME TWO

"Immortality may be a double-edged sword, but it's one the intoxicating Jo wields with a boundless grace in this addictive page-turner."

- Publishers Weekly

sleeper

"**SLEEPER** is a perfect noir story that just happens to star people who can do fantastic things."
- ***io9***

"**SCENE OF THE CRIME** is one of the very few books in the entire world to make me growl 'Ugh, I should have thought of this!'"
- **Brian Michael Bendis**

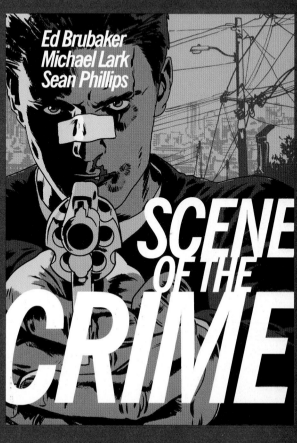

Ed Brubaker
Michael Lark
Sean Phillips

SCENE OF THE CRIME